ESCAPE FROM
OBLIVION

Toby Smith

ISBN: 1-4196-9665-3
ISBN-13: 9781419696657

Visit www.booksurge.com to order additional copies.

Dedicated to the light spirits – you know who you are.

Introduction

This book has been written in urgency to create a safe home. As adults, people find it increasingly important to create a home which will shelter and comfort them from the elements in society which undermine their emotional and physical well-being. Consequently, this book represents a safe place, an environment which constructively addresses complex issues.

The best homes are based on visions. The vision may be nothing more than just a gleam in the future owner's eye, but homes are bought and chosen with respect to an imaginary dream house. Just like a home, this book is based on a vision. The idea for this vision came as the result of a movie called "On a Clear Day". The movie was about a psychology professor who fell in love with a past reincarnation of one of his hypnotized students. It wasn't the idea of reincarnation that provided the inspiration, rather it was the idea that a person could attain such an understanding of themselves that all the pieces of events from the past, present, and future would fit together like a puzzle and present a vision of life so awesome and comprehensive that one would never question their place in the universe. Everything would be seen and understood for its own sake and life would just simply be enjoyed.

Initially this vision existed solely in the imagination. In order to achieve this vision the limits prescribed by time and space must be transcended. In the imagination the past, present, and future can be fused together in one single moment. Once a place exists in the imagination for the vision, then the individual thinks of ways to make their imagination a reality by changing their environment.

This ability to affect and change the environment somewhat can be termed as the god-monkey duality: the god creates and the monkey imitates. For example, give a child some paper and crayons, and watch the child draw his/her universe. Give them some blocks and see them build their world, then destroy it. Yet, if mother leaves out her make-up or father forgets to put away his shoes, guess what the tot will be wearing next? Adults, on the other hand, generally imitate those who they also respect and create heroes specifically for this purpose. Even this type of imitation is limited and often a little more creativity is needed in order to succeed; when heroes fail, consult the muses.

So after musing over the challenge of transforming visions into reality, an individual resorts to the traditional means of achieving this, otherwise known as 'the human quest'. Defining the human quest as a search for meaning in life through the interplay of creation and imitation, it can be pictured as a succession of people standing on the shoulders of the individual who came before them in time or effort. With each person the overall view of the world increases in scope, because each person can see a little bit further beyond the horizon than the next. As a result, the base from which one chooses to stand influences the viewpoint extracted. The only problem with the perspective gained by standing on another's shoulder is that there comes a point in the hierarchy where the individual begins to lose site of the original position.

However, clear day visions differ from human quests in that they are more comprehensive. These visions require more than just the combined interplay of creation and imitation, they also recognize the individual's bond to the environment. Moreover, they are like instant camera shots where the flash of insight is so brief that if one wasn't aware they would miss the significance of the impression on the senses. These impressions enable individuals to remember who they are and what they want out of life during the dark storms of confusion and self doubt.

Scientists have developed several physical explanations of clear day visions. Some physiologists refer to them as adrenalin produced highs. Other professionals claim that the vision occurs when the neurological impulse on one side of the brain becomes so forceful that it passes through the analytical side of the brain (without even a blink of an eye) and registers within the emotions connected to the abstract portion of the brain. Yet, a third group of scientists claim that clear day visions are a simply another mode of knowing. This description seems to most accurately account for the type of information perceived with clear day visions.

A psychologist from the third group, Robert Ornstein, asserts that there are different modes of knowing as concluded from his electroencephalogram studies of the brain. The different modes of knowing correspond to the functions of the left and right brain. In his book, The Psychology of Consciousness, Ornstein claims that western societies use only one-half of their mental capacities because of the emphasis on language and logical thinking. Eastern societies tend to develop the left hemisphere of the brain through their intuitive and mystical cultures. He stresses that there are alternate ways of knowing which are ignored in the West:

> "...As a result of this preoccupation with isolated facts, it is not surprising that we face so many simultaneous problems whose solutions depend on our ability to grasp the relationship of parts to wholes... Split-and-whole-brain studies have led to a new conception of human knowledge, consciousness, and intelligence. All knowledge can not be expressed into words, yet our education is based almost exclusively on its written or spoken forms... But the artist, dancer, mystic have learned to develop the nonverbal portion of intelligence."

Clear day visions result when the two modes of knowing unite in one mutual understanding, and it is one of those phenomena in life which one must accept in the imagination before making it possible in reality. All the trivial day to day details such as making breakfast, fighting the traffic, and getting to work on time, assume a new significance when placed in this bird's-eye perspective. Major worldwide events such as war, hunger, and famine lose their despairing effect. Personal issues can be understood and accepted in a new light. Everyone has the capacity for clear day visions; the choice to utilize this perspective depends on the individual. What matters in life is an individual's response to reality because it generally reflects what one chooses to value. The story on the following pages reflects certain values, including a belief in clear day visions.

Chapter One

On a clear day
Rise and look around you
And you'll see who you are...

"On a Clear Day"
Lyrics by Alan Jay Lerner
Music by Burton Lane

On one clear, very clear summer's day in Wichita Falls, Texas, a group of twelve year old girls in racing swimsuits gathered at the edge of a crystal blue twenty-five meter pool.

"Swimmers take your mark," barked the man behind the megaphone. He stood along the side of the swimming pool which faced Carrie. The shimmering water at her feet mirrored the reflection of the cloudless sky above.

Eight ten year old girls who had been anxiously standing at the edge of the pool curled into starting position. Each reached firmly for the bottom of the block with every muscle cocked for the firing of the pistol.

The man holding the megaphone pointed his pistol upward and abruptly fired into the air.

Go! Carrie silently echoed as her legs automatically unfolded. Her arms embraced the entire distance of the body of water awaiting her. She gently greeted the water with a series of swift arm pulls and dolphin kicks.

"The water is warm," she thought, registering the temperature internally. She hated starting a race in cold water. Although extensive practice caused Carrie's body to react as a finely tuned machine, she abhorred the sudden sensation of cold water on her body. She relied on her body to win the race; her psyche provided the drive and determination. It was as simple as that.

Carrie felt an instant release of tension as her body recognized a familiar habitat --- water. She loved the buoyant feeling and the ease of movement associated with her aqueous friend. The water felt alive and rejuvenated her senses. She kicked and pulled her way through the sparkling blue liquid like a newborn emerging into a another world.

Time stood still for a few seconds while all movement became slow motion. Carrie felt her body glide over the water like a hydrofoil. Everything moved according to its own rhythm: people followed biorhythms, planets twirled on their axes at predictable rates, and light bounced in a pattern prescribed by its color. The universe was like a ballet of diversified participants, all dancing to their own beat, while remaining consistent with the universal pattern. Somehow for the present she managed to match her form to the relative rhythm of the liquid. The water and Carrie assumed the same wavelength as her body skimmed the surface without ever seeming to touch the pool beneath her.

She opened her eyes and surveyed the unbroken blue ahead of her. Although she was in the lead, her position in the race no longer mattered. As spellbound as Icarus by the idea of flight, she was totally absorbed by the sensation of swimming. Sometime within the same minute, she fell back down to earth. Carrie became conscious of the cheering spectators and her arms began to feel heavy.

"Spirit is willing but the flesh is weak," Carrie mused as she adjusted her stroke to compensate for her tiring muscles. She took a deep breath, closed her eyes, and thrust her head into the water.

Her arms rapidly circled over the water two more times. Squinting through the splashes, she estimated the remaining distance before the finish. She was almost there.

More strokes. More kicks. Only three more strokes until the end of the pool!

Holding her breath she fought her way through the waves. Time to give it all... No more time for joyriding... Her arms gave one final stretch for the wall. The race was over.

She felt exhausted. She floated on her back and allowed the water to support her body. Then Carrie returned to the end of the pool and lifted her weary body out of the water. It was time to face the clock and the reality of her efforts. The moment of reckoning had arrived. Had she been as fast as she had imagined? Had she actually beat the clock?

Chapter One

"Looking good!" yelled Coach Gramm who was standing among the crowds surrounding the pool. His words meant a lot to her. He was a firm but easygoing coach, never placing any undue pressure on a young swimmer to compete. He was one of the few coaches she knew who fostered a true enjoyment of the sport in his swimmers. Some coaches resorted to intimidation and peer pressure to squeeze faster times out of their swimmers, but Coach Gramm challenged his swimmers while they were relaxed and not even thinking about racing. This enabled swimmers to concentrate on their own ability to achieve success, rather than rely on external sources for motivation.

Carrie smiled back at Coach Gramm before glancing at the times posted behind the starting blocks. She was happy with her time! It was her fastest ever! Now she was qualified to compete in the state championships!

Her feelings concerning the event corresponded well with her time. Much had occurred within a minute and a half. Recalling the peace that she had enjoyed while gliding over the water, Carrie savored the experience of a clear day vision. It was as if the water and her were one, possessing the same body, mind, and spirit. A fast time could always be faster and won by someone else, but the memory of the event was hers to keep. That clear day underneath the scorching sun in Wichita Falls, Texas increased in significance and importance later in her life, giving her a sense of belonging in the universe. The impression gleaned from this hot summer's day would help her remember who she was and what she wanted out of life during the dark storms of confusion and self doubt.

Chapter Two

Bless the Beasts and the Children
For in this world they have no voice
They have no choice...

"Bless the Beasts and the Children"
Barry Vorzon and Perry Botkin, Jr.

Long before the experience during the swim meet, the Nightmare haunted Carrie. As far back as she could see, she had always lived with it. This Nightmare had many forms and it appeared at significant turning points throughout her life. The forms mirrored the way Carrie's world had changed, reminding her of a link to something dark and ominous in her past. Sometimes she knew this mirror as oblivion, sometimes as darkness, and sometimes as a light so white and bright that it hurt her eyes to see. Whenever this Nightmare occurred, all of Carrie's senses were annihilated, obliterating her perception of the present and coldly leaving her for the world of the dead.

In spite of its threat, this Nightmare made Carrie feel very sane because the Nightmare recognized her real feelings about the present. The Nightmare exposed her deepest thoughts and revealed what was most significant in her life. Nobody seemed to understand Carrie like this Nightmare; it told her the things that she should know about herself and the world. She never understood why it terrorized her. She never could see any motive behind the Nightmare. It was just there. She could not ignore it. She always resented the paralyzing effect on her senses; all Carrie could do was lie down and watch the Nightmare play out like some sort of judgment imposed on her. It was difficult to explain to other people; nobody seemed to have the capacity to realize its meaning. Carrie only knew that she was not the cause.

One of the most vivid manifestations of the Nightmare occurred when Carrie was seven years old. During this time period in her life, Carrie lived in a brown stucco house located about a half-mile away from the Los Angeles International Airport. In this house Carrie shared a bedroom with Ellen, her younger sister by one and one-half years. A braided oval rug in the middle of the wooden floor separated their beds in opposite corners of the room, and the walls were painted in turquoise. Despite being located next to the closet door, Carrie liked being as far away from Ellen as possible. Ellen always tore the heads off the dolls she played with and left their twisted naked bodies lying on the floor in front of her bed. She made the community of dolls look as if godzilla had visited them.

One day Carrie had arrived home from school and found her doll lying face down among the stark bodies. Wincing at the sight, she was sorry she had not been wise enough to hide the doll from Ellen's grasp. Only two others remained untouched by Ellen, Carrie's male doll and the life-like baby doll sitting on the dresser between the window and Ellen's bed. At least Carrie's male doll was safe in his case underneath her bed.

After checking underneath her bed for the sight of his doll case, Carrie walked over to where the baby doll sat and examined it. It was in the section of the room that Carrie had let Ellen take over, but its position on the dresser was too high for Ellen's reach. This doll looked like a real live baby; Ellen didn't like it very much and never tried to reach it. Carrie searched the doll's face for any sign of expression over the hideous play which the doll had witnessed while Carrie was at school. The doll seemed so life-like to Carrie that she still could not decide whether this baby was really a boy or a girl. She couldn't tell; it was just a baby. Carrie lightly ran her fingers across the doll's face and tried to close the doll's eyes. The painted eyes would not close. Then she touched the doll's forearm, letting her fingers trace down the skin and fall into the doll's little hands. The doll felt hard and cold to Carrie. She always cared for the doll as best she could without being obvious. If she showed that she liked it, then Ellen might cry for it and that would be the end of her nice doll.

After Carrie straightened the doll's light blue dress, she went over to the closet near her bed. Carrie opened the door and sat down in the darkness. Clothes hung all around her and the small closet barely had enough room for her. She had to move aside a few boxes to make herself comfortable. Ellen had taken over most of the bedroom for her activities and things, while Carrie had retreated to the closet for a safe place. Carrie knew that Ellen would not follow her there because Ellen was afraid of the dark.

Gazing at the arrangement in the closet, a wonderful idea sparked her imagination. She would become an astronaut and make the closet her spaceship. For the next few days Carrie concerned herself with the project of converting the closet into a space capsule. She created an instrument panel with a chalkboard and colored chalk. The chalkboard served as the viewing screen, while Carrie drew in her destinations to all the various planets as she traveled through the galaxies. She simulated space travel by closing the closet door and turning on a flashlight which illumined the instrument panel. Ellen became fascinated with Carrie's spaceship, forgetting the fear of the dark as she claimed her share of the closet. In order to avoid an argument, Carrie reluctantly let her younger sister into the spaceship and made Ellen promise not to report her to her mother. Ellen began cooperating with Carrie under the circumstances.

However, it was the Nightmare that interrupted Carrie's spaceship travels rather than Ellen's endeavors. The first Nightmare came after the family's visit to their friend's house. Carrie and her friends had enjoyed a small hike in the foothills surrounding the city. The hiking group consisted of Carrie and her friend named Kerry, Kerry's father, Kerry's little brother, Ellen, and Carrie's father. Sometime during the excursion, Kerry and her father came across the body of a dead animal and motioned for the rest of the group to stop.

Never before in her life had Carrie seen anything dead.

Underneath a young tree laid the deteriorating carcass of a small lamb. Wisps of soft, wooly white hung on the quiet bones like cotton. Curiously Carrie studied the animal skeleton in the yellowed blades of grass, and saw nothing frightening about the appearance of death. Tucked quietly in the oak grove away from the grazing flock, the remains blended with the natural elements in peace and she never would have seen it without the aid of the other people on the hike.

"Probably died because it strayed from the pack," Carrie's father remarked as he looked towards her.

Evading his glance, she shrugged and stepped back and closed herself within the ranks of the rest of the hiking group.

"Yes, it probably was lost and a wolf or some other wild animal killed it," the other father said, gazing sorrowfully at the dead lamb. He knelt on one knee as if to pay his last respects. A painful thought flickered across his countenance and he immediately rose. Fearing the separation associated with death, he discreetly pulled his children safely towards him with his eyes.

"Let's head back now. It's getting dark," he announced with his hands protectively on his children's shoulders.

Together they hiked in an invisible subgroup with Carrie's father being the only exclusion. Kerry's father smiled at her as Carrie followed alongside his family. He seemed to understand her choice. Feeling temporary relief from her father's words, Carrie happily noticed Ellen following close behind her.

The hikers returned to the familiar ground of suburbia just before the sun sank behind the hills. The lights of the neighborhood twinkled cheerfully in the twilight and welcomed them to civilization. Gazing back at the distant hillside one last moment after the trek was over, Carrie discovered that there was something which still concerned her. It wasn't the experience of finding the dead lamb that bothered her; death danced to the natural rhythm of life and music of the hills. It was her father's remarks which concerned Carrie. She really didn't understand his malice towards her. Separating her father's actions from the rest of the hike, Carrie fondly remembered her time on the hillside.

Two days after the visit to Kerry's house, she began having a nightmare connecting the dead lamb, a human skeleton, and her closet. The closet contained a hidden passage connecting a skeleton to the site where the dead lamb had been found, and this skeleton threatened to wrap Carrie in its bony embrace. Tonight someone had left the closet door open before turning out the bedroom lights. Carrie laid in bed as the skeleton came to see her. Then skeleton seized her body with its hard cold penetrating grip until Carrie was filled with so much pain that she could feel no more.

She tried to escape, but she could not move. She hated the touch!—the fleshless contact which violated every inch of her body. Through the stare of its hollow black eyes the skeleton laughed as she cried and tried to escape.

Closing her eyes, Carrie attempted making the skeleton go away in her mind. She wanted to sleep, but it would not leave her in peace. There was nothing she could do to stop it; she could still feel the blackness creeping its way out of the closet towards her. Her mother would reprimand her if she was caught out of bed. Silent tears rolled down her face as she succumbed to the terror.

A sharp blow from out of nowhere struck her across the forehead, pinning her body to the bed. The blow caused her to regain her senses. Carrie opened her eyes and peered at the darkness left in the room. Sinking back into their cavity underneath the strain of another sleepless night, her eyes weighted her head like a couple of stones. She didn't want to see anymore. In the vague dark mirror of her room Carrie saw that she had begun to resemble the hollowed out skeleton. Immediately, the skeleton departed from her bed, leaving her to take its place amongst the greenish-blue walls of her room.

Boom! Crunch! The mildewed wall next to her bed seem to crash down on her, breaking her spirit, destroying everything nice about her until the deathly smell of the collapse permeated her life's breath. The crash left nothing untouched; nothing sacred remained standing.

She stayed in bed and silently waited for the first rays of sunlight to appear around the shaded window. Still shivering from the cold of the dark night, Carrie remained frozen in the devastation. Although she had no power over her motionless body, she could see. She let her eyes move for her and take in the room's former appearance. Carrie saw that she did not like the room. She felt no attachment for her world; there was nothing in it that moved her or could bring her back from the world of the sleepless dead.

More light entered the room as the wee hours in the morning steadily passed. Carrie's world awoke from the darkness, and she tried wiggling her toes underneath the blankets. Yes, she could still feel life there. She was glad that her mother never noticed that she had quit wearing socks to bed. Her mother always wanted her to cover them, though Carrie enjoyed experiencing the world through her feet.

Bounce! Bounce! Squeak! Squeak! Now she could hear her baby sister Samantha moving around in her crib in the room next door. Soon Carrie's mother would turn on the light in their bedroom and tell them to get ready for school.

When Carrie's mother had flipped on the light in the bedroom, Carrie hopped out of bed and retrieved her school uniform from the closet. Using the power of daylight to her own advantage, she carefully examined the contents of her closet and looked for the skeleton's secret passageway. She realized that she was playing a game called hide-and-go seek with the Nightmare.

Chapter Three

Yesterday, all my troubles seemed so far away
Now it looks as though they're here to stay
Oh believe in yesterday.
Suddenly, I'm not half the man I used to be,
There's a shadow hanging over me
Oh yesterday came suddenly.
Why she had to go I don't know, she wouldn't say.
I said something wrong, now I long for yesterday.
Yesterday, love was such an easy game to play,
Now I need a place to hide away,
Oh believe in yesterday...

"Yesterday"
John Lennon and Paul McCartney

For the next few weeks Carrie made sure that the closet door was closed before the lights were turned out at night. In spite of these precautions, there came one night when Carrie forgot to check. This time somebody had left the closet door opened six inches instead of three. As a result, the skeleton arrived at her bed even faster than the previous night. Carrie wanted to quickly close the opening, but was afraid of being caught by her mother for getting out of bed.

As soon as the skeleton reached her, Carrie felt it inflict blow upon blow. In her dream, Carrie saw her mother's thick wooden brush, the stick that was used for punishment. Carrie wished that the stick would break so that her mother would be forced to discard it. She hated being hit on the head. It was the feeling of her mother trying to hurt her that bothered her most of all. Years ago, about the age of four or five, she remembered staying up all night crying over her mother, who would punish her and put her to bed for reasons that she never understood. She yearned to talk to her mother and hoped that she would return to reassure her that everything was alright again, but her mother never came. Carrie's hot tears turned to soft whimpers in the night.

Almost a year later, Carrie found her words and confronted her mother during a verbal joust in the kitchen. "You don't love me," she finally told her mother. "I'm running away."

Her mother taunted her, "Good."

Carrie didn't like the way her mother toyed with her emotions, so she started packing a paper sack with peanut butter ritz cracker sandwiches. Ellen saw her and wanted to come along. After Ellen had filled her paper bag too, Carrie and her sister climbed the five foot white picket fence to unleash the latch on the gate. The gate swung open and the two little girls walked out. The neighbors on the corner asked the girls where they were going. They replied that they were running away with peanut butter cracker sandwiches.

Rounding the corner up the hill, darkness began to settle on the subdivision. Two houses down the street, Carrie spied her mother and father walking towards them with their family dog Fluffy. She felt a little disappointed. Nobody said much except that it was time to go home. No apologies made. No resolution of the disagreement.

Now she fell prey to the black hollowness inside the skeleton's eyes, where she died in their depths. The feeling broke Carrie, shattering her heart. When the skeleton disappeared, Carrie wept for her mother. In her pain she wanted to find her mother, but Carrie never left her bed out of respect and obedience.

"I'm seven years old," she quietly told herself one day. She sensed that something had change. Scar tissue had formed over the wound in her heart. Rapidly entering the cortical stage of development, Carrie could now confront her peers and world with cool intellect. The world of imagination and make-believe no longer entertained her thoughts these days. She felt ready to move beyond it.

Carrie bravely looked at the opened closet again. She recalled the beautiful blue fairy from the story Pinochio. The kind blue fairy told the wooden boy that she could help grant his wish to become a real boy. Somewhere in her depths Carrie felt the compassion of the blue fairy stirring inside her. Reaching for her twirling baton below her bed, she managed to pick it up without ever stepping on the floor. Although the baton was a shiny blue, the blackness of the night muted its brilliant color. Carrie hid it under her blankets. Now she had her own stick, a magic wand, and unlike anything else in her room she was attached to it. Carrie waited a few seconds before making her move with the wand. While listening cautiously to her mother's movements inside the house, Carrie slowly retrieved the baton from the blankets. Her mother would only be able to hear her from the living room. Luckily, from the sound of her mother's footsteps in the house, Carrie could tell that her mother was in the kitchen now and well out of hearing distance for Carrie's bedroom. Without making any sounds she extended the length of the baton to the closet and pushed the door shut.

Carrie sighed with relief. "Won't get out this night."

Armed with her shiny blue baton, Carrie fought her paralyzing fear. She reasoned that she might be able to change her circumstances with some pretending and a wave of magic from her wand. If she acted less like a puppet child and more like a real person, then her predicament might change. She rolled out of bed and ventured cautiously from her bedroom. She found her mother sitting in the nearby living room. Carrie's father was away for the evening. Her mother had become entranced by the late night movie on T.V.. She scarcely acknowledged Carrie's presence when she wandered into the room.

"Can't sleep," Carrie murmured, quickly mimicking her mother's stare at the television screen.

"It's a good movie," her mother replied. She seemed to appreciate Carrie's company and made no motion for her return to the bedroom. Relieved to be out of her room for at least part of one night, Carrie felt very fortunate in the bright and cozy living room. She had broken the puppet strings and could begin to think and act for herself.

"Do you like skeletons?" Carrie cautiously asked at the commercial break. She hoped that her mother might be able to help her get rid of the skeleton in the closet.

"No," her mother responded absentmindedly. She could tell that her mother was deeply absorbed in her own thoughts about something else. Though her mother wasn't willing to offer any advice on the matter, at least she wasn't becoming angry.

"I don't either," Carrie decided and dropped the subject. She didn't want to open the door on anything that might upset her mother. She shuddered at the thought of the skeleton leaving the closet and haunting the place where she slept. She didn't want to go back to the cold, lonely room. Although she wasn't interested in the movie, Carrie focused all her attention on the T.V. program and watched the entire show.

"Time for bed," the mother announced, turning off the set when the show ended.

Carrie rose slowly from her place on the carpet. She had broken the pattern. Her experience with the other father and the dead lamb had moved her. She found that the reality of death haunted her relationship with her parents. Now she could imagine a world where parents didn't allow skeletons to grow in their kids closets. She glimpsed a place where relationships were more than just structure; parents protected their children out of concern rather than duty. The Nightmare had lost some of its potency and she didn't feel so scared anymore. The wound inside her heart could heal. She was growing up fast, maybe too fast, but for the moment it didn't matter.

The next morning Carrie rose from her bed, retrieved her clothes from the closet, and ran to the door between the living room and her sister's bedroom. Before dressing in her baby sister's room Carrie always peered inside to make sure Samantha wasn't asleep. Sure enough, her one and a half year old sister was already jumping in her crib. She smiled at Carrie when she spied her older sister through the slight opening in the door.

"Jeepers! Creepers! Where did you get them peepers!" Carrie sang as she burst into the room. She ran to Samantha, rubbing noses with her until both blue eyes were level with the other sister's, and dramatically ended her song: "... where did you get those EYES!"

Samantha laughed and rubbed her tiny hands together. Carrie loved seeing her sister cheerful and ready for action in the morning. She could dress by the heater in the small cheery bedroom as opposed to the coldness of her own adjoining room. Taking off her flannel nightgown in the warmest corner of the room, Carrie continued to hold her sister's attention, "Good morning, Samuel Peeper! How's the peeper doing today? What's Sammy up to?"

Sammy was her mother's nickname for Samantha. Carrie readily adopted the name for her own term of affection. The idea of calling Samantha by a boy's name appealed to Carrie because it made Samantha seem so much more alive. Having a lithe form, long curly blond hair, and blue eyes, Samantha strongly resembled her two older sisters. As the oldest of the three girls, Carrie understood the dangers of being mistaken for a live doll. Although Carrie never really felt pretty, she feared being turned into a doll. She didn't want to be fussed over, made to sit still, and look pretty. She would rather run around and play.

As Carrie finished dressing, she resumed her song for Samantha,"... jeepers, creepers, where d'ja get 'em peepers!..."

Meanwhile, Samantha leaned on the crib rail and bounced in time to the music, becoming more animated when Carrie started singing and dancing with her yellow chick. Carrie flew the little bird across the wooden bars of the crib until the toy was well within Samantha's eager grasps.

"This little chick with the soft yellow fur reminds me of Samantha most of all. You're the chick with the yellow fuzz on top," Carrie smiled at Samantha. All her sisters had blond hair and blue eyes like their father.

Samantha caught the tiny chick in her arms and drew the stuffed toy towards her as gracefully as her awkward limbs would fly around the object. Once she had encircled the soft toy, she cooed and giggled at it.

"It goes "peep, peep,"" Carrie corrected her. "All little chicks go "peep, peep" at the world when they break through their eggs."

Thump! Samantha threw her chick on the floor below her crib. Then she leaned far over the edge to inspect the results. She leaned so far towards the ground that Carrie became alarmed that she might tumble out after the bird.

"What?! You want someone to pick up your chick for you?! OK, Sammy Peeper, I'll show you how to pick up chicks!" Carrie announced. Then she quickly bent over the chick, so that Samantha would stay in her crib. Curious, Samantha watched her closely. When Carrie handed her the bird, she tossed it across the room again. Noticing how Samantha's eyes followed the toy after it had landed, Carrie felt sorry for her sister confined in the crib. Carrie picked up the bird again for her.

"You're only peepin' at the world," Carrie observed. Then she paraded the chick in front of Samantha's reach. The ruse worked. The dancing motion of the small yellow bird captivated the infant's attention. Samantha tightly grasped the bird by its yellow fur and brought it to her opened mouth. Slobbering over the stuffed toy, she sat down inside the crib. Carrie happily watched how much the little chick absorbed Samantha's attention. Satisfied that she wouldn't have to play "pick up the chick" again, Carrie left the room to finish getting ready for school.

Chapter Four

...Sunny, thank you for the truth you've let me see...

"Sunny"
Bobby Hebb

Although the Nightmare persisted well into Carrie's adult years, there were other memories of her youth that guided her through life. These cherished gems of unique experiences shined through life's storms and gently reminded her to trust whatever seemed to come her way. She used these precious moments to restore her clarity and perspective. Usually there was something in her own nature that helped her identify these gems, because their discovery depended on her own prospecting.

Carrie found one such gem at the very young age of five. He was a playmate named Kenny who lived across the street. Being one year older than Carrie, Kenny seemed much more worldly. He often brought a welcomed sophistication to their child's play.

"Wanna try a puff?" he asked her one day.

Admiring Kenny's latest prop, Carrie watched him elegantly smoke a cigarette on the end of a long holder. "No thank you," she decided. Carrie knew her parents would disapprove and she was not willing to test her mother's eyesight from the living room window.

Kenny nodded his understanding and continued to enjoy his puffing alone. They always played very well together, so well that his mother sincerely believed that they would marry each other when they became older. Sometimes Kenny would walk with her to school and show her where he had his first grade class. When the other boys called her "Kenny's girlfriend", Kenny only smiled and firmed his grip on their interlocking hands.

As one of the their favorite games was "Batman and Robin", Kenny and Carrie unconsciously stayed in these characters throughout their relationship.

Even when playing doctors, they still kept their hidden identity as Batman and Robin. Kenny played the role of Batman, whereas Carrie played his partner Robin. Since she was a girl, they created a different Robin; their Robin was a woman just as wise and capable as Batman. She became Batman's companion rather than the ward of a wealthy guardian. Though Kenny and Carrie played many other games such as cowboys and indians, pirates, army, and doctors, their favorite game was "Batman and Robin". Kenny possessed a clever imagination and artistic sense that flourished in his repertoire of costumes and props. They both relished making their play as realistic as possible. Wearing his black Batman cape, Kenny often cruised in Carrie's driveway with the announcement: "Let's go, Robin!" Quickly she'd hop on his bike and they would zip down the sidewalk in caped crusader fashion.

One day during a game of army doctors, Kenny proposed the idea of listening to Carrie's breathing with his stethoscope. He wanted to be just like a doctor, and one of the most important activities of being a doctor involved listening to a person's breathing. Carrie eagerly nodded her head. Kenny's idea of being a doctor sounded like a lot of fun. As soon as she had given her consent, he asked, "Okay if I undo the buttons that are on the back of your shirt?"

"OK," she told him.

"I'll be careful," Kenny assured her.

They were as quiet as church mice. Carrie felt Kenny's gentle fingers unbutton the top button. "Breathe deeply," he whispered softly. His fingers felt warm on the back of her neck. She took her deepest breath and slowly released it.

"Again," he quietly demanded while listening through his stethoscope. Because he was so close to her, she could hear Kenny's breathing as well as her own. Determined to be a real doctor, he directed his curiosity in a very professional manner. Releasing only the top three of her buttons on the back of her blouse, his examination remained gentle and deliberate. Carrie felt touched by the amount of care and concern Kenny demonstrated, treating her as if she was a prized jewel.

Kenny took off his shirt when Carrie's turn came to be doctor. He looked very handsome and she earnestly wanted to treat him as wonderfully as he had cared for her. She tried to be as delicate in her touch as possible while still exhibiting the same degree of skill as he had done. Noticing his smooth tan body go limp with the motion of her hands, Carrie observed the effect she desired. She felt very pleased and proud that he enjoyed her efforts.

As if by magic, her perception of her environment changed at that moment. Looking across the backyard, Carrie watched the crystal dew drops dance underneath the sun's warmth on the green grass. The skin on her forearms tingled with the air's fresh spirit as she heard the birds sing their morning songs like a dozen tiny bells echoing through the atmosphere. Immediately she became conscious of another part of her existence, of life and death, the freedom and tranquility associated with nature. The children discovered that they were not alone; they had heard the breath of life.

Carrie stopped as they both listened to the music in the air surrounding them. Resuming their play of army doctors, they seemed intent on preserving life in a war that they could only feel but not see. It was the mid-sixties and there had been adult whispers of revolutions going on in the world. They had found something very real in their game of make-believe. When the time came for Kenny to return to his home across the street, they smiled as two good friends and waved their goodbyes. Both had been deeply touched by the experience and left with the sensation of having peered across the threshold at some wonderful secret concerning man and woman. They never played doctors again. The play seemed too trivial for what they had felt. Like Batman and Robin, they never ventured into any encounter where they weren't prepared.

Chapter Five

It comes so fast...
All I know is that I love you

"All I Know"
Art Garfunkel

After Carrie's eight birthday, the family moved to a small town in Texas. The scenery changed from hippies, peace signs, psychedelic murals along the beach to craven cowboys, Jesus Saves signs, and herds of slow grazing cattle. In Los Angeles, Carrie had spent entire recesses with her friends pretending that they were horses and would run to avoid being captured and tamed. The rugged Southwest terrain suited her taste for the wild as well as her adventurous spirit. The boys called her "speedy" because she could run faster than any of them. Carrie relished being a maverick on the plains and excelled in her academic pursuits as well. The years passed quickly and soon she entered high school.

During the early autumn of her sophomore year in high school, Carrie's class decided to construct a class float for the homecoming parade. The high school totaled approximately **2800** students and was divided into three rival classes; Sophomores, Juniors, and Seniors. Of the three, the Sophomore class was the largest and the most disorganized, a condition which made class projects impossible. Their youth and lack of experience earned them campus ridicule, which undermined their class spirit even further. As a result, Carrie's class, developed within itself a cocky sense of pride in order to get the job done.

"Hey, Mike we need some more tissue paper over here!" yelled Shelly, the leader of the section where Carrie worked on the class float.

"Come-ing!" hollered Mike as he hurried off to retrieve more sheets of paper. "That section looks re-al good," he told a busy group of assembly line workers.

"Gosh, it sure is nice of Margaret's parents to donate their driveway for this Sophomore class float," observed Lisa as she stopped her task for a moment and surveyed the rest of the operation.

"Yes, they won't be able to use it for the next month. The Sophomore float for Edison High School is being constructed next door to my house. They have students working in their backyard twenty-fours a day," Carrie commented.

"What! You live in Edison territory!" Shelly exclaimed.

"Only a block away from the school," Carrie acknowledged. Edison High School was River Heights High School's fierce rival. "I wanted to swim at River Heights so I transferred school districts. Edison doesn't have a swim team," she explained. Many of Carrie's friends on the team were transfer students also and she had known them since she was ten years old. Fortunately, most of the neighbors in her block respected her desire to excel in swimming and overlooked the rivalry. Carrie had attended the local school the previous year and had earned their friendship.

Mike arrived with more paper to fill in the holes of the chicken wire mesh. The float would consist of a series of wire sections which fitted a design. Each hole in the wire section had to be filled with colored paper according to the arrangement of color in the overall pattern.

"We're gonna be one of the first Sophomore classes to win the float competition," promised Mike. "I heard that the Juniors' float is three-quarters finished and looks pretty crummy."

"Well, things are moving pretty slow here," sighed Lisa.

"Maybe we should start working twenty-four hours like Edison's Sophomore class," suggested Shelly.

"We should have someone guard it too. Some of Edison's Seniors are threatening to burn the Junior's float. A few Juniors from our school stole their spirit stick. Somehow they managed to lift it from the school office and walk off campus with it," Mark said with a hint of worry in his voice. Although a spirit stick was simply a baton painted with the school's colors, it symbolized the high school's honor. The baton was a coveted possession and was given to the class which demonstrated the most spirit at the weekly pep rallies.

"Ya, we can't expect Margaret and her family to stay at home all the time," Carrie added.

"We could have a major gang war on our hands," Lisa frowned. As class president, one of Lisa's duties consisted of representing the Sophomores as a group of civilized students.

"Let me know what is decided," Carrie told Shelly. "My father is supposed to pick me up at eight o'clock and I must go now... See ya tomorrow!" Carrie waved at the group. Then she walked down the long driveway to the street's curb and waited.

Her father never came. It was not unusual for Carrie's parents to be an hour or two late. Since her mother would not return home until after ten, she decided not to risk abandoning her post. Her father might be in a bad mood when he arrived and Carrie wanted to be able to leave the gathering as quickly as possible if this proved to be the case. Whenever her father arrived late, he was usually very irritable. So Carrie was cautious in her dealings with him. She was secretly afraid of him and didn't always know how to handle such situations in public.

About fifteen minutes after everyone had left the gathering, Carrie started the three mile walk towards home. It wasn't a safe walk even in the daytime, but she really didn't want to call home. For whatever reasons, she knew that her mother would be upset once she learned that Carrie's father had not arrived.

"Get in!" Her mother shouted as she drove up beside Carrie and opened the passenger door. Carrie had only made it halfway up the block before her mother's arrival. "Why didn't you call?" her mother angrily continued.

"Dad agreed to pick me up," she reminded her. Her mother knew of Carrie's arrangements, having set them up herself.

Her mother drove a block down the street and stopped at a four way stop sign. Suddenly her father's car emerged from the street to their right. He turned and stopped alongside her mother's car. Opening his car door as if to rescue her from her mother, he calmly said, "Get in, Carrie."

Carrie didn't move. She didn't trust her father either, and his words and actions seemed strangely inappropriate considering the circumstances. Carrie's mother quieted. As soon as his attention focused on his wife, Carrie quickly locked her door so that he would not be able to pull her from the car if he became angry.

"I'm picking her up," her mother told him. Her mother and father argued feebly for a few minutes, while the time passed like hours for Carrie. Then her mother drove away and her father followed a few blocks behind them.

"He's been out this whole time. You should have called me. He has probably been drinking," her mother yelled at Carrie as she accelerated down the familiar streets towards home. "There are too many things going on at home. See what happened tonight!"

After parking the car in the driveway, she continued talking while Carrie quietly walked through the front door. Carrie ignored her and quietly marched towards the room she shared with Samantha, She left Carrie in the darkness and hurried to her own room without anymore verbal assaults. Once Carrie heard the cold click of her mother's bedroom lock, she sighed with relief. She finally felt safe from her mother's harangue. Soon Carrie's father arrived and turned off all the lights in the house. He slept in the living room.

In the quiet black comfort of the night, Carrie cried. Like a swimmer caught in a fast moving river, she seemed helpless against the events which seem to direct her life, unable to defend herself even verbally with her mother. There was something about her parents which trapped her and killed her inside. She didn't know how to explain herself; it was hopeless to try. Carrie's mother would ridicule her if she ever admitted being scared of her father.

Her parents reminded her of the Nightmare. Tonight, Carrie knew the Nightmare in a different form. Staring at her from the darkness of her confusion, she saw the face of death accusing her. She wanted to flee from its coldness, but she could see no other options before her.

Carrie felt more tears roll down her cheek. Whatever it was that trapped her also had the power to kill her. Realizing that her emotions concerning the Nightmare were lethal, she decided to cut them off before she gave into them. Was the Nightmare really her fault? Carrie would die if she was to blame. Why bother trying to survive with the Nightmare?

Somewhere in the back of Carrie's subconscious stirred the memory of a teenage boy who once lived at the far end of her block. He had included Carrie in one of the neighborhood baseball games at a crucial moment during her early teen years. Although Carrie was about four years younger than the rest of the players, she loved playing ball and welcomed any opportunity to play. Unfortunately, she had difficulty being accepted by other kids on the block, because she attended a different school at the time and was perpetually considered the new kid on the block.

While the older kids were busy organizing the teams, Carrie observed the chaos from the curb. She didn't want to commit to their aggressive antics. Besides being rather reserved, Carrie disagreed with about seventy-five percent of the capers that most of the older kids pulled, and she wanted to play ball without any getting involved in their monkey business.

Everyone waited for a fellow by the name of Brian to join the group as if they couldn't play without him. Evidently Brian possessed some special quality that captivated the attention and respect of even the roughest bullies.

"Where's Brian?" someone asked.

"Go get Brian!" another commanded.

"Will Brian play?" they questioned.

Brian piqued Carrie's curiosity. What did people see in him? She studied Brian as he exited the house at her right. He casually strolled across the grassy front lawn in his bare feet and greeted his friends waiting on the street. He appeared to be carrying a slight weight on his shoulders and his clothes hung on his delicate athletic form. When he saw the gang of players eager for coed baseball, his face immediately brightened. It was his desire to be with people rather than his enthusiasm for the sport that had lured him away from his bedroom sanctuary. His eyes surveyed the appearance of every individual in the group as if he held a personal interest in their wellbeing. No one seem to be aware of his gaze. Content with having won him as their prize, the teams ignored his presence and continued their frolic. Nonetheless, Brian held silent leadership status in the group, and no definite decisions were made without his consultation.

Maintaining a slight distance from the rest, Carrie stood almost directly to his right and pondered the social game. When he turned towards her, Carrie met his gaze. He smiled at the her and instinctively puffed out his chest proudly. Swept by his gesture, she returned his smile and instantly fought the compulsion to turn her head away. Carrie preferred meeting males on equal ground, no matter how cute they seemed. Of all the boys that she had ever played baseball with, Brian had been the first to acknowledge her feminine attributes rather than her baseball skills. Her heart immediately soared to her head. She flew over to the team that selected her as if Brian, himself, had drawn her closer under his wing.

After the baseball game, Brian and Carrie went their different directions. The five year age difference discouraged a relationship. Carrie contented herself with being an admirer. The following year Brian went away to study at a university four hours from his home. Sometime during the next spring Brian fell to his death from the heights of the university stadium. The local newspapers headlined the controversy surrounding his death.

Never bothering to read the newspaper articles herself, Carrie heard enough about the story from her parent's conversations. Although the medical examiner ruled his death a suicide, some of his family and close friends vehemently protested and claimed that the young man was victimized by the physicians who had been treating him for depression. For several years, Brian had undergone drug therapy without any positive results. Those who knew him insisted that the prescribed drugs destroyed his perception of reality and emotional balance, causing him to fall unintentionally during a confused state.

Since many of the family's relatives lived by the college where the young man had died, the funeral was held in the same city. A memorial service was given at the parish church a few days after the funeral. Since the young man's parents were nonpracticing parishioners, the priest seized the opportunity to bring the family back into the fold. He counseled the parents during their grief, blaming Brian for his own tragedy and relieving the parent's guilt.

Carrie attended the memorial service to pay her respects. Only one other person besides herself and Brian's younger sister represented the kids from that day of the baseball game. Relieved that the casket ceremony had been held elsewhere, Carrie intended to remember Brian for the spirit she had known. Before the end of Mass, his younger sister approached the lectern and expressed the same intention.

"I want to remember Brian as I knew him. He always enjoyed playing his records in his room. There is one song that he loved to play all the time, it best describes the Brian that I knew." Then she left the podium before her tears choked her. Kneeling over the phonograph with a microphone attachment, she placed the needle on the revolving record.

The song "All I Know" by Art Garfunkel, embraced the entire congregation. Serving as Brian's self-defense for his own murder, the words and melody embodied Brian's spirit, the same spirit which sang with Art Garfunkel and pierced the hearts of those who listened:

Chapter Five

It comes too fast...
So fast that...
All I know is that I love you...

Looking around the congregation, Carrie noticed that many people were quietly rocking themselves with their tears. Those who cried understood Brian and his passionate struggle to create love in a world of pain. Like a young Icarus, he had dared to escape the circumstances of his existence and had flown too high in his quest, a pattern often characteristic of the desperate. Through his death he stirred the sleeping Daedalus inside those who also flew on the wings of love, and they awoke mourning for their lost son.

Her mother's friend, Grace, who came with them to the service also wept when she heard the song. During the drive home she recalled how Brian had helped her locate her missing child when he worked as an usher at the local movie theater.

"He was different than the rest. He cared enough to go out of his way and help me find my son. He understood my concern as a mother." Then she looked down at the floor of the car, shaking her head at the recognition of another son. It was Brian who was missing now.

"There is something about our society that seems to kill those who are most beautiful and sensitive... the good die young," she continued shaking her head in frustration and grief. "Yes, he was too good," Carrie's mother added sadistically while smiling at the clouds in the sky.

* * *

The memory Brian struck Carrie like icy cold water thrown across her face. No wonder the Nightmare represented death for Carrie; she identified with Brian's struggle in her own family. People like her parents would have killed Brian just to get him to heaven sooner. With this revelation Carrie forgot her thoughts on suicide and suddenly remembered her low tolerance to pain, her queasy stomach, and the fact that she went into shock easily at the sight of blood. Her senses flooded with memories of all the good times from the past; there had been many people that she had known and loved. People like Grace lived in the world, as did others who were just as nice as the kids that she worked with on the Sophomore float. She had to make contact with the people who were unlike her parents; the ones who could feel for Brian and help him live. If only she could survive the despair of this night and see the dawn of a new day, then her spirit would rejuvenate with the sunrise.

With the intention of staying afloat in this crisis, Carrie inventoried the effects of her emotions on her body. She felt physically exhausted; in order to survive the next day, she required a good night's rest. Because the sinking portion of her feelings had to be left behind, a part of Carrie needed to die in the rebirthing process. These emotions were dragging her down and she needed to sever her ties from their weight or else perish in the depths. So she took three aspirin and committed an abbreviated version of hari-kari. Carrie knew that three aspirin would not kill her; nonetheless, she wanted to capitalize on the knockout effect. During the night, the portion of Carrie which had been formerly tied to the fate of her parents died.

The next morning, life resumed as usual without any reference to the stresses of the previous night. Carrie broke the silence at the breakfast table and confessed some of her feelings from the previous night to her mother. While Carrie cried, her mother told her that she'd surely go to hell if she ever considered acting on her feelings. Carrie's father stood at the kitchen counter ready for work, ignoring their conversation as he slowly sipped his orange juice while staring out the window. Carrie didn't feel any better after talking with her parents.

She never worked on the class float again, and the project died after the float mysteriously burned to the ground a few weeks later, the arson target of either high school rivals or competing upper classmates. Concentrating on other flotation devices for self preservation, she buried herself in her studies as her only hope for an independent future. Carrie minimized her reliance on her parents and obtained a driver's license on the same day she became the legal age of sixteen. Using the license to provide dependable transportation for herself and sisters, Carrie judiciously limited contacts with friends to school hours. These temporary changes helped Carrie cope with her home situation.

Chapter Six

People, people who need people
Are the luckiest people in the world
We're children needing other children
And yet, letting our grown up pride
Hide all the need inside...
Acting more like children, than children.

"People"
Lyrics by Bob Merrill

By the time she was a teenager, Carrie had painfully buried the Nightmare in her subconscious. The feelings associated with it were too deadly for further examination. However, bit by bit, she began the process of gathering information for herself that might help her unravel her tangled emotions. Often Carrie's best resources were the youngsters in her swimming classes.

"I don't wanna swim," cried the two year old boy. "There are sharks in the water," he concluded after scouting the chlorinated swimming pool.

Carrie studied the youth intently while thinking of a way to quiet his fears before he became hysterical. Once a two year old became fearful in situation, it became nearly impossible to deal with the main issue. Fear in a such a very young child had to be considered seriously, because it might permanently affect a child's attitude towards swimming. Two and three year old children generally took longer to recover from unpleasant experiences, much less make another attempt.

Carrie taught many children who had feared the water, and discovered that these fears usually affected self esteem and confidence in other areas of their lives. These students proved more challenging than others because an instructor confronted the psyche in addition to merely teaching a physical skill. As the psyche healed, the child became more assertive in the aqueous environment and swimming became fun.

From earlier lessons, Carrie had noticed how well the boy got along with other children his age. He possessed a certain type of charisma that enabled him to relate well with his peers. He did not appear to be a whiner, a brat, or a child with excessive anxiety. However, Carrie knew that he had something on his mind besides flutter kicking when he said on the first day in class, "My Daddy's up in heaven. My Mommy says that he's an angel."

Feeling that there wasn't too much that she could offer verbally, Carrie listened to the boy's mimicked explanation of an event that he was still trying to understand. After the lesson, a day care teacher confided to her that the boy's father had perished in a house fire earlier that spring.

Now she stood waist high in the water trying to find the key which might release the youth from his feelings of entrapment. Apparently, swimming was a life or death issue for the lad. Unlike most children, he was very much aware of the sink or swim phenomena, and felt more attuned to the dangers of being physically attacked while swimming. She personally knew many adults who shared the same fears as the boy, especially after viewing the movie "Jaws" this year. Carrie felt that the boy had a legitimate concern. As a swimming instructor, it was her intention to nurture the consummate swimmer—someone who could swim comfortably under rough water conditions. Chlorinated swimming pools were just simulated models of oceanic and freshwater environments in which the chances of attacks were not remote. In freshwater a swimmer had to be alert for water moccasins and other poisonous snakes.

Besides the basic life and death question, vulnerability or the sense of being a powerless victim in a life threatening situation seemed another important issue. Recognizing the tragic loss of his parental guardian to circumstances beyond his own control, the youth realized his own vulnerability and demonstrated his refusal to involve himself in a situation that taxed his physical and psychological capacity. As she heard the boy's adamant stand from the nearby steps, Carrie couldn't help but admire his courage. This fellow's wisdom compensated for his puny external frame; he was vulnerable, he knew it, and almost damn well proud of it. He knew what he was talking about.

She did too. She could recall her own experiences of vulnerability. Now Carrie was faced with the prospect of going away to college at the end of summer. Her parents had been separated for over a year now. Although the home scene had quieted, there was still a definite lack of support which caused her to be a little bit apprehensive about making such a major change in her life.

Well, she asked herself, what does one do when confronted by sharks in the water? Carrie recalled a wildlife special that she had seen on T.V. about scuba diving and shark attacks.

"They say that the best way to beat a shark is to poke 'em in the eyes and hit them on the nose. Just pretend you are like one of the three stooges, make a peace sign with two of your fingers, and then jab the shark in the eyes like this," Carrie said as she punched an imaginary shark in the water to convince herself as well as the boy.

The youth picked up this skill in self-defense very quickly. "Like this...!" he burst exuberantly while making peace signs at several imaginary underwater sharks.

"Yep, you've got the right idea," she answered, being careful not to encourage him too much. Her intention was to communicate several ideas to the boy: His fears were legitimate; he had the power within himself to cope with adversity and fear; and he had the right to protect himself and fight back.

The boy jumped excitedly off the steps, submerged his head underwater, and stabbed a few more pretend sharks. Having discovered a weapon he could safely rely on, he attempted a frontal glide complete with flutter kick. He kicked remarkably well for a two year old; the boy proved to be a natural swimmer.

Carrie sighed with relief. It would have been a shame to have the youth remain imprisoned with his hopeless fear of sharks. Who knows when he would have ever entered the water again? Carrie was so glad she had found the key concept for the boy and had seen the T.V. special. She also, had wondered what to do in case of a shark attack. The boy's enthusiastic response had showed her just how far a little imagination and self sufficiency could go. Any shark that ever attacked either of them would be pounded into dog meat.

Chapter Seven

You, who are on the road
Must have a code that you can live by...
And so become yourself
Because the past is just a goodbye

"Teach Your Children"
Crosby, Stills, and Nash

Carrie began her first year at a small liberal arts college, nestled deep in the wooded hills overlooking a nearby football stadium. The University remained cloistered from the affairs of the civilian world by location as well as ideology. A slogan spray painted on a campus water tower herald the University's philosophy: Home of the Fighting Phenomenologists. While walking on the wide brick mall that united the main buildings on campus, Carrie often felt as if she had entered another time zone. The founders of the University wished to create an old style European environment that contributed to the study of classical literature and art. Anachronistic in terms of architecture and core curriculum, the University ignored most literature following the eighteenth century with emphasis on Greek, Roman, and medieval studies.

Less than one month after the school year began, Carrie encountered a Sophomore cross country runner named Marty. Their relationship just sort of happened, or rather they mutually walked into each other's life as if there had been a space waiting for them. Carrie met Marty at one of the first dances held at the start of the school year. It was a warm summer night and she didn't know many people at the University. Carrie spent most of the evening chatting with her new college acquaintances outside on the veranda.

"Would you like to dance?" asked the tall, wiry man with the mane of strawberry blond hair. Given another fifty pounds and a helmet, this gentleman could have easily passed as a viking.

"Yes, I would," Carrie smiled. For over an hour Carrie had been amusing him with tales of her white water canoeing escapades, while Marty had entertained her with stories describing the antics of the University cross country team. She could not recall ever having spent so much time talking with one particular individual without stopping the conversation to throw a football or softball.

Marty and Carrie made their way through the crowd to the dance floor inside the glass building. Carrie could feel the strength of the drum beat vibrate inside her body and stole a quick look at Marty before giving way to the motion. Noticing how easily his eyes betrayed his emotions, she started to dance with his movements. There had been no ready defenses in their eager blueness, and for this reason Carrie suspected that he shared the same degree of inexperience as she did. Carrie glanced at his face again to be sure of meaning in his expression. This time he met her gaze, allowing his body to sway to the music's time. His eyes danced with happy disbelief.

"He likes you, Carrie," she thought to herself. Her heart moved with excitement. Everything about this guy seemed right for her. They danced together for the remainder of the evening, never leaving the dance floor until the band stopped playing and started to pick up their equipment. After the music stopped, Marty motioned Carrie to the veranda which offered a view of the sleeping city lights.

"So you and your roommate are going to drive cars for the rental agency tomorrow," he said with a big grin.

"Yeah, Richard is supposed to drop by in the morning," Carrie replied. She was eagerly looking forward to the new experience. The idea of driving for the car rental agency seemed fun to her. The company hired University students to transfer cars between the many rental agencies scattered across the state. Carrie had met Richard earlier at the party. In addition to working for the car rental agency, Richard ran cross country and was Marty's good friend.

"My roommate Ernie is the one who handles the arrangements between the campus and the car rental agency. You'll meet him in the afternoon. He's going to pick up everyone who drives for tomorrow. ...Ernie..., he's an alright guy," Marty reflected, cocking his curly head to one side with his thoughts. "Sometimes I think he studies too hard and drinks too much, but he's one of those premed types. They all study hard and party hard. Most everyone here is like that."

"I don't study near as much as the others," he wryly observed. "I have never been drunk to the point where I got sick or passed out. I have contro-o-ol," Marty smiled as he leaned backwards and shook his finger at Carrie.

Then he moved towards her and softly asked, "So tell me about you..."

"Well, I am premed..., but I believe that there is more to life than studying my brains out... I don't like beer and I have never been drunk to the point where I lost control or became sick," Carrie told him. "But I like to play hard," she teased, leaning forward to return his taunt.

Grinning from ear to ear, Marty reached for Carrie. Placing his arm around her waist he remarked, "You're just my type."

Suddenly realizing they were the only ones left on the veranda, the tone of their encounter grew serious.

"Mind if I walk you to your dorm. It's not so safe around here...there were a few incidents last year," he asked as he held Carrie's hand in concern. She felt his fingers tighten around her palm. They did not want to let go of her and told her more about Marty than anything else at the moment. She could feel his warmth. Carrie did not want to let go either.

"I would like that very much. I prefer to play it safe," she replied.

Marty firmly closed his hand around hers and led Carrie down the backstairs of the veranda. "Have you been by the Art department?" he asked. "There's a really nice walkway that goes through the woods. It goes directly to your dorm. People don't use it much, though. I guess they don't like walking through the woods. The University is full of the studious types that like to stick to the main paths."

Carrie looked beyond to the soft clay lights illuminating the path before her. Dark green vegetation cloaked the trail while moonlight glistened off the leaves, inviting Carrie to follow the swirling trail in front of her.

"Yes, I like the woods and I haven't seen the Art department yet," she told him in almost a whisper.

They stepped on the white gravel covering the walkway. The softly lit path beckoned them to another world, a place where time followed the course of nature. Carrie quietly walked with Marty to an alcove hidden amongst the shadows. Leaving her one step higher than where he stood, he took both of her hands inside his. Then he softly kissed her lips.

Closing her eyes, Carrie returned his kiss. She could feel his heart racing against her breast. His gentle breath swept through her body like the wind. Parting from their embrace, they stood back for a few seconds. Marty's face shone with joy. Carrie trembled slightly with excitement. She could feel his radiance. Then she and Marty closed their eyes once more, melting into the warmth of the summer night with a soft kiss.

In their fervent embrace she felt Marty's hands seek their way past her shoulders to the curvature of her body. Slowly he ran his trembling fingers over her skin, gently lifting the clothing away. Cupping her breasts into his hands, Marty tenderly caressed them with moist lips.

She sought him underneath the shimmering moonlight. In the whorl of emotion flooding her senses, Carrie's fingers unbuttoned Marty's shirt and freely explored his strong chest. Then their eyes met. She felt different as she began to see herself through his eyes. His sweet gaze swept over her breasts as he sensed the the proud trembling heart beneath. His eyelids dropped with the flutter of his own heartbeat, exposing the strength of his own vulnerability.

At two o'clock in the morning, Marty and Carrie said their good byes on the steps leading to the dormitory hallway. Since men were only permitted inside the building during certain hours on the weekend, they lingered for awhile on the stairs.

"What are you doing tomorrow night?" he asked as he kissed her.

They made arrangements to see each other the next evening before Carrie hurried to her dorm room. She expected to find her roommate already asleep in the room. However, a quick glance at her empty bed informed her that her roommate was still out for the evening.

Carrie awoke the next morning and dressed before Ernie picked her up to drive for the car rental agency. She had fallen asleep before her roommate's return last night. It was nice to know that they had similar lifestyles, because no excuses would ever be necessary for staying out late. She looked in the mirror as she washed her face and thought about Marty and her feelings of the previous night. She had not even come close to crossing that threshold past virginity. There was no need. Marty had kissed her body as if she was some sort of goddess and she still tingled from the experience.

Carrie reflected on the inconsistency concerning societal rules and her studies: they were required to study lovers like Odysseus and Penelope, Aeneas and Dido, Antony and Cleopatra, and coerced into settling for second hand knowledge regarding passions of the heart. This attitude didn't make much sense to Carrie. How did she know whether these people were truly lovers or just dysfunctional?

Carrie and her roommate met Ernie at the front of the dorm and drove together to the car rental agency. Another cross country runner by the name of Mike joined them there. Their assignment that day consisted of retrieving some stolen rental cars at the city pound. Ernie drove them to the city pound and inquired about the stolen cars. There were a few minor bureaucratic delays, but soon everyone in the group had a car to transport back to the agency.

Ernie led the procession while the rest of the drivers followed him through the industrial and business sections of town. Carrie soon learned that these drivers went through red lights and averaged eighty miles per hour in a forty miles per hour speed zone. These boys seemed protected by an invisible shield. It was a challenge to maintain a close distance behind Ernie, because he drove past her comfort zone. She could keep up with the boys or drop out. Deciding that she wasn't quite ready to drop out, she resolved to never get into a situation like this again. Never before had she broken so many rules in one afternoon, and perhaps it was the first time she had broken any.

Finally reaching their destination, the drivers swerved into the agency parking lot and handed the keys over to the agency's mechanics. Then the group hopped in the back of Ernie's white truck for the return trip to the University. Reclining leisurely in the bed of the truck, Carrie watched the autumn sun sinking in the late afternoon glow and savored the grandeur of the day. The truck sped onto the main highway and she felt a gentle breeze tug at her hair, reminding Carrie of her evening plans with Marty. She looked forward to being with him again.

In the evening Marty took Carrie to a pub where they listened to a local rock band. While they sipped drinks and munched on nachos, they entertained each other with more stories about their interests and activities. The magic of the preceding encounter still remained. Without any conscious effort Marty and Carrie slipped into each other's lives as lovers. Afterwards, throughout the semester they met each other at dances, parties, between classes, and in the cafeteria without any formal arrangements. People immediately treated them as a couple and revealed where one could find the other without being asked.

Sometimes Marty and Carrie spent their evenings studying together, taking a break about midnight for a late evening stroll. One night, as they were walking across the campus esplanade, Carrie nudged Marty's arm and whispered, "Let's climb that piece of modern art."

There were several metal sculptures scattered randomly around the campus for aesthetic purposes. Being outside always made her feel more peaceful and she loved to climb, enjoying the view that accompanied her efforts. Carrie knew that the sculpture would be a challenge to her abilities and she watched Marty amble up the huge black iron sculpture with the ease of his six foot three length. Obviously he enjoyed climbing too. He offered Carrie his hand and she joined him on the platform that stood about eight feet above the ground.

"Look at those stars!" Carrie exclaimed.

Marty smiled. The dark shadows of the sculpture camouflaged them from the wanderers on the mall below us. They sat down on the platform and watched several figures walk across campus, completely unaware of their high perch.

"There goes Joe Romero probably on his way to see his girlfriend in Siena Hall," Marty whispered. Marty seemed to know everyone on campus and they all seemed to know him. "And here comes Frank and Tony...," he continued.

"Looks like the library just kicked everyone out," Carrie observed as she counted a few dozen students trickle out of the building. "That means that it must be 1 am," she concluded.

"This makes a good study break," Marty yawned, drawing attention to their own little world residing on the sculpture's platform.

After talking about their studies, classroom anecdotes, and other newsy tidbits, they eventually drifted to the subject of philosophy.

"Ever read Bob Pitt's novel?" he asked.

"No, I haven't."

"I must give you the book sometime. It's about this guy who works on his car as if it is himself. He tours the country with his son while searching for meaning in life or what he calls the "Is"."

Marty continued with a hint of sadness in his voice, "There's something I ought to tell you. Sometimes I have periods of time when I withdraw into a shell. I have a hard time believing in all the things that other people do like God, religion, people, peace, love...; people, especially the religious ones, are such hypocrites. I just can't stand it. And love, what is love? How do people know when they are happy?"

Marty recounted some of his frustrations with the members of his family and their ignorance of subjects such as philosophy. He claimed that most people were money-oriented and he cited his last girlfriend as an example. Apparently she had dropped him for a wealthier fellow. Marty explained how different he was in comparison to other people he knew. He referred to himself as a cynic, because he felt unable to accept and enjoy the happier aspects of life. Everything seemed to be a facade; nothing seemed real or tangible.

Carrie gripped the rim of the iron platform so that she wouldn't fall off. She watched Marty smile as he shook his head over his version of the world's affairs. He seemed to be enjoying his ideological isolation and his attempts to find the errors in his logic were feeble. She wondered whether his former girlfriend had actually left Marty for a boyfriend with a richer perspective on life. Carrie loved Marty; regardless of her own feelings towards life, she didn't question his. She sensed that Marty didn't really believe his own convictions, but she was unaware of the extent which stubborn ideology could influence an individual's actions. In comparison, her attitude towards life in general was much more optimistic, and she couldn't agree with Marty and Nietzsche that God was dead.

"I'm waiting for a revelation, a vision," he told her. "Then I'll change my mind. I'm open to new ideas and experiences that contradict my own. But, how does one really know without having a revelation confront them? It takes a revelation to change a person. Ever have a revelation?" he asked as he teasingly nudged Carrie's arm.

"Well, I have vision, my ideas...," she admitted cautiously.

"Like what?" Marty asked, still eager for a revelation.

"Nothing really earth shattering. Mostly just a series of isolated events that wouldn't have much significance if I never bothered to string them together in a manner that provided meaning for me. It's hard to explain. I guess it just takes a lot of faith to believe in ideas and give them meaning. They become like a revelation for me, but I've never had one big experience that I could claim as a real revelation."

"You'll have to tell me about these ideas sometime," Marty coaxed with a gentle grin. Hearing the chimes from the campus tower sounded the two o'clock notes, they began their descent from the sculpture's platform.

"Looks like you're getting back to your dorm late again," Marty observed.

Fortunately, there was no curfew.

Chapter Eight

Carry on my wayward son
There'll be peace when you are done
Lay your weary head to rest
Don't you cry (don't you cry no more)

"'Carry on my wayward son"
Kansas

For the entire semester Carrie experienced life without the Nightmare. When Marty left with the other half of his Sophomore class to study in Rome for a semester, the Nightmare returned. The new ideas raised in her classes and her relationship with Marty forced Carrie to confront the Nightmare. She questioned the Nightmare's existence and tried to decide whether it was something that existed only in head. She tried to make it go away with some of the logic learned in her classes. Eventually the Nightmare assumed another form besides death. It had become a burden. Carrie learned that it was easier to carry this burden rather than deal with its death. She soon realized that this weight contained the burden of proof.

However, Carrie found that she could relieve some of this weight in the letters she wrote to Marty. Little did she realized that she was also formalizing the concepts which would eventually free herself from the Nightmare. Though she had always trusted Marty's insight, the distance in their relationship forced her to rely on her own intuition. She had to understand her own concepts before she could write them down in a letter to Marty. As a result of their ongoing dialogue, Marty and Carrie wrote each other many letters of great philosophical length throughout the entire semester.

For Christmas he had given her Bob Pitt's novel and she read the book over the holidays. The book proved excellent preparation for the Metaphysics class that she took spring semester. All undergraduates were required to take

Professor Fritz's class on Metaphysics. Many students referred to the instructor as "MetaFritz" as they enjoyed watching the professor's absurd antics as he exhorted logic. He'd roar at the class and wave his cigar as if he was doing a Groucho Marx routine. "It's a paradox," he'd utter, chewing on a cigar which he later hurl at the class.

His tests were simply exercises in literal regurgitation; so it was important to memorize the concepts using the professor's same vocabulary. Rather than submit to this zombie state of affairs, Carrie developed her own concepts concerning Metaphysics and exchanged her ideas with Marty. She desperately needed to derive a satisfactory ideology which would allow her to come to terms with the Nightmare that haunted her. There was no explanation for the Nightmare's existence in the philosophies she studied in class. MetaFritz's paradoxes failed to relate to the reality of the physical world, which made the Nightmare seemed even more elusive. Consequently, Carrie diverged from what she had been taught and came up with her own brand of Metaphysics to plot her course. She wrote Marty about her philosophy:

Dear Marty,

...finished reading Bob Pitt's book over the holidays. Seems that the car mechanic could have saved himself a lot of gas and energy if he had bothered to ground himself in human relationships before beginning his journey. I think the key to the story can be found at the end of the book when the mechanic realizes the importance of his relationship to his son. In the final episode, the ghost vanishes as the mechanic's relationship to his son materializes.

The story reminded me of a question that you asked me sometime ago during last semester, "what is truth?" I think that truth and love go hand in hand. MetaFritz has been discussing the pursuit of truth with regards to Aquinas' concepts of Being and Essence, and he loves referring to "Paradoxical Structure of Existence". He seems to relish leaving the class hanging in paradoxes while he discusses aspects of being and nonbeing. Evidently, he can live with paradoxes in his life.

I don't particularly care for paradoxes myself, and view them as an indication that further questioning is needed for the sake of a resolution. Like life's little ironies, sometimes paradoxes reveal more about the nature of life than a straightforward answer, but they aren't an answer. I consider paradoxes to be similar to the koans offered by the zen masters where one actually must measure the reality of the situation in order to find it.

First I feel that truth does exist in today's world and finding the truth merely requires the application of a few basic principles. In discerning truth three properties must be examined: Esse, essence, and existence. Aquinas refers to Esse as the supreme essence of the object. I think of Esse as the single identity of an object in relation to its universal nature. Some zen artists might call it the "One". Essence refers to the nature of the object. Some might call it the "Many" because an object can have many different natures at once and still be the same object (Esse). The third property of existence describes the relationship of the object to the universe by virtue of its function and activity.

Seeking the truth forces the pursuer to employ these three properties. The next step involves the act of prescinding or cutting away valueless information concerning the subject. Care must be taken so that important information regarding the subject's nature (essence) is not overlooked. In other words, those who wish to delve in the heart of the matter must examine the subject in both its One and Many forms; truth is found in the correlation of a subject's existence to its Esse and essence.

Then, there is the question of finding truth in the form of concepts and ideas. The two properties examined in this instance are context and content. Content refers to the subject's matter. Context describes the relation of the matter to its universal whole. Once again both properties must be considered in terms of the One and Many. The prescinding operation must be utilized, waste discarded, and bammo! Truth emerges. I think MetaFritz, Aristotle, Aquinas, and Pitts make it harder than it has to be...

Within the next few weeks Marty sent Carrie the following reply:

Dear Carrie,

I agree with your idea that the book calls attention to the fact that one must find a ground in human relationships in order to comprehend meaning in life. Pitts takes a long time to reach this conclusion, and I feel that the book should have gone into this concept in more detail. It's so important.

Spent the spring break traveling alone through Northern Europe. I'm going through one of my blue funks again. Wish you were here. The architecture of some of the churches and museums is really spectacular. The weather is very cold, but the people are warm and friendly. Stayed at a youth hostel in Sweden and learned of a castle in the area that serves as a learning center for Nietzsche's studies. I was impressed but I'm not sure if I can agree with all of Nietzsche's philosophies on life. The center seemed pretty open-minded though, and I had a good time rapping with the rest of the people there. I look forward to seeing you when I arrive in a few months.

Love,
Marty

Chapter Nine

Sunshine go away today
I don't feel much like dancing
Some man has gone, tried to run my life
Don't know what he's asking...

"Sunshine"
Jonathan Edwards

Marty returned from Rome a month after the spring semester ended. As Carrie met the passengers on the arriving flight from London, she easily distinguished Marty from the crowd by his long lean frame and bushy red beard which had grown during his travels. She ran to Marty immediately and wrapped him in her arms. Filtering from head to foot like a powerful light, an enormous smile flashed across the tall man's face.

"Hey, what's happening?!" he greeted, apparently overwhelmed by Carrie's attention but enjoying it nonetheless.

"Good to see you!" Carrie answered before he swirled her around in the air with a mighty hug.

"Same here," he sighed as he put her down. "I've missed you. ...Like the beard?" he added. Then he made a funny face and tugged the hairs on his chin.

"Yes," she laughed. "Now you really look like a viking."

Marty stayed a couple of days at Carrie's house before driving home to St. Louis. They had much news to tell each other and spent many hours discussing the events of the past semester. Anxious to hear his thoughts on the ever-changing world, Carrie particularly enjoyed listening to Marty's tales of his European travels.

"This is my favorite place," he told Carrie, handing her a postcard of Killarney, Ireland. "A friend and I camped one night in a pasture near Kerry. It's so peaceful in southern Ireland, not at like Belfast... And here, I brought this back for you." Marty pulled an Irish pound from his assortment of curios inside his traveling bag. "Ireland has very beautiful paper money," he commented while handing her the note.

"You're right," she commented. "This isn't money; this is art."

"Ya, I know. Look at the English pound," Marty replied as he pulled a wrinkled sample from his pocket. "Although the English receive more U.S. coins for their money, the Irish pound looks more valuable."

"The Irish pound is much prettier. I think I actually like it the best," Carrie laughed. "Thank you very much."

"The artwork portrayed on the money has its own value," he observed. Then he began rummaging through the stack of travel booklets inside his case. After he found what he had been searching for, he handed Carrie a green pamphlet. "Oh, I also brought you a historical map of Ireland."

Carrie unfolded the map and laid it on the floor in front of her. Feeling the currency underneath her fingers as her direct link to the pulse of the country, she imagined what would be like to live in the foreign land. Meanwhile, Marty sustained her imaginary transition with a narration of his journeys there.

"My great grandmother came from southern Ireland," Carrie recalled after Marty had finished. "Sometimes my grandmother would tell me stories about her mother who immigrated to America. She told me how the Irish survived the potato famine. For dinner they placed a photo of a plate of food on the table before them. They stared at the picture and went through the motions of eating as if they were actually eating from a real plate. It required a great deal of concentration, but it prevented them from feeling the pains of hunger."

"How did their bodies handle the malnutrition?" Marty asked.

"She said that they still starved to death. They only fooled their bodies into blocking the pain."

"Mind over matter," Marty observed.

"Only to soothe the mind itself."

* * *

"To soothe the mind itself," Carrie murmured under her breath as she stood squarely on the end of the diving board high above the swimming pool. Alone in her world on top of the diving platform, Carrie broke from her silent thoughts to survey the scene below her. Like the others waiting patiently behind her, the party held no interest for her. A few people at the pool party stopped and watched the parade of divers in the crisp night air. The rest were deeply absorbed in their conversations and paid little attention to the small group of divers perfecting their flights over the blue waters.

"One swan dive in perfect grace and form," she told herself before she began the motion.

Bbberrummph! The diving board echoed as Carrie sprang off its edge and flew into the beauty of a starry night. With her arms held wide in the air to accept all the warmth the dark air could offer, she strained every muscle against the earth's gravity. Once she achieved maximum height she let the earth catch her. Then she arched her body until the head was lower than her feet, maintaining straightness and poise throughout the motion. Carrie entered the water like a knife slicing through the waves with the lightest of splashes. Deep below the surface, she flipped her feet around her and pushed off from the pool's bottom. Within a few seconds Carrie appeared on top of the surface like a cork bobbing in tub of water and swam to the water's edge.

One swan dive with grave difficulty, she quietly told herself as she heaved her sopping wet body over the pool's tiled wall. Her thoughts came from the memory of high school diving meets where the judges always announced scores after every performance. Tonight in her solo competition Carrie played all the roles: judge, spectator, coach, and diver.

As she waited her turn on the high board her thoughts returned to the other concerns in her life at the moment.

"I'm not sure I can say 'I love you' anymore," Marty had told her inside the empty restaurant during a midsummer's evening. Though his words stunned Carrie, she decided not to press the issue. At the time Carrie had wanted to give him freedom to air his emotions regardless of the pain she felt. Realizing that Carrie wasn't going to question his feelings, Marty immediately relaxed and sought her hand.

Placing her hands on the cold steel ladder leading to the diving board, Carrie began the ascent for another dive.

Marty was far away from the University now. Over the last summer, he decided to major in computer science and transferred to a state university two hours away. With this new sense of direction Marty appeared much happier with himself. He enjoyed his course of study and no longer brooded over heavy philosophical diversions. In spite of the positive changes in his life, Marty continued to bury himself in his habitual shell, pushing Carrie away from him in the process.

Reaching the top of the metal diving platform, Carrie stood upright and waited for the previous diver to exit the area directly below the board. She felt a cool breeze brush across the pool's surface. She wanted to catch a ride with the moving wind as soon as possible. Quickly Carrie sprang off the diving board. High into the air, she felt her body float through the atmosphere until hurling past the water's hard surface.

Deep in the blue depths more thoughts about Marty entered her head. Often during their discussions, Carrie assumed the positive and fought the negative while Marty accepted the negative and questioned the positive. The issues Marty raised were echoes in her own mind, They both knew that their debates with each other were also debates with themselves. Carrie played the part of the optimist whereas Marty chose to be the cynic. They played their roles very well, each trying to convince the other of their own argument; and most of the time the debates ended with the two laughing at their predictable responses.

The night with Marty in the restaurant had been different. There had been no prescribed roles or responses; they had been dealing with reality instead. It marked a turning point in their former light-hearted relationship.

Another dive. Carrie didn't want to be dragged down by her emotions anymore; she wanted to rise above the surface of this present existence. Stretching high above the pool's surface, she rose above the scene below her. Then she plummeted to the depths, breaking the surface's impact with her fists to save herself from the effects on her skull.

"I can't say 'I love you'," Marty told her in the restaurant that night. His parents had divorced that summer and he allowed it to touch their relationship. Carrie recalled his words as she pulled out of her underwater descent.

"That's it!" Carrie thought as she swung over the pool's ladder. "I'm taking too much impact with these repeated dives. I should enter the water with my fists like all the high divers. Otherwise I'll have to quit diving tonight on account of a headache."

Then she focused on Marty. She could not change him. Her parents had also divorced, but she was still optimistic that there were people who could say "I love you" without denying it or turning it into a philosophical debate. Other people were willing to take the plunge.

After climbing to the height of the board, Carrie paused briefly before starting her next dive. She wondered if this is how Brian felt during his jump off the stadium.

"I just want to fly too," Carrie told herself. Here it was safe as long as she concentrated on what she was doing. "I have con-tro-o-ol," Carrie mentally reminded herself as she tensed certain muscles for the timing of the dive.

Attaining total muscle control on this dive, she later felt the waves rush over her rapidly submerging form.

For her next dive Carrie imagined being Brian. "All I know is that I love you!" she called to the world during her silent flight. She wanted to feel the impact of such a love. She wanted to remain conscious of its effect. As she struck the water below, Carrie watched the waves crash around her head and rip past her body. She concluded that Brian must have been in a daze to attempt a dive from such heights.

Carrie hurried to the top of the ladder again. Brian was dead now. Carrie still lived with the Nightmare. Like a dive, it could be fatal if she wasn't careful. Standing perfectly still at the far end of the board, she steadied her form and concentrated on the dive before beginning her next attempt.

"Yes, you can fly whenever you wish," she reminded herself. "Just keep your motions free and safe. Protect yourself from injury in your form."

Executing this intention high over the pool, Carrie assumed the grace of a spirited swan. The dive was finished in a matter of seconds, fast and unrestrained. She exited the pool and stepped onto the concrete edge. She had mastered her dives. She could control their momentum almost like automation. As a result, theory had become reality. Soon she might even be able to face the emotional force of the Nightmare without being threatened. "Brrerumph!" roared the diving board as another diver flew over the pool. Carrie turned and watched his effortless motions. She curiously wondered what other divers thought about during their jumps.

Chapter Ten

Oh baby, baby it's a wild world
It's hard to get by just upon a smile.
Oh baby, baby it's a wild world.
I'll always remember you like a child...

"Wild World"
Cat Stevens

While Carrie mastered her emotions and physical body in the blue heights above the swimming pool, the physics lab encouraged her to define her perceptions of the physical world through controlled experiments. The Nightmare complicated her life. Like most physicists, she craved simple explanations. The notion of reducing all the affairs in her life to mathematical equations encouraged Carrie to take a different approach. Unlike metaphysics, physics brought the intangible world within her grasp so that she could understand it in simple terms. Physics sought an inherent understanding of the universe. The discipline pursued the root causes of phenomenon. When it came to questioning the universe, Carrie felt that the physicists had the most fun; they applied principles they learned in class to the experiences of their own lives, breathing life into their academic experiences.

The Physics department at the University consisted of two instructors. Professor Max, a gracefully aged Romanian, served as chairman. The youthful assistant professor was affectionately known by his students as Dr. C. The teaching style of the two men differed immensely, but those who were fortunate to study under both discovered that the different approaches complemented each other.

Carrie studied under Professor Max for her second semester physics class with eight other students. After growing accustomed to the thick Slavic accent, she only had to follow the professor's metaphysical diversions. "Phee-zeeks" according to Professor Max was the most truthful of the sciences, following behind philosophy and mathematics in the hierarchy of disciplines which studied the dynamics of the universe.

More than any other scientist Carrie had ever known, Dr. C. knew how to enjoy the rules in the physical universe. The young, silver-haired physicist from an ivy league school was occasionally seen climbing the science building to retrieve the various gadgets set in flight during the course of his lecture. His lectures were the results of his raids on toy departments at local dime stores. He possessed a mechanical bird that could fly with the help of a wound-up rubberband and conservation of energy. He tossed frisbees to demonstrate principles of angular momentum and inertia. Once he even held class at the local honky tonk to discuss the special physics of beer bubbles. More concerned with the pragmatic side of physics, Dr. C.'s toys demonstrated the importance of physical knowledge in the world.

Having realized the value of adult play in the world, Carrie marveled at the manner Dr. C. played this knowledge to his advantage. She noticed how Dr. C. seemingly bent the rules of the physical universe during the process. With the professor's aid she discovered the usefulness of such fantastical pursuits, especially for individuals with limited resources. For this topic in physics Dr. C.'s most instructive hour usually came during the week when students raised money for charity. Traditionally, one day of charity week was devoted exclusively to the disruption of classes. Both students and professors could have their instructors or classes thrown into jail for a fee determined by the size of the class. These circumstances often pitted students and faculty into direct financial confrontation. Some students skipped class, some professors cancelled class, and others eagerly paid the price to send the other party to jail. Stalemates were broken by the highest bidder and often nobody knew who had won until the jailers hauled them away.

Dr. C. always tried to cut expenses with his attempts to outsmart the jailers (who were usually members of the Knights of Oblivion) with his physics tricks. His first experiment made its debut two years ago, when he showed how a handful of rope and a small four ounce pulley could support a chair and one Physics professor clutching a Physics book. The advanced Physics majors tested the apparatus with a nonmajor before suspending the instructor to a height of twentyfive feet. When the jailers arrived to seize the professor, they found him conducting class from his swing over the lecture hall. After making many futile attempts to coax Dr. C. down from his perch, the jailers resorted to spraying him down with a garden hose from the campus grounds. Then they carried the drenched professor to jail.

The next year Dr. C. resorted to electrical power as a defense. Armed with an electric cattle prod, he encamped himself behind a network of barb wire standing in the lecture room. His position placed him beside the electrical wall outlet and enabled him to prod the jailers as they entered the room. The only recourse for the frustrated jailers was to pull the circuit for the entire building. Without the least hesitation or consideration for other ongoing classes in the building, they turned off the power source and hauled the professor away in the dark.

By Carrie's sophomore year, Dr. C.'s class act became even more elaborate. He rented a white limo to drop him off at the front of the lecture building, and emerged from the car attired in a white suit with matching white cowboy hat and boots. From the crowd of students curiously gathered around the limo, there appeared six Physics majors dressed in black suits and masked in dark sunglasses who stood next to Dr. C. and escorted him to class.

In class Dr. C. explained the Faraday principle and later proved that a electrical charge could indeed reside on the surface of a closed conductor. Underneath his white suit Dr. C. had clothed his body in a shield of aluminum foil. This suit of aluminum foil served as Dr. C.'s closed conductor. After directing his mafia to guard the room's electrical socket and the building's circuit breaker, he plugged the Van der Graaf generator into the guarded wall socket and placed one hand on its silver globe.

After spending twenty minutes overcoming the Physics majors guarding the circuit breaker, the jailers that reached Dr. C. received a blue spark that arced at least a foot. The professor also hurled a few streaks of lightning at nearby metallic objects for dramatic effect. Again the jailers pulled the circuit breaker for the entire building and Dr. C. lost his charge source. The jailers, ignorant in the basic principles of physics, lunged for the professor when they realized that the generator had been turned off. Since a charge will continue to reside on the surface of a closed conductor until that conductor is properly grounded, the first few jailers touching the professor were shocked with a dazzling blue arc. Consequently, they served as the human ground for discharging the electrical energy from the professor's metallic suit. Without suffering any personal discomfort during the entire episode, Dr. C. had enough juice to zap four jailers after losing his power source. It took a moment for the puzzled jailers to recover from their bewilderment and resume their efforts in capturing the professor. Eventually, they succeeded and led Dr. C. away to the cardboard prison in the student activity center. There he joined a few students and faculty members who were just striking up a poker game, while a philosophy professor practiced on his violin in another corner of the enclosure.

Under the silent fatherly eye of the department chairman, the student physicists continued to mimic Dr. C.'s fun throughout the year and create an active learning environment for participants. The only other female Physics major lived just down the hall from Carrie's dorm room. Phyllis was a junior level Physics major. For her birthday someone decorated her room in lengthy swirls of toilet paper. The culprit left a message inscribed in red lipstick on her mirror: Happy Birthday, Betsy! XX Dr. C. Dr. C. vehemently denied any involvement with the room papering when confronted with the evidence. People believed that Dr. C had been framed and the identity of the joker remained a mystery.

As a result of these paper capers, it surprised no one except Dr. C. when he unlocked his office door one morning and walked into a forest of multicolored bathroom tissue. Dr. C. was speechless and to prove his point he sat at his desk all morning flashing a large poster with the message "Help!" to whomever happened to be walking down the hall. Even the brilliant professor admitted that whoever had been responsible for the caper was a master artist; there was no conceivable way to enter the office except through the locked metal door.

Only Professor Max proved exempt from these feats in the Physics department, though the adjoining city of Dallas became an unwitting participant. Students who spent late evening hours in the laser lab would sometimes take the helium-neon laser outside for a midnight stroll. They discovered that many spectacular effects could be produced by bouncing the monochromatic light beam at the clouds hovering over a nearby football stadium. The laser light produced a show similar to what one might see at a science fiction movie. The experiment caused traffic to slow down on several of the freeway systems crisscrossing the area. Some of the cars even stopped and pulled over to the side of the road. Although the class never read about the results of their experiment in the newspapers the next day, they couldn't help wonder whether people on the highway could distinguish a laser show from a unidentified flying object.

Yet, when it came to demonstrating the wizardry of physics, Professor Max reigned. The older professor taught Carrie the importance of being able to approach life's challenges from the perspective of a physicist. At the beginning of every year, Professor Max shook the dust from boxes containing the most famous experiments in the history of physics. Then he handed the boxes to his students with the instructions to repeat the observations. Everyone in class, including Carrie, learned that the most significant breakthroughs in physics were simply a matter of faith and obstinacy on the part of the experimenters.

Carrie never could decide what motivated Millikan to painstakingly spray a charge on a tiny oil drop, suspend it in an electric field until the oil drop was motionless, and then measure the charge of an electron by determining the electric force needed to hold the drop stationary. Millikan became the first to record the charge to mass ratio of an electron. What was it that caused him to initially consider the possibility? What led him to believe that his experimental approach to the problem would ever succeed? What kept him going through all those years of trying to balance an oil drop in an electric field? She experienced only a portion of the frustration in the university laboratory; and she already knew the results.

Of course, Carrie wondered whether the forebears of physics actually created their own reality through the design of their experiments. Was it possible for the scientist to affect the outcome of the experiment with his expectations of what the results should be? Conceivably, anyone could cause an experiment to produce the results one wanted. Could one find the truth also by simply swearing an oath or pretending to be an impartial observer? Could mere faith find the truth in spite of human limitations?

The Michelson - Morley experiment upheld the notion that truth exists on its own merit. They proved that imagination could not affect the final outcome of an experiment, because the results of their experiment were beyond anyone's wildest predictions. Scientists once believed that electromagnetic waves such as light were propagated in a medium called "the ether". Light moved through the ether in the same manner that a person swims in a stream; the time required to cross the stream depended on whether the individual swam with the current or against it. The ether wind or current was caused by the revolution of the earth around the sun, analogous to the wind a person feels when hanging an arm outside the window of a moving car. Michelson and Morley wished to detect this ether current by measuring the velocity of light moving parallel and perpendicular to this stream. The differing velocities in these two courses of travel would be due to the motion of the ether. Surprisingly, Michelson and Morley failed to detect a change in the speed of light as it moved through the ether. There was no ether wind to disrupt the flow of light. It didn't matter whether the ether actually existed because the speed of light remained absolute; one could only acknowledge what affected one's universe. Many people repeated this same experiment because they personally disagreed with the implications. Many added their own variations. Some tried it at different parts of the world. Some performed the experiment at different times of the year. Others propagated the light travel at different angles with respect to the ether stream. Everyone obtained the same results: the earth moved at rest relative to the ether like a motionless car without gas.

These astounding results forced reevaluation of Newton's mechanical universe. The acceptance of this experiment did not guarantee the understanding the phenomena. Twenty years elapsed before a satisfactory explanation was found in Einstein's special theory of relativity. No longer could the universe be viewed from a mechanical perspective; it had many dimensions and apparently some absolutes.

Armed with a historical perspective, Carrie learned to believe in the unseen universe, and realized the usefulness of her imagination in devising experiments and equipment that placed it within her view. With this ability to separate imagination from intuitive reality, she developed a sixth sense for the feel of her physical world through scientific methods. Then all of Carrie's senses, intuitions, fantasies were transformed into experiences that could be analyzed by her intellect. She learned how to make the impossible seem valid by just conjuring the possibilities; thereby, learning how to decide what really could not be.

Chapter Eleven

...Hope you guessed my name, oh yeah
But what's confusing you
Is just the nature of my game
Just as every cop is a criminal
And all the sinners saints
As heads is tails
Just call me lucifer
'cause I'm in need of some restraint
So if you meet me...

"Sympathy for the Devil"
Rolling Stones

Carrie learned to accept the Nightmare's reality without bothering to prove the Nightmare's existence. She was beginning to believe in power of her own capabilities, after Professor Max and Dr. C. made it all seem so easy. Yet, in spite of the strides Carrie made in dealing with the various intangible realities in her life, some events occurred which brought her dangerously close to the Nightmare's death grip. Though Carrie could greatly control the physical environment of the swimming pool and laboratory, there were other events in her life which she could not alter. As consequence, she did not foresee what would happen on the night of freshman initiation or do much to avoid the circumstances. This single event catalyzed a turn in her life, one in which the Nightmare nearly won.

One early autumn weekend, Marty and Carrie spent the afternoon at a state park located two miles North of campus. Many towering oaks filled the park making it an ideal birding habitat. Jays and robins hopped in the brush as raptors circled above them. The couple hiked several miles inside the park before deciding to stop for a picnic.

"The park ranger knows every bird call from the golden eagle to the Concorde jet," Carrie told Marty. "We met him when our biology class hiked through here last spring."

"Looks like things are getting run down," Marty remarked as he noticed the beer bottles lying in the brush nearby.

"Yeah, it was much cleaner for the spring class. I wonder what happened over the summer," Carrie replied as they approached the trail sign at the end of their hike. After a moment's reflection, she explained as she stooped down to pick up some litter, "They started holding rallies last August. My sister took a detour down some dirt roads in the valley. She was returning home from work one night. There were a bunch of men in white sheets burning crosses..."

"Are you kidding?" Marty asked.

"My sister got out of there really quick." Then she continued, "Erin mentioned last year that they were burning crosses on people's lawns in her hometown." Carrie looked at the eagle soaring in the sky overhead. Then she peered at Marty. "When I was in high school, we had incidences of hangings and dead cats in local cemeteries. The town newspapers traced it to some sort of satanic cult that had fascinated a few teenagers in a wealthy neighborhood." Carrie walked on, "I know the cemetery. Its just a little pioneer graveyard like all the others scattered around the Chisholm trail that went through my backyard."

Carrie and Marty reached the trailhead at the park's entrance and put down their packs for a break. They examined the sign for a map, however some odd scripted letters and symbols caught Carrie's eye on the back of the wooden sign. "Oh no!" she exclaimed as she took a step back. "It looks like the satanists have been here too!"

Marty fearfully eyed the writing on the back of the sign. He and Carrie hurriedly grabbed their packs and began hiking towards the road.

"That park ranger won't be happy to see those engravings on the back of his park sign. I wonder if he has seen it yet," Carrie commented, breaking the silence once they were a quarter of a mile down the road. "Connie told a bunch of us in the dorm last week about stumbling across a satanic group in one of the men's dorms. Connie was in a study group with AJ and Tony and they went to that dorm because it was relatively quiet. I don't think even AJ or Tony know about it. She warned us not to go to any study groups there. She wouldn't go into details... she was pretty shocked by what she saw."

"Which dorm was it?" Marty quizzed her.

"Ignatius," she told him.

"It figures," he remarked. "Those guys study too hard."

"John, the Biology teaching assistant, said that the local priest was pursuing some black rose cult on campus."

When they reached campus, they went straight to Marty's car in the parking lot. Over the summer Marty had transferred to a state college an hour 's drive away. He placed his pack in the car and sat behind the wheel as he inventoried the contents. Then he rolled down his window and sought Carrie's kiss.

"I'll see you in two weeks," he said when they finished. "Are you going to see the Senior's skits tonight?"

At the beginning of every year, some upperclassmen in the women's dorm would perform a series of skits on how to survive life at the University. Although they called their show "Freshman Initiation", it offered friendly advice without any hazing. Many representatives from all classes, men and women, came to enjoy the hilarious satires.

"Yes, I'm going to meet Erin and Connie and walk over to the women's dorm at eight tonight."

"Have fun," Marty waved as he backed his car out of the lot and sped off.

Later that evening, Carrie and her friends walked to the lobby of the women's dorm. The room was filled to capacity. Carrie personally knew several of the seniors conducting the presentation from her grade school days, and marveled at their sophisticated interpretations of campus affairs. They always impressed her.

Just before the performance of the last skit, a low rumble was heard from outside the dorm.

"It's the K of O," Erin whispered. K of O referred to Knights of Oblivion, an illicit fraternity which met every Thursday night to lose sobriety. The meetings were held in the woods surrounding the campus at a location marked by an enormous bonfire. Usually by their sophomore year most men on campus had attended at least one K of O meeting. Many men sought to assert their masculinity through alcohol consumption.

Occasionally some of Carrie's male friends attended the meetings to obtain a free beer, but they never bothered to linger. They claimed that the K of O was a pretty rough bunch who become rowdier in direct proportion to the amount of alcohol consumed. Women were not allowed at the meetings and were physically threatened if they ever wandered close to the bonfire. Most of the women on campus would have preferred seeing the group disbanded because it promoted an inane type of machismo that disrupted relationships on campus. Many men had difficulty choosing between their girlfriends and the bottle.

The K of O had their own violent version of freshman initiation, though their commitment varied from year to year. Some years they never even bothered with the rite. Their rite consisted of intoxicating all the men on campus, freshmen in particular, and marching to the women's freshman dorm. Adhering to the late medieval style of the Goths and Vandals, the K of O would hose down the surrounding terrain with water and create a giant moat around the dorm. Then they would pelt the building with rocks and mud balls. Men from their ranks would be assaulted as well. Once they broke into the dorm, they would drag its inhabitants outside and stone them. School leaders were prime targets.

This year the K of O seemed more rabid than previous years for the resident assistants were drug from the dorm within only fifteen minutes. Resident assistants were always the first to go. This rendered the dorm defenseless, creating confusion and panic among the terrified freshman. The key strategy for the building's inhabitants involved securing all possible entrances and exits to the dorm until the mob quieted and left. Freshmen usually hid in their rooms.

Suddenly the low rumbling noise was replaced with horrified shrieks. The Knights of Oblivion burst through the doors in the main entrance and grabbed anybody standing near the entrance. Kicking and screaming, the victims were carried outside and thrown in the mud. Those in charge of the dorm were pursued first, leaving the inhabitants in a disordered panic.

"Lock up the side entrance!" Someone shouted. "We can't let them get in!" Meanwhile, other people rushed to protect the front entrance. By the second attack all of the seniors and resident assistants had been captured. The remaining juniors and sophomores assumed responsibility for the welfare of the people inside.

A volley of rocks and wooden poles shook the building. Instantly, all the lights went out as the K of O cut off the electric power. A series of screams greeted the black-out and continued to echo throughout the two floors in the dormitory.

Through the dark shadows Carrie followed Erin and Connie down the hallway and to the building's side entrance. They joined the efforts of several others who were pushing the door closed, while Carrie gathered some metal poles that would brace the door shut and relieve the group's hold. More heavy objects struck the walls of the side entrance.

"Oh no! They're gonna break the windows!" Someone whispered. Tall plate glass windows towered above the heads of those defending the entry hall. If any window shattered, the entire group would be one bloody mess.

"I heard that they were not going to come this year," Carrie mentioned to a student council representative who was helping her gather the poles. Her words could hardly be heard above the din.

"Me too," she said. "Joe Cotter said that some of the guys really got blitzed at the bonfire in a mean sort of way. Joe was there and watched it all... He left early to warn the dorm. Somebody should call campus police... Liz!" she hollered while hurrying to the door that was about to be attacked for a second time. "Call security!" she authorized.

Just as Liz left the vicinity, the door was suddenly jerked from the hands of those trying to keep it closed. Twenty to thirty men dressed in the medieval garb of the K of O rushed at the small group in entry hall. Carrie was seized by a gang of six men and flung high into the air. They carried her into the mayhem outside and hurled her in a pit of dirt and mud.

Thrashing wildly as the men wriggled her into the ground, Carrie fought those trying to hold her down. Out of the corner of her eye she noticed two other members of the K of O come towards her with their arms full of mud and gravel. Then she turned her face away from the onslaught of stones and dirt. As she remained pinned to the ground she felt two men separate her legs and rake mud over her. Other members of the K of O tore at her breasts and abdomen.

Carrie closed her eyes, spinning her body like a hurricane against her attackers. Some of the mud contained glass fragments and the embedded pieces in her skin stung her movements. In spite of her blindness and pain, she swung her limbs wildly at those attempting to hurt her. They became immediately discouraged and left.

After her attackers went away Carrie remained motionless in the mud for several long seconds. She wondered how many people had been assaulted that night. She imagined that the initiation for freshman boys had been worse, because the Knights of Oblivion seized more liberties with their own gender. The symbolism of the mud and the sexual tone of the assault jarred her consciousness. One month they were roughing people up in the name of charity and in the next month they were harassing both genders. Carrie quickly leaped to her feet as she surveyed her surroundings.

What had began as a fun relaxed gathering for coeds had turned into a ghastly event. People were slinging mud all around her, but none of it seemed aimed for her. She was just another grime-covered body in the throng and relatively safe now. Carrie searched the crowd for signs of the group who had been drug from the side entry. She wondered what had happened to them. Instead of leaving, she launched a counter-attack and decided to rejoin the throng. Picking up a handful of mud, she threw it at a man preparing to pole open the entrance to the dorm. The man dropped the pole when the wad hit him on the side of the face. A group of women from the dorm windows cheered Carrie. Carrie ducked and gathered another mud ball. She threw another in the man's direction and missed. Despite the missed shot, the women in the dorm screamed with delight and muted the frenzied howls below. The man turned towards Carrie and sighed. The happy yells supporting Carrie's attack had taken the steam out his. Some men who had been assaulted fought for the pole. Another grime-covered woman appeared to Carrie's right and slapped a hand of mud on the head of a nearby Knight of Oblivion. The women from the window quickly became inspired and started dropping buckets of water on the heads of attackers.

The mob went away. Some Knights of Oblivion doggedly continued as if in a trance. Carrie watched the hate and sadness in the eyes of the attackers grow and grow, emptying the spirit like a cancer. Dorm defenders exuberantly danced around them and toppled the deflated attacker into the mud. The defeated men didn't get back up so easily.

Carrie turned and walked up the ridge behind her. As she started to climb the slope she spotted Mike, a friend of Marty's. Still wearing his running shorts from cross country practice, he slowly sipped a beer while maintaining a watchful eye on the chaos below.

"Hi," she said, tossing a friendly mud ball in his direction. She purposely missed him.

"Hi," he replied, returning the mud toss without malice. A few seconds of silence elapsed before she joined him at the top.

"It's pretty wild down there," he said grimly.

Carrie turned around to survey the activity after she found a safe distance from the scene below. She had broken the pattern by leading the counter attack. Future K of O assaults would be opposed. She noted the difference between this University and other schools. Students at other colleges experimented in love-making; this one regressed to barbaric medieval rituals.

"Ya, I'm going back to my dorm," she decided in a hushed voice. Her body still shook from the trauma of the experience and her legs weakly supported her stance.

Without saying another word, Mike escorted Carrie over to the other side of campus. He left her alone at the water faucet where she hosed the blood and dirt off her body before entering the dorm. Although Carrie still felt emotionally drained, physical damage amounted to a few cuts and bruises. The water felt warm to her touch and it restored strength to her aching limbs. After rinsing her body, Carrie turned off the water and sat down on a nearby concrete step.

She looked up from the earth's darkness for the soft white glow of the moon. It was still there in the middle of the star studded sky. Carrie sighed as she began to feel safe in her world again. The magic of the moonlight filtered through the night and soothed her wounds and emotions. Then she rose and limped up the stairs leading to her room in the dorm.

"What happened to you?!" her roommate asked Carrie.

"Freshman initiation... turned into a real fight...," Carrie gasped as she headed straight for the refuge of a hot shower.

The next morning she attended classes as usual and saw Erin and Connie in the cafeteria during lunch. Following their cue, nobody mentioned the event of the previous evening, except noting the muddy footprints found in the dorm's hall this morning. Connie revealed that security had arrived shortly after she left. Although, the Knights of Oblivion continued to be an institution on campus, their activities faded into obscurity.

Chapter Twelve

The captain of Carrie's intramural volleyball team was an African American named Darlene. Darlene was also in Carrie's third year calculus class, and she sat at the back of the class with several other outspoken individuals, keeping tabs on the instructor's calculations. When they weren't busy watching the instructor, Darlene and her compatriots were goofing off. Sometimes they even had a poker game going amongst themselves. Despite the distractions caused by this group, the professor thrived on their attention. The mild heckling remained jovial and rescued the class from a dry lecture.

One of Darlene's friends was a tall, skinny fellow with a scraggly beard who endlessly toted a camera around his neck. He usually came to class attired in a Greek sailor's cap, black leather jacket, and dark glasses. He reminded Carrie of an ex-motorcycle rider who had been dropped by his gang for wearing a cheesy smile. When he wasn't busy taking pictures for the yearbook and school newspaper, he played volleyball with a team called the "Swans" or followed Darlene around. Darlene was the coach for the "Swans", a motley group of sophomore men who named the team after a fairy tale about a young princess with six brothers.

Carrie had always been fascinated by the fairy tale of the princess and six swans. According to the story, an evil witch transformed the six princes into swans. In order to free her brothers from the enchantment, the young princess sewed six shirts out of star flowers within six years. She could not speak or laugh during this period. In spite of her silence, she managed to marry a King and give birth to three children. However, the evil queen stole the children and claimed that the princess had killed them. Just as the princess was to be executed for the crime, she threw the shirts on her brother swans and transformed them into princes again. The princess proclaimed her innocence, the evil queen died in a freak accident, and the children were returned to their parents. Although the fairy tale ended happily, there remained one minor problem; the princess had been unable to finish the sleeve of the sixth shirt and the youngest brother kept a swan wing.

Carrie was delighted with the men's adaptation of the fairy tale. She learned that she wasn't the only one who juxtaposed fantasy with reality for amusement. Sometimes Carrie felt she could identify with the mute princess. Other times she could relate to the prince with the remaining swan wing. When practicing her high dives, Carrie tried to be as graceful as a swan. She could admire the princess' determination to knit a happy endings into the given situation.

It was obvious that the Swan with the cheesy smile was infatuated with Darlene, his volleyball coach. He seemed to follow her almost everywhere, about two steps behind. Darlene enjoyed his company but declined a romantic interest. During a campus blood drive, Carrie became better acquainted with Darlene's swan.

Though Carrie had donated blood before without any adverse effects, she felt more anxious than usual while lying on the table waiting for the extraction of the usual pint. Her blood seemed to be pumping slowly and she noticed that she was feeling lightheaded as well. Taking her mind off her predicament, Carrie initiated conversation with the guy who was lying head to head with her. Neither could see each other.

"Ever done this before?" she asked him.

"No," he answered.

"What class are you in?" Carrie continued, feeling encouragement.

"Sophomore. What class are you in?"

"Sophomore."

"Going to Rome?"

"Yah, I plan to go early and travel through England and Ireland. I've always wanted to visit those countries. Do you know Claire McDonald and Jan Smith?"

"Yes," he said excitedly.

"We plan to fly together to London. A lot of people are meeting in London. Mike McNeil is throwing a party on January 10th. Any University traveler in England is invited. After the party Claire, Jan, and I plan to buy a BritRail pass and go to Ireland. Then we'll ride the Eurail to the Rome campus... By the way my name is Carrie Jackson."

"Brent Wright. I haven't really made any plans for my travels yet."

"You're welcome to see my maps on the countries. I can give you directions to Mike's place and we can arrange to meet in London. If you are interested in going through Ireland, you could even travel with us to Rome."

"I like your plans. Could I look over your maps this afternoon?"

"I'm free at one o'clock but I leave for work at three. I'm a lifeguard for the campus swimming pool," she told him. "My room number is 324 in Patrick Hall. Just give my room a buzz and I'll meet you in the lobby. Where are you from originally?"

"Vermont. My parents own ten acre farm near the mountains. We have a few cows and chickens, and grow our own fruits and vegetables."

"What brings you to Texas?"

"I have a scholarship. I plan to get a master's degree in applied solar engineering after I complete my Physics degree. I'll graduate in three years instead of the usual four years. Because I'm interested in Engineering, Professor Max is allowing me to substitute some Engineering courses from a state university for some of my Physics work. After I return to the States, I plan to spend the summer in the area. I already have several jobs at the University waiting for me in addition to the two or three courses I'll be taking this summer."

"I'm interested in studying solar energy too. In high school I built a solar-powered radio for a science fair project. By using an earphone I minimized the amount of power drawn by the amplifier... It actually worked! I heard music from some of the bigger stations... Last summer I made a solar oven."

"How hot did you get your solar oven?"

"400 degrees Fahrenheit on a typical summer's day of 100 degrees Fahrenheit. I never tried to bake anything in it, though. I ran out of time."

"My father and I built a solar greenhouse last summer. We added some ventilation to the original design because the greenhouse became too hot. I did it just like a real Engineer," Brent said in a voice suggesting that he was still awe-struck by the accomplishment. "I drew the blueprints and had a city inspector approve my design before ever beginning the project. We used fiberglass for the sides and made an insulated base from styrofoam. Originally, we planned to heat the house by opening the structure to my parent's bedroom window. But Mom doesn't like the earthy smell of a greenhouse, so we closed the opening. Now my Dad grows his tomatoes and starts seedlings for his garden inside the greenhouse."

"That sounds neat!" Carrie exclaimed. She was impressed by this unidentified talker. Then she added, "I'm a Physics major also. I'm about a course behind because I changed my major from Chemistry. I'm making up for lost time with summer school. Do you have Dr. C. for any of your classes?"

"I'm taking his electromagnetics course. We papered his office about two weeks ago."

"So you're the one who pulled it off!" Her blood donation had become a serendipity.

Without being asked, Brent excitedly volunteered the intricacies of the prank. "I popped the ceiling panels above the electronics lab and crawled over to his office. The lab is adjacent to his office and all I had to do was remove a ceiling panel from Dr. C.'s office. I landed on his desk... It helps to be tall and skinny. Then I unlocked the door and helped Betsy paper the room. She supplied the paper; she wanted to get even with Dr. C. for papering her dorm room."

"But Dr. C. insists that he wasn't responsible for that one."

"I know... I did it," he confessed. I opened a window from the room next door and walked across the outside ledge. Betsy left one of her windows open, so I crawled through it and papered her room. Then I left a message in red lipstick on her mirror and signed Dr. C.'s name. I knew she'd accuse him first regardless of the message."

"So who did our room?"

"Fred Morris, Connie's younger brother. He always uses computer paper. For my birthday they filled my room with millions of tiny paper dots from the computer sheets. I found paper dots in my drawers, my socks, my shoes, my books, my camping gear,... I'm still finding caches of dots in my things."

"Looks like you're finished," a blood technician announced as she walked over to Brent.

"You seem to be going rather slowly... keep pumping that blood," coached the technician as she glanced at the measly amount in Carrie's bag. Then she left.

Finally able to solve the mysterious identity of the adjacent conversationalist, Brent hopped to his feet and walked towards Carrie. She recognized Brent as Darlene's Swan. He flashed her a cheesy grin and said, "See ya at one o'clock. Take it easy, lady." Then he left to relax at the recovery station.

She glanced at the bag of blood hanging over her right arm. It wasn't even half full. Oh, why wouldn't her blood pump any faster so that she could get out of this place?! It already had taken much longer than anticipated. Everyone else seemed to be donating at a faster rate.

After forever had passed, a technician finally came and pulled the needle from Carrie's arm.

"You're done," she said. "How are you feeling."

"OK," Carrie responded, anxiously glancing at the clock. She had been on the table for over thirty minutes. Brent had donated in less than fifteen minutes. Though she possessed low blood pressure like most athletes, Carrie really felt that a half hour was too much for a donation.

She slowly rose from the table and walked towards the recovery station. Carrie never made it that far. Within the same minute she collapsed on the floor and awoke staring at the white collar of a priest. Much to Carrie's relief, he never asked her whether she wanted the last rites. She wasn't sure which shocked her more: the presence of the seminarian hovering overhead or her prone position on the ground. At any rate, she left the premises as soon as her legs were strong enough to support some weight.

Late in the afternoon Brent came by her dorm to see Carrie's maps of Ireland and England. "You have quite a collection here," he commented afterwards. He was impressed by the thoroughness in her travel plans.

"I'll meet you in London after Christmas!" he decided. Then Brent flashed her one of his cheesy smiles and exited the dorm's lobby.

Chapter Thirteen

There's a little black spot on the sun today,
It's the same black spot as yesterday...

"King of Pain"
Police

Carrie never made it as far as London.

"What is going on here? What about your scholarship?" Carrie's mother demanded without waiting for Carrie to answer. "We'll talk about this when I get home." Then Carrie heard the click on the other end of the phone.

For several seconds Carrie remained frozen and then slowly replaced the receiver on the hook. Her mother's anger frightened her and Carrie could barely think. The college authorities had left her no time to break the news to her mother gently. Carrie numbly gathered her things and called a taxi. She'd leave on the next flight to Florida. There she knew she could find a warm climate and some old friends. She had to get-away on her own.

When the taxi arrived Carrie hurriedly loaded her gear in the back and settled in the passenger seat.

"Airport," she instructed the woman driver who looked like she had been a runaway herself once.

The driver never required any further conversation and Carrie enjoyed the silence as the road-hardy station wagon sped along the airport freeway.

"I've never felt so alive!" Carrie softly murmured. "I may not know where I'm going, but at least I'm really living." The woman across the seat smiled and nodded at Carrie, while the car accelerated through the traffic. Though the driver could not possibly hear Carrie's thoughts, she seemed to feel them.

When the car passed Carrie's high school, she stole a final look at the campus. On the other side of the freeway stood the Radio Shack store where

Carrie had worked as a sales clerk last summer. As she left these memories behind, Carrie's thoughts sadly turned to the present circumstances.

Ever since the encounter with the Knights of Oblivion, her stamina had rapidly deteriorated. She quit eating regularly and lost too much weight for her athletic frame. Many of the things she was compelled to learn in her classes added to the sick feeling in the pit of her stomach. the campus experienced an epidemic number of rapes after the incident involving the K of O and the women's dormitory. It bothered her that the school officials would not take the necessary steps to protect its student population. Carrie felt like an easy target for another assault; there was no guarantee that it would not happen again. Before entering the University, her supervisor at Radio Shack, had cautioned her about the problems with sexual assault on the Rome campus. He knew several women who had attended the University and they had told him of their experiences there. Being in a foreign country, the women on campus had even greater difficulty in getting the University officials to address the problem. Carrie's future at the University appeared futile. Not only did she lack the confidence to successfully present her different points of view with the instructors, but she noticed difficulty in regurgitating their fixed views in her term papers.

Carrie checked her baggage and walked through the smoky glass corridors towards the gate. As she anxiously stood in the area waiting to board her plane, Carrie gazed out the brown-colored windows enclosing the terminal. Yellow winter grass dotted the plains beyond the runway. The broad blue expanse in the sky promised her a safe flight from her former home. Once she was in the air no one would be able to stop her until she landed at her destination. Pressing her face closer to the glass to hide from a policeman who was walking by the terminal, Carrie suddenly recalled the incident with her mother which had hurt her so deeply a month after the assault.

It had happened as the result of a warm cup of Bailey's Irish Cream.

"You've been drinking! I can smell the alcohol on your breath," her mother hissed at Carrie in the dimly lighted University parking lot.

Carrie slammed the trunk lid down on the things that she had just finished loading into her mother's red Subaru station wagon. She was going home for the weekend to visit her teenage cousin who was in the hospital. Her cousin had nearly died a week ago with a collapsed lung.

Chapter Thirteen

Carrie turned and faced her mother, "It was only one cup of Bailey's Irish Cream." It was the weekend. Carrie's roommate had offered her the warm drink before her mother had arrived at the dormitory. The alcohol had relaxed Carrie enough to get in an extra hour or two of studying before facing pressures at home.

"You're just like your father," her mother screeched at Carrie as she put her things in the car.

Carrie stepped back. She felt like she had been hit. The words had a staggering effect on her and there was nothing more she could say.

During the stay at home, Carrie's mother added, "No longer can you call this house your home anymore. You are like your father... you don't belong here with us."

Stunned by this harsh comparison, Carrie never defended herself. Her mother's rejection tore her in half. After the policeman left the terminal, Carrie heaved a sigh of relief. She didn't want to be pressured into returning home or to the University. Her life seemed to be rolling into one assault after another.

Carrie hurried onto her plane when it arrived, hopping quickly into her seat. She knew that everything would be okay if she could just see the ocean again. The rolling waves would speak to her and remind her of how life goes on and on; she knew she could find this message in the water's motion on the beach. Carrie just needed to feel it one more time. Her own will to survive depended on it.

Her friend, Donna, seemed very happy to hear Carrie's voice on the phone. "Your mother called the police," she told her. "She thought that you might come and see me. The police have even been looking for you at the airport... Your mother was worried that you might have killed yourself."

"I'm doing just fine," she assured Donna. Carrie was surprised at how little her mother understood. "I needed a break and some time to sort things through. I just wanted to see the ocean again...," she added without admitting that she had been afraid of meeting her mother that afternoon.

During the five days spent in Florida, Carrie stayed with Donna and her family for a few days. Observing their interactions, she noticed how differently the family behaved from her own. They showed genuine concern and care for each other. Carrie felt so happy that she could have hugged the grocery store when they went shopping. She experienced the greatest joy in the most mundane activities—washing dishes, playing pool, shopping,...etc. Parallel to Carrie's conscious desire to see the ocean existed the unconscious burning of a single question: Was her idea of a loving family fact or fantasy? Like her visit to the ocean, she just had to know that it was there.

"You can't just disappear," Donna told Carrie. "Look at you, you're as skinny as a rail."

"I was hoping that my mother wouldn't try to find me," Carrie dryly answered. She had not been aware of her weight loss until she landed in Florida.

"Well, she did and she is coming to take you home. She called everyone she knew, and now they all know that you are here," Donna told her. "Where else can you run?"

Because she simply lacked the strength and energy for further struggle in life, Carrie reluctantly returned to her mother's house by the end of the week. The Nightmare had caught up with her.

Like the others who knew her, Marty was surprised by Carrie's sudden departure. Feeling personally concerned, he met Carrie at her mother's house the same afternoon she arrived from the airport. During Carrie's absence Marty had spent many afternoons with Carrie's sisters at the house, waiting for news of Carrie's whereabouts. He fitted in well as an older brother and her sisters like his company. They often invited him to stay for dinner, and Marty usually accepted their offer of a home-cooked meal.

After dinner that night, Marty and Carrie disappeared for a private stroll.

"I sure am glad to see you," he started long after they had past the first streetlight on the corner of the block. "You had me worried for a little while."

Having spent the last several minute walking quietly, Carrie appreciated his words, though they had no effect on her feelings. They turned the corner of the next block and continued down the paved road. Cars from the nearby highway roared softly in the background wind.

"You know, Samantha suspected that something was up all along," Marty continued, shaking his curly head at the pavement. "She said that you were too tired to play football with her over the holidays."

Carrie felt tears rush to her eyes, but she immediately took a deep breath and pushed them back. "I'm sorry I couldn't tell you. I didn't think you'd understand," she explained.

Marty stopped, looked Carrie directly in the eye, and cocked his head to one side. "Why did you think that I would not understand?" he stammered in frustration.

"Because you're a cynic and I'm an optimist, remember?" Carrie firmly replied without sadness or anger. Then she looked away at the distant blue stars shining in the black sky. The hint of a winter wind brushed her jacket, but Carrie remained motionless on the concrete street. For the first time in several months she felt as solid as the pavement, an impenetrable wall with a position as fluid as the dark sky above her. Something had shifted inside her since the trip to Florida.

"I told you how rough things were going," Carrie reminded Marty when she returned his gaze. Then she paused for Marty's slow nod before continuing. "I have my dreams, my visions,... these things I believe for my own sanity. I want something better for myself," she announced. "I was dying inside and had to get away before it killed me. You were part of the problem. I can't confide my deepest secrets in someone who can't tell me they love me. That's just the way I am."

Marty and Carrie resumed walking. Without a word Marty looked reflectively ahead of their steps. Staring at the space for a moment, he glanced sideways at her and nodded again; Carrie knew he understood now. Having made her point, she was glad Marty never told that he loved her that night.

Chapter Fourteen

It is the night
My body's weak
I'm on the run
No time to sleep
I've got to ride
Ride like the wind
To be free again

"Ride Like the Wind"
Christopher Cross

The next morning Carrie lingered in bed, waiting for her mother and Samantha to leave for work and school. Carrie sighed, slumping back against the headboard. She had watched the lives of both her parents evolve through the years. For the first ten years of her life her family moved almost every year. When she was very young her father had earned his living as carrier for a moving company. Now he had an MBA and worked as a systems analyst for a military-industrial complex. Her mother had obtained a degree and started work as a teacher for a rural middle school just before Carrie's final year in high school. During Carrie's first year in college, her parents finally divorced after a long and messy battle over the house, debt, and blame for the marriage's demise. Regardless of their difficult financial situation, Carrie's mother kept the house and lived in the same middle-class neighborhood where the family had spent the last nine years.

Carrie overheard her mother instructing Ellen to watch Carrie and prevent her from leaving the house that day. Once she heard her mother's Oldsmobile roll down the driveway, Carrie hurriedly stretched across her bed to the front window and peered through an opening between the shutters. She wanted to be sure her mother was gone.

When Carrie saw the car make a quick right at the stop sign, her heart began its active beat and her eyes flickered open. She looked around her room and blinked. Despite her consciousness, Carrie found that she still felt numb. She had never expected to be in this room again. Even in her panic, the decision to leave and never return had been absolute, a decision as final as death itself. Now that she was back in her room again, she felt the weight of that decision bearing down on her as if she were a trapped animal. As a result, she had fallen into a state of shock like a captured rabbit when she felt the jaws of an inevitable fate close around her. Accepting the mercy which with nature mysteriously compensates those who fall prey, Carrie became limp in her struggle at home instead of allowing herself to be devoured by the pain she felt. She noticed that she was having difficulty feeling much of anything these days. She felt as if she had come back from life to live with the dead.

Her thoughts were interrupted by the familiar sound of her cat, Cleo, forcing her way past the bedroom door. Bump! Squee-ea-ek! Bump! Soon Cleo arrived on top of the bed and met Carrie with a happy purr. The noise reminded Carrie of the good things in life which refused to change with time and events. The little Siamese cat assumed its favorite curl in Carrie's lap as Carrie ran her fingers over the soft fur. Carrie could tell that Cleo had already been outside that morning because the black limbs of the cat's body felt cold. Automatically Carrie started warming the tips of Cleo's tiny ears with her fingers as if she was another cat licking life into her.

"Oh, Cleo!" she wept softly. The appearance of the little cat moved her. During her flight she had forgotten Cleo, her inconspicuous source of comfort. How many times had she dried her eyes with the black tip of Cleo's tail! "It's OK to cry now," she murmured so quietly that even Cleo couldn't hear. A stream of tears rushed down her face and landed on the cat.

"Now Mom thinks I've been brainwashed," Carrie said, sadly shaking her head over the cat and feeling helplessly little inside. Try as she might, she could not find the strength to stand up to her mother and convince her otherwise. Carrie, herself, had a hard time believing that she was okay, that she was good inside. Now faced with the possible emergence into adulthood, Carrie wanted to leave home before she became a threat. A responsible adult would only cause problems at home. Though she knew deep inside that she had not really done anything wrong in running away, there was still a part of her that wanted to destroy herself out of frustration. Before the gut instinct which had caused her to run became any bigger, Carrie felt pressured to kill it. Otherwise, Carrie sensed seizure by a pain so deep that she'd collapse like some mystic in a hypnotic trance and float away to oblivion.

Shuddering at the thought of oblivion, Carrie shook the tension out of her body like an athlete keeping her muscles loose. She looked thoughtfully at Cleo, stroking the little cat's furry body. Although Cleo was a house pet, Carrie was well aware of Cleo's independent mind. Oblivious to Carrie's woeful lament, the cat continued purring and nodding her wedge-shaped head in well-grounded euphoria. Carrie quieted as she watched the cat's response to her touch. In spite of her despair, the cat's ecstatic response amused her. Evidently Cleo was amused by Carrie, so the relationship was mutual. Carrie swept the cat into her arms, holding Cleo as tight as she could without harming the tiny beast. "You're just a bundle of love! You really don't know much of anything else," she agreed with the cat. "You're my lub-dub."

Carrie rubbed her face against the cat's head and listened to the sounds of Cleo's existence: the purr, the breathing, the rapid thumping of Cleo's heart, the brushing noise of fur, whiskers, and skin. Carrie could still find the beat of her own heart by listening to Cleo. Then Carrie released the cat into her lap and began absentmindedly drying her eyes with the black tip of Cleo's tail.

* * *

Carrie and her mother met Carrie's father at a psychiatrist's office later that afternoon. The moment the strain of the suspense became almost unbearable, Carrie's father emerged from the psychiatrist's office. Leaving the waiting room, she ventured down the hall to the psychiatrist's office where daylight splashed the walls of the room from the windows on the western side. After adjusting her eyes to the light outside the waiting room, Carrie took a deep breath and examined the office.

Propped up behind an enormous metal desk in a luxurious black sofa chair, sat a ruddy-faced platinum-haired woman. Everything else in the room seemed made out of glass or metal, and the only plant in the room, a spider plant hanging by the window, had begun to resemble the brown carpet below it. The woman's face reflected the luster of her objects, hardened by the displays of power decorating her office. Carrie noticed that the woman appeared moved from the session with Carrie's father.

The psychiatrist glanced at Carrie as if she was just another object and waved her to one of the insignificant chairs in the room. Frowning at her desk, the psychiatrist intently wrote more notes with the silver pen in her hand. The lack of direct eye contact gave Carrie the opportunity to settle into the sterile room without subtracting from the rigidity of its appearance. Once Carrie situated herself amongst the competing objects, the psychiatrist looked up from her notes and spoke. Without moving from her position behind the desk, the psychiatrist formerly introduced herself and explained that she wanted to ask Carrie a few questions.

"Did you say you had a vision?" began the psychiatrist after she finished the introductory conversation.

"Well, yes," Carrie replied truthfully as the psychiatrist shook her head and wrote more notes. "It's sort of a inner vision, coming from my own imagination..."

Carrie gulped, choosing to remain motionless in her chair. In spite of the consequences she would not shrink from her position on this matter which was dear to her. Whatever story her divorced parents gave the psychiatrist already had made a strong impression.

"Have you ever heard voices?" the psychiatrist persisted.

Hesitating a few seconds before answering this question, Carrie tried again, "They aren't voices as you might think. Sometimes I carry on dialogues in my head as if I am writing a play, sometimes I even coach myself, and sometimes the flashes of insight into a math or physics problem seem so certain that it is like a single voice."

Meanwhile, Carrie calmly noticed the lack of color in the passionless room. Any color which did exist seemed muted.

"Have you ever done drugs? Smoked pot?" the psychiatrist asked.

"Never. I hate drugs," Carrie told her.

"Is it possible that anyone could have dropped some sort of drug in your drink or something?"

Carrie became more uneasy with the psychiatrist train of questions. She didn't like their insinuations. Rather than be moved by the rude questions,

Carrie inspected the psychiatrist's pinned perfect attire and wondered about the psychiatrist's own personal habits.

"None of the people I hang out with do drugs," Carrie replied as she politely crossed her legs at the ankles. Any motion in the room now belonged as part of Carrie's statement.

"Why did you run away?" the psychiatrist finally questioned, shifting in her chair and looking away from her notes.

"I needed a break, a chance to get away from it all."

* * *

Two days after the meeting with the psychiatrist Carrie's mother deposited her at a city hospital. There they met Carrie's father who was waiting for them at the reception desk.

"It will just be for a week or two," both parents told her. "The doctor wants to run some tests. You'll be out in plenty of time for the Rome trip if you decide to go."

"Sign here for being admitted on a voluntary basis," the admitting nurse instructed. Dressed in civilian clothes, only her name tag identified her affiliation with the hospital.

"It shows that you are mature enough to know when you need help," everyone coaxed her.

Sitting down beside the reception desk, Carrie picked up a pen and carefully read the fine print at the end of the paper. Her left hand heavily brushed the bounce out of her hair as she thought. Did she really have much of a choice?

Looking up, Carrie read the faces of those who were urging her to sign and thought for a moment. At home Carrie's mother and sisters watched her every move, so that she'd be easily caught if she ever tried running away again. Where would she go if she ever managed to escape? No friend or relative would have her. On the other hand, Carrie knew that she would have a slim chance of survival if she tried making it on her own in the streets. She felt an ironic relief when she heard the metal door lock behind her. It was a ruthless and crazy way to leave home, but the hospital provided some refuge from her parents.

Chapter Fifteen

...And I don't know how you do it
Makin' love out of nothing at all
Out of nothing at all...

"Makin' Love Out of Nothing at All"
Air Supply

Scarcely a week after Carrie entered the hospital, another patient came to the ward. The new patient, a trim gentleman in his mid-forties endlessly paced the circular hall which joined all the rooms in the unit. The steadiness of his walk reflected the strenuous revolution of the gears in his head churning over some mighty question. His thinking processes were so focused that Carrie almost ran into him as she crossed the hallway from her room.

"Excuse me," he politely offered when Carrie searched his face for the meaning of his intense walk. The gentleman matched Carrie's glance and their eyes met. Looking deeply into his shiny almond-colored eyes, she found the omniscient spirit of a sea captain, an old salt who had skillfully guided his vessel through many of life's storms. Almost immediately a hurt shone through their strength, revealing their pain in a desperate plea for help. Without even daring to ask, the eyes called for human contact.

Carrie shyly looked at the floor. The man was very handsome with olive skin and distinguishing lines of silver through his black hair. She was only a teenager, a female at that. How would a middle-aged man with such a square jaw accept anything she had to offer? She looked at him again and her eyes caught the dark spot on his white turtleneck sweater. Although his attire indicated that he took pride in his appearance, he seemed like a waif in his present state. Carrie wished that he would put aside his quest long enough to care for himself. The man ignored her without denying his weakened state; some things were even more important than himself. He turned away abruptly and continued his journey around the hall.

"Who's that?" Carrie inquired as she met Eric, a teenage male four years her junior, just inside the door of the lounge.

"That's George," Eric answered, shaking his head in bewilderment. "I heard that he wants to get into alpha."

"Alpha?" Carrie murmured. She couldn't imagine what was so special about a pursuit that would land an individual in a hospital.

"It's one of the mind's deepest levels of thinking," Eric explained solemnly.

Carrie pondered Eric's explanation for a few moments. What was so important about thinking such deep thoughts? Remembering the desperation in the man's face, Carrie decided that she would help him if he ever approached her again.

Her opportunity arrived within the next few minutes. It appeared that George had heard her silent thoughts, because he entered the lounge on his next turn around the ward. Carrie stopped chatting with Eric and his friends and turned towards George. He approached the group, attempting to articulate a question, but his deep thoughts proved too difficult to verbalize. Then he motioned the teenagers towards a chalkboard on the wall where he could communicate in writing. The adults in the room moved away to the opposite end of the room, feeling uncomfortable with George's inability to speak and hopeless gestures.

Carrie stood at the man's left shoulder as she watched him pick up a piece of chalk with his right hand. He examined the chalk with a slight smile, wielding the powerful communication tool that was now in his grasp. This writing instrument would be the key to his thoughts. Raising his arm over the black board, George paused briefly as he tried to remember the feel of writing before making a mark. For a few seconds he made circular motions in the air until he connected the motion of the chalk in his hand to the motion of thoughts within his head. Then he glanced sideways at Carrie to be sure that she was still with him. Carrie quietly nodded her readiness before George quickly glanced at Eric who stood on his right side. Encouraged that his attempt in communication would not be in vain, George commenced with the yellowed chalk.

He drew a slow, careful white oval against the blackness of the board. "How can an egg be a triangle?" he asked, finally finding the words.

Briefly, Carrie stepped back and wondered whether she should censor her answer. She was accustomed to such questions in her philosophy and calculus classes as frenzied professors wildly lined the board in a few seconds. Clearly, this was not the work of a madman. Compared to their ranting and raving, George appeared rather sane. He also seemed more sensitive to his audience.

Feeling encouraged, she picked up a piece of chalk and drew her answer on the board. In the tradition of western thought, the triangle illustrated the three different aspects of a single entity: body, mind, and spirit. Generally the symbol was used in a male context of father, son, and spirit. Likewise, the egg could represent a female version of how three distinct parts formed a single entity like the parts of an egg : yolk, white, and shell.

"See, it fits inside easily," she observed, rounding the egg inside the triangle she had drawn. "It touches all the sides." Besides female maturity, the circle symbolized continuity between alpha and omega, the beginning and the end.

Doug, a lanky seventeen year old male standing at the far corner of the board, proposed his own drawings to Carrie when she stepped back to double-check her figures. He suggested the biological symbols for male and female. Carrie blushed at his overt flirtation, politely shaking her head at the hot-blooded philosopher. He had a good point, but sex wasn't just a matter of biology or religious necessity.

Wishing to incorporate some romantic chemistry between the biological symbols, Carrie considered some figures which could relate more freely to the other. It bothered her that the triangle must conform to the size of the enclosed circle for the sides to touch. The circle, on the other hand, was constrained by the size of the triangle. So Carrie proceeded to draw a strong and wide O on the board. Such a nice O, Carrie believed, deserved a big strong 1. After completing her 1 as handsomely as she could, Carrie studied the figures together. The desire between the two figures seemed very natural and strong. In fact, the desire for the other form was so strong that the figures sought each other.

Satisfied with her answer Carrie left the board, separating herself away from the group while leaving her answer intact. George smiled and waved his hand at Carrie as he stayed at the board with the male teenagers. Carrie nodded back and left the lounge to return to her room for the night, still contemplating her latest drawing. Mostly, she thought, George just wanted someone to listen and relate to him. It seemed that the answer to his question was the fact that she had responded, not only offered solutions.

Because Carrie's therapist generally discouraged interaction with the other patients, Carrie's schedule prevented her from seeing George and the others until a week later. Meanwhile, the psychiatrist increased Carrie's medication, severely impairing Carrie's motor functions. Carrie spent her spare moments recuperating from the effects of the drugs, lying painfully sprawled across the bed in her room. One drug, known by the patients as the roller coaster, compelled Carrie to run out of her skin one minute and made her drowsy the next minute. Another drug immobilized her, while creating a trembling in her limbs so heavy that she exercised all motions with extreme caution. Carrie felt like crying every time she noticed the shaking in her hands, a sharp contrast to the finely-tuned body that she had once known. She had spent much of her life taking care of her body as an athlete. Now she was watching the doctors destroy it.

As a result of the medication, Carrie felt very sick and tired when she visited the lounge again. This time she spotted George, Eric, Doug, and some of the others sitting at a table across the room. George raised his hand and smiled at Carrie. He was wearing a clean shirt and seemed very alert as he chatted animatedly with those around him. On his right sat a very attractive olive-skinned woman with deep dark eyes. The beautiful woman, apparently George's wife, sparkled brightly at Carrie and whispered to George, "Is this the one?! She's beautiful!"

For a few seconds Carrie beamed with the woman's approval. Then she stared sadly at the hospital floor while measuring the painful effects of the hospital on her body. This was not the time nor the place to encourage friendships or develop attachments. Carrie felt that the people whom she admired deserved better meeting places than mental wards; they did not belong in hospitals.

Declining the invitation to join the group, Carrie chose a nearby chair in a quiet corner of the room. There she read her book, while keeping her ears tuned to the conversation at the table. She wanted George to concentrate on leaving the hospital.

In the days that followed George used his talents as an executive salesman to make the hospital a better place. He successfully captured the ear of the head nurse and organized a committee to voice patient grievances and protect their rights. Because of his persuasiveness, the hospital installed an air filter in the lounge to clean up the cigarette smoke. Carrie admired his courage and learned from his diplomatic style as he voiced his concerns over the head nurse's patronizing responses. He became Carrie's silent champion and Carrie wished that some day she would be able to do the same about the things which concerned her.

Another woman who entered the ward only a few days after George was as equally vocal as George about patient rights. This woman was hiding in the hospital to avoid being killed by someone who had threatened her life. The woman was the owner of a supply store and had aroused the wrath of some man she refused business. This woman and George became fast friends and Carrie quietly enjoyed their company whenever she made it into the patient lounge. Although she felt too physically sick to ever participate in the rapport, she always sat close enough to listen and watch.

One day, while Carrie was waiting to speak with one of the nurses at the nurse's station about the increased dosages the psychiatrist was prescribing for her, Carrie spotted her patient chart lying opened on the near desk. Skimming the contents, Carrie learned that the section had been written by the portly male nurse on the day of the chalkboard drawings. Although the male nurse professed to be a born-again-christian, Carrie was still surprised by the references to John the Baptist in his interpretation of the encounter. His poetic license appalled Carrie, confirming her suspicions that the patients were completely at the mercy of the nurses' fantasies. If she and some of the other patients didn't be more careful around the nurses, they'd never be well enough to match the nurses' expectations and leave the hospital.

The discovery convinced Carrie to maintain discrete contact with George, Doug, and some of the others. They followed her cue and immediately realized the hostile situation. They began accepting the roles given to them by the hospital staff like actors and actresses, in order to save their real spiritual dimensions from scrutiny and oppression. George's physicians diagnosed him as manic depressive and released him within two weeks. The other woman left two days later. Despite the lack of direct contact, Carrie wept after George and the woman left. Though she was happy to see them leave the hospital, she missed them very much. She had never met people with such warmth and it was difficult to be without them.

As the effects of the drugs became more pronounced with each passing week, Carrie learned more about how the psychiatrist and therapist viewed her case. Nobody had spoken to her about what to expect in terms of hospital therapy and Carrie felt lost in the environment, living patiently from one day to the next without any apparent reason for remaining there. After having stayed at the hospital for a month, the therapist gave her a few clues.

"Historically, every culture has its list of topics which are treated as taboo," the counselor from Argentina lectured in her German accent. As she listened to the therapist's lengthy discourse, Carrie rummaged through the corners of her mind for an appropriate reply. The effect of the drugs heavily bound Carrie to the chair like chained weights and she had difficulty focusing. She carefully eyed the therapist in front of her, one of the people presently responsible for making her life so miserable and painful that she scarcely had the energy to remember how to read or write, much less remember her life before the hospital. Finally, Carrie realized the reason for the lack of direct communication concerning her case; she was the taboo subject.

When the therapist finished, Carrie offered a taboo subject, "A long time ago, when I was six or seven, I found an injured baby blue jay in the backyard. Some kids from the other side of the fence claimed that the bird belonged to them and that they were taking care of it. After I gave the bird away my mother came outside. She hit me for handing the bird over to the older children on the other side of the fence."

Carrie paused for a moment as she felt a tear escape. Then she softly explained, "My mother told me that mother birds kill the baby birds that are touched by humans. She told me that the baby bird would die because I had touched it."

Then Carrie glanced at the therapist for her response. Failing to make the connection between the past and present circumstances, the therapist murmured something incoherent and stared at the floor. A few seconds later the therapist looked up, handed Carrie a tissue in a token gesture to wipe away the tears Carrie had incurred during the moment, and eagerly began writing in the chart book. Without bothering to dry her eyes, Carrie held the tissue in her hands. She felt relieved that the information had satisfied the therapist and hoped that the therapist would not require anymore tears from her.

Chapter Sixteen

...Tell you about a dream that I have every night
It's in dolby stereo but I never hear it right
Take me for a fool well that's alright
Well I see the way to go but there isn't any light
I don't know why I'm scared of the lightning
Trying to reach me...
You're lighting a scene that's faded to black
I threw it away cause I don't want it back
But I don't care it's all psychobabble rap to me...

"Psychobabble"
The Alan Parsons Project

The months slowly passed in the hospital while the details concerning the intent of Carrie's therapy remained vague. The psychiatrist failed to choose a diagnosis for Carrie and had even greater difficulty dealing with her parents. Carrie eventually accepted her weakened physical condition and concentrated on those activities which would appear innocuous to the hospital staff. Determined not to become a casualty of boredom in the environment, Carrie devised many ways to entertain herself. She played her guitar in the lounge for the others and went walking or jogging whenever she could obtain a pass to go outside. She learned how to crochet and tried all sorts of artistic endeavors during the open hours of the art room. These activities enabled Carrie to tune out the more obnoxious patients and hospital staff.

"This place is just like a WWII concentration camp," yelled Bill, one of the patients, at several of the nurses in the ward. Then he remarked to those inside the art room, "The staff are like Nazi guards and the patients are the prisoners."

"Do we need to ask Dr. Sloan to increase your medication?" threatened the head nurse, a blond possessing the same facial luster as the psychiatrist in the metallic office.

Carrie dropped the paint brush she was using and switched to a thicker one. Usually this chubby middle-age man chattered about his sexual preference for pre-adolescent males. She noted that Bill was beginning to make progress in recovering from his own control issues. After her second month in the hospital, Carrie started treating most of the hospital staff as stooges from Soviet gulags, and ironically they responded by showing her greater respect. They probably never would have realized how she really felt about their abusive need for power, but they unconsciously responded as admission of their complicity. It was a double-edged sword; she observed them as much as they watched her. Carrie mastered a philosophical approach to the situation and just continued to feed their plays as if they were caged animals in a zoo.

She tilted her head back and critically eyed her acrylic painting. At least now she had time to paint; she had sorely missed the activity while she was a college student. This present painting showed signs of recovering from the initial shock of being in the hospital. The trees in her landscapes looked like something a two year old might paint. As much as she tried she wasn't satisfied. The turning point came when she started treating the hospital staff like gulag stooges. Having mastered the art of escaping the hospital system for her benefit, Carrie was pleased to see her artwork regain its former sophistication. Carrie chose another brush and blended more colors on her wooden canvas while the head nurse and Bill quietly argued in the hall.

Another patient rushed into the art room. "Cory is gone! He escaped again!" Mary Arnold whispered excitedly. Mary Arnold, a slightly mentally retarded woman who had been abused by her mother, grandparents, and medical professionals, loved talking about Cory.

"I helped him the last time," Mary Arnold boasted, "...when he hid inside the lunch cart and was wheeled downstairs to the kitchen."

Surprising the bewildered kitchen workers, Cory had quickly jumped out of the cart and bolted out of the hospital.

"It's one of those crazies from the fourth floor!" a black cook had hollered at him. Cory laughed when he heard her.

Cory, a nineteen year old all-American boy, had been hospitalized for attempting suicide after his girlfriend broke up with him. His first attempt consisted of dashing past the male nurses when someone opened the metal door to the ward. In his second escape, Cory hid in a lunch cart going back to the kitchen and ran out of the hospital. The fire department caught Cory in an abandoned field. They hauled him back to the hospital where he was stripped nude and locked in isolation.

"He popped a ceiling tile and tried crawling out over our heads during the group session," continued Mary Arnold. "The fire department is chasing Cory inside the crawl space now."

Two hours later, Carrie watched Cory jubilantly stroll into the patient lounge. "They are going to let me go home," he announced.

This time the hospital decided against imposing any punitive measures. Cory sat down in the rocking chair beside Carrie and excitedly rocked. "My Dad is buying me a car. My buddies and I are taking it on test drive to New Orleans next weekend... can't wait to see how it does on the highway."

Carrie nodded, knowing that Cory's father took delighted pride in his son's hospital escapes.

Then the teenage boy shook his head and stared at the floor between his knees. "No girl is worth committing suicide over. Nobody is worth that much."

Carrie sensed, though, that a girl was only part of the reason for Cory's suicide attempt. Cory's actions reminded her of the value of freedom. Carrie felt compelled to assume minor risks for her own sense of human dignity.

"Do you have a moment?" Marianne interrupted Carrie at the desk beside her bed.

Carrie nodded and quickly put away the pen and paper she was employing for the moment on a writing project. Then she left the desk and sat down next to Marianne on the bed.

"How's it going?" Marianne started. "Was that your sister who came with your mother for the visit with the therapist yesterday?"

"Yes, that was Samantha," Carrie remembered with a smile. Then a sadness flickered across her face.

"How did it go?" Marianne continued.

"It went OK," Carrie replied before explaining the technical results of the encounter. To Carrie, all the details of the meeting seemed trivial and inconsequential. She still felt like she had lost contact with Samantha, who had continued living at home while she was away at college.

"I came because I wanted to give you a hug," Marianne offered with her palms opened towards Carrie.

Carrie reached for her and felt Marianne's arms close around her with a gentle rock. Marianne's gesture surprised Carrie, because it was unusual for staff to make any sort of physical contact with patients as if the patients had been deigned untouchable.

"You are a very strong young woman," Marianne commented in a hushed voice.

The words pierced her and Carrie immediately started sobbing. When she became aware of a weakening in Marianne's hug, Carrie withdrew and quieted the violent shaking within her abdomen. Carrie turned away from Marianne as the tears continued to softly stream down her face. A look of regret flashed across Marianne's face when she realized that the moment had been lost. Carrie faced her again, drying her tears. For a few minutes they sat together in silence. Then a young male nurse arrived and told Marianne that she was needed at the nurse's station for a meeting.

"I'll be alright," Carrie assured Marianne as she rose from the bed to leave.

"I know," Marianne smiled, nodding at Carrie. "Thanks for the hug."

Carrie eagerly nodded her response and Marianne left the room.

Several weeks later, the hospital finally discharged Carrie on the conditions that she never return to either of her parents' homes and continue therapy as an outpatient. Carrie had stayed at the hospital for four months. There had been financial incentives for keeping Carrie in the hospital for longer than the initial two week period. In addition, the psychiatrist had become a third party in the bitter power struggles between Carrie's divorced parents. She used her control over Carrie in dealing with the parents. Eventually she finally found a diagnosis for Carrie which satisfied them. She dubbed Carrie "manic depressive", implying that the problem was biological and hereditary.

Although she had found a job and a place to stay, Carrie returned to her mother's house a week after her release. In making the transition from the prison of the hospital to the civilian world, Carrie realized that she needed a familiar world to restore her confidence. It would take time for the effects to wear off.

Chapter Seventeen

Maybe it's you, maybe it's me
Maybe it's just the constant rhythm of the sea
Maybe it's just that I've never been the kind
Who can pass a lucky penny by
Maybe it's wise, maybe it's not
Maybe it's you who brought the caring I forgot
Isn't nice to talk about the special way
You smile whenever I'm around
Rising on the shore the ocean came
Walks along the waves of velveteen
His only thought was love for me...

"Maybe It's You"
Words by John Bettis
Music by Richard Carpenter

Initially, Carrie's relationship with her family proceeded smoothly. Eager to become self-sufficient as well as minimize her family contact, she immediately found work as a grocery store cashier which paid very well. She assumed a second job at the community college where she earned nine credit hours during the summer. Though the college workstudy position didn't pay as much as grocery store business, Carrie enjoyed the comradery that the print shop offered.

Meanwhile, she severed relations with the University, maintaining friendships with only a few close individuals. Most of Carrie's classmates thought that she had simply dropped out of school, except for one student who pursued her sudden disappearance.

On a midsummer's afternoon she received a phone call from Brent, her head-to-head conversationalist from the campus blood drive.

"Hi, this is BW!" said the familiar voice.

"BW?!" Carrie answered perplexed.

"Brent Wright," he rejoined. "BW is a nickname."

"Oh...," Carrie said slowly as she quickly connected the name and face to the sender of some mystery letters that had been sent to her home.

"I missed you in Europe. How are you doing?" BW asked.

"Oh, I'm doing alright. I landed in the hospital and had to cancel the trip to Rome."

"I'm sorry to hear that," he said quietly. "I've tried calling you, but I had to look up the number in the phone book. There are quite a few of you with the same last name. I called most of them. Did you get the letters I sent?"

"Yes, I did. Thank you very much. I'm afraid to say that I wasn't in much of a position to respond. I was having a rough go of it."

"I'm glad to hear that you're doing much better." Changing the subject, Brent simply asked, "Would you like to see the musical "My Fair Lady" this Saturday?"

"That's the one showing with Rex Harrison...," Carrie commented while weighing the possibility of dating someone else besides Marty. The friendly voice at the other end of the wire touched Carrie with its sincerity. She was impressed that he had tracked down her phone number. Carrie decided to take a chance with this man who obviously didn't give up so easily.

"Yes, Saturday sounds fun," she answered. Brent didn't fit the regular mold of typical dates; he was too honest about his feelings. As she replaced the receiver on the line at the end of the conversation Carrie wondered what would happen next with BW.

＊ ＊ ＊

Brent arrived at 7pm on Saturday. Assuming the role of hostess, Samantha opened the front door and invited Brent into the house as Carrie finished dressing. Donning a cool cotton tan dress for the summer night, Carrie hoped the flesh color of her hose would cover the red marks on her legs, the result of the worst shaving job in her entire life. She felt nervous about getting out again. Then she hurriedly fastened her feet into a comfortable pair of dress sandals and ran to save Brent from her family's scrutiny.

"How are you doing, lady?" Brent met Carrie with a smile.

Unconsciously, Carrie looked directly into his eyes and noticed a few tears welding inside their blueness. This surprised her; apparently, she affected this man's life more than she realized. Carrie immediately sat down on the couch before the trembling in her legs betrayed her giddiness. He had used that word again, "lady", and she felt disconcerted by his respectful endearment.

Noting the absence of his Greek sailor's cap, Carrie studied Brent's formal attire of plaid slacks and shiny yellow shirt. He dressed in same the harmonious fashion as an artist displaying his paintings. Admiring his appearance for the sensual maturity it projected, Carrie looked forward to spending more time with Brent.

Stepping down from the front porch, Brent drew Carrie's attention to a '67 Volkswagon beetle with splotchy green paint and red headlight fender.

"Meet Maxwell," he said as if introducing her to a roommate.

"Maxwell, the physicist?" Carrie grinned, giving the bug a second look. This was no ordinary car.

"Ya, the one responsible for the famous Maxwell equations in electromagnetic theory," he said as they got into the car and began the forty minute drive to the city music hall. "My father and I picked out two VW bugs at the local auto yard," Brent explained as he sped over the highway. "We plan to convert them to solar power. My father found the plans in a magazine and sent away for them. The car can be built from a VW chassis. One guy managed to drive his solar powered bug over the Rockies. He stopped every two hours to let the batteries recharge."

Carrie had never even considered building a solar powered car. Carefully, she examined the insides of Maxwell while contemplating the intricacies of such an undertaking. Then she noticed the handmade wooden knobs on the doors, glove box, and stick shift.

"My dad made those," Brent interjected proudly, observing her curiosity. Carrie noticed that he was watching her more than the traffic.

"I made the one on the glove box. It keeps falling off," Brent explained while reaching across the car to demonstrate. Carrie anxiously glanced at Maxwell's swerve on the highway.

"I need to glue it in place. My dad has a shop in the basement. The original handles were broken so we just whittled some new ones," he continued.

"I like the workmanship. What else do you make?"

"Most everything. We make our own butter, soap, applesauce, cider, vinegar, wine... Daddy tried making champagne once, but it had too much fizz. He produced two cases worth. Of the twentyfour bottles of champagne: the first cork put a hole in the kitchen ceiling, twenty corks cleared the telephone wires outside, and the remaining three bottles exploded in the basement."

Carrie looked at Brent with amazement. She had been raised on instant cake mixes and homogenized milk.

"How did you learn to do these things?" she asked.

"My father raised us on a farm. He and Mom bought an old farmhouse with ten acres the year after they married. He learned about running a farm by trial and error. He also works as a test engineer. On vacations he loves to go fly fishing."

Carrie commented, "There's not much fly fishing around here. We do a lot of pole fishing."

She elaborated further, "My high school chemistry instructor and I wanted to paint our lures with glow-in-the-dark paint. I found the recipe to make fluorescent calcium sulfite in a chemistry book. It makes glow-in-the-dark paint."

Hesitating a moment to be sure she had Brent's attention, Carrie continued her story: "So I crushed some oyster shells, mixed the powder with sulfur, and heated the mixture in an old butter dish while the family was away. The hood above the stove collected the fumes and the experiment went along fine. However, the stuff wouldn't glow. My instructor and I tried the experiment at school, and the results were the same. Evidently, the oyster shells didn't contain enough impurities. It's the barium and zinc impurities that cause the stuff to glow. We never did get a chance to try it out on the fish."

"We'd consider that cheating," Brent grinned as the wind from a small side window threatened to tousle his curly dark hair. "Fly fishermen just use a hook. The secret is in the wrist motion of the cast; it makes fishing a real sport... and you must fall in the stream at least once, otherwise you can't consider it a real fishing trip," he added while adjusting the window's opening to save his hairstyle.

"I'll have to try that some time. There's little opportunity around here for fly fishing; the streams only move fast when it floods. I suppose that's why we cheat when we fish. We have to outsmart them instead of outmaneuver them," she replied.

Leaving Brent speechless for a brief moment, Carrie ignored the healthy wind currents rocking the Volkswagon and proceeded with another topic.

"There's something I've been meaning to ask you...," Carrie started. "Are you the same BW who sent the photo and letter to my Mom last fall?"

"Ya, that was me," he proudly smiled. "Should have seen the photos of Tim Sullivan and his girlfriend that I sent to his parents. It was a series of shots with the last frame showing his girlfriend sitting on his lap. His parents loved it; Tim did too. They wrote me a really nice letter. Jan Smith's parents wrote me also. Parents like to hear how their sons and daughters are doing away from home. It's a lot of fun and it makes a lot of people very happy. My job with the yearbook gives me access to the addresses of all the parents."

Carrie searched the innocent face of the mystery writer and swallowed hard. So it was Brent! She never bothered telling him that her mother disliked the letter, being suspicious of an any outsider's interest. Carrie didn't wish to complicate Brent's world; it was too precious. For the remainder of the evening, Carrie let Brent do most of the talking. She enjoyed listening to his version of the world and Brent liked talking about it. They spent a wonderful evening together at the musical.

The following week Carrie invited Brent on a hike and picnic at one of her favorite nearby lakes. The trails changed seasonally and she enjoyed staying in tune with the changes in the same manner one maintains contact with a friend. According to the amount of rainfall received each month, the lake would redistribute its waters with respect to the varying topography. Every time she visited the site Carrie always discovered something new and different in the lake's biosphere. The quick recovery of the terrain corresponded with its ability to accept change. Carrie noticed that nature often compensated with the dramatic growth of certain species of wildlife and vegetation which restored the biosphere. Watching the continuity of these cycles in the web of life inspired Carrie with a sense of connection.

Today she wanted to show this environment to Brent. Carrie led the way over the winding green trails as Brent and she hopped over tiny streams and scurried through gullies to the music of croaking frogs and chirping crickets. Brent toted his camera around his neck and occasionally tried enticing Carrie to pose for a few snapshots. She discouraged him by directing attention to their surroundings.

After feeling a raindrop brush her face, Carrie stopped abruptly and peered at the darkening sky.

"Brent, do you feel any raindrops?" she asked while testing for the droplet amount with her palm extended to the sky. No sooner had Carrie asked the question, then they were bombarded with a flurry of water. This marked the advent of a summer storm, the kind that could bring every kid in Carrie's neighborhood outside to swim in the torrential street gutters.

She watched Brent's face for an expression of his feelings; they were both waiting for the other to decide on a course of action. She quickly assumed the initiative, "I think that we should make our way back to the car. There's no telling how long this downpour will last and I'm cold."

Minutes later, hail the size of popcorn pelted them from the clouds and rain poured in buckets. The tiny streams Brent and Carrie had crossed earlier reached the full extent of their gullies, forcing them to create a new route to the car. Brent followed closely behind her. Carrie appreciated the trust in her capabilities. Most men she knew would have insisted on carving the route to the car themselves, regardless of their unfamiliarity with the area. These macho rituals escaped Brent. This man was definitely more advanced.

While they wandered through the mud and blinding rain, Brent reached out and placed his Greek sailor's cap on her head.

"Wear this," he instructed. "You're getting chilled; I can see the goose bumps on your arms... a person loses ninety percent of their body heat through the head."

Accepting his chivalrous offer, Carrie grinned and adjusted the fit of the cap. Not only did she have his trust, but she presently sported one of his most prized possessions. She turned around and continued the journey as the rain transformed into a light sprinkle.

When Brent and Carrie reached the car, they ignored the vehicle and decided against canceling the picnic. While dark clouds hurried across the sky, Brent and Carrie basked in the intermittent sun bursts. The sun's warmth penetrated the sopping dampness of their hiking clothes and dried their skin after the showers ceased. Brent and Carrie loitered on a series of nearby rocks where Brent stole a few photographs of her. This time Carrie submitted to the whims of his photographic art without feeling overly self conscious.

The summer storm had removed her awkwardness with Brent. They found a dry spot underneath the swaying branches of a weeping willow for their picnic. As they relaxed and chatted over the assortment of food in the picnic basket, Carrie looked at Brent for what seemed to be the first time. A veil of guise fell from between them. She observed the man before her as if she had a pair of new eyes. He was wearing jogging shorts and a tank top which revealed wiry muscles on his lean frame. Brent brightened as if he could sense her silent appraisal. His slow deliberate actions nourished her admiration, calling further attention to his form. When she realized that Brent had been observing the subtle movements of her own body, Carrie became conscious of her own motions. The swimmer's analogy no longer could describe the physical attraction in their relationship.

Brent took her home later in the afternoon where Carrie said goodbye and hugged him warmly on the porch steps. No longer was he just a guy she knew from college; he was rapidly becoming her friend. He accepted Carrie's embrace with a gentle smile and returned to his mechanical pal, Maxwell, for the drive back to his apartment.

Chapter Eighteen

Gotta get off, gonna get on,
Gonna get off this merry-go-round...,

"Valley of the Dolls"
Alan Jay Lerner and
Burton Lane

A few days later Carrie saw the therapist, whom she had been seeing weekly since her first day at the hospital.

"How's did it work out with Marty?" the therapist asked after Carrie settled into chair facing hers.

"I broke up with him a few days ago," Carrie admitted.

"Oh you did..," the therapist commented, while scrutinizing Carrie's face for the justification. Carrie had done the opposite of what she had been encouraging Carrie to do. Last week the therapist had suggested that Carrie take advantage of the sexual freedom afforded by modern methods of birth control.

"I wanted to make a clean break...," Carrie explained as she squirmed uncomfortably in her chair. She knew that the therapist would not understand her relationship with Marty, so she quickly drew the therapist's attention to a more pertinent problem. "There's something else...," Carrie began as her hands sought the letter inside her purse that she had received from Brent only a day ago. She painfully shook her head over the letter, running her right hand over the top of her forehead.

"The letter is from Brent, the friend from school who sent me all those letters that I never answered. He's the one who looked me up when he returned from Rome," Carrie sighed heavily. A look of worry haunted her features. Putting the folded letter away by her side, Carrie announced, "I don't think I should see him anymore."

"Why?" the therapist demanded in her thick accent.

"There's something wrong about it. I don't understand his letter. This guy must be strange or something."

"May I read it?" the therapist asked, her curiosity aroused. Carrie immediately handed the letter over, feeling relieved to get it off her hands. The therapist devoured its substance. Finishing, she leaned back in her chair and grinned with her eyes half closed. "He loves you."

"He what?!..." Carrie stared at her in disbelief. She had felt the attraction with Brent, but love was another question. "Are you sure?" she gulped.

"Read the letter again!" She instructed, tossing the letter on Carrie's lap.

Feeling like a fool, Carrie skimmed over the words. Brent's emotions were definitely on the paper; though, he never actually wrote "I love you" his clumsy sentences verified the sincere attempt. Of course! That is what he had been trying to say to her.

"What am I going to do about being manic depressive?" Carrie pleaded, her head drooping over the letter laying on her lap. "It's not so good to fall in love with me...," she whispered as tears welled inside her eyes. For a moment she forgot the counselor was listening; this was the real issue that concerned her about the letter.

"I think you should tell him. He already knows something is up," the therapist suggested with a confidant puff of cigarette smoke. Then she leaned back in her chair again and took a long drag off the skinny cigarette. She nodded until Carrie agreed with her.

Carrie straightened in her chair with the advice, resuming her composure. The therapist was right; she would have to tell Brent sometime... and the sooner the better.

After the meeting with the therapist Carrie went home and called Brent that same evening. She invited Brent over for the following afternoon, telling him that she needed to talk with him about something important. Brent accepted her invitation, happily promising Carrie his ready assistance on any matter which concerned her.

When he arrived the next day, Carrie answered his knock on the front door and ushered him into the living room where she had arranged a plate of brownies. She had chosen a time when she knew her mother and sisters would be absent from the house for a few hours, away from hearing distance.

"Have some brownies," Carrie offered as they sat down on the living room sofa. Having heard that the quickest way to reach a man's heart was through his stomach, Carrie desperately wanted to take full advantage of the effect. She watched in delight as Brent eagerly picked up a couple of brownies from the plate.

"Would you like some milk?" Carrie asked, disappearing into the kitchen before Brent answered. She still felt easily flustered around Brent.

"That would be wonderful!" he exclaimed, standing up after her. Carrie glanced at the enthusiastic skinny frame waiting for her in the living room. There was no need to capture this guy's heart by serving brownies and milk; it was already hers.

She joined him in the living room and handed him a glass of milk to accompany the brownie that he held in his hand. Slowly they resumed their former seats on the sofa as Carrie started, "Brent, there's a few things I need to tell you."

Brent sipped his milk for a few seconds and then politely placed the glass on the coffee table.

"What is it, lady?" he asked, moving his body closer to hers.

Surprised that the brownies could produce such dramatic results, Carrie backed away from his approach. She could not honestly respond to his nonverbal cues until Brent knew about her circumstances. Carrie continued, "Well, you know the city hospital? ...My parents put me in there because I ran away."

Brent protectively placed his arm around Carrie, demonstrating his refusal to be scared away by her information.

Carrie remained motionless underneath his arm and explained further, "The hospital diagnosed me as manic depressive and told me that I would need medication for the rest of my life. They said that I had a chemical deficiency."

True to the spirit of a male protector, Brent straightened and lightly squeezed Carrie. "It's alright," he assured her. "I'm on your side."

Carrie disregarded his knightly offer. "Thanks for your support," she answered without emotion. She never returned his embrace, indicating that she preferred dealing with her own problem alone. How could she expect someone else to understand the recent events of her life when she scarcely understood them herself?!

"There's something else... I'm not sure if I'm up for the astronomy party at the University. It hurts to go back because not everyone understands," she admitted. "Some of the memories there aren't so pleasant. I keep my story a secret; there's a lot of stigma involved and I don't like feeling as if I'm some sort of freak."

"If there is anything I can do to make it easier on you, let me know," he offered. For some reason Carrie felt that she could trust Brent's words and she let him take her hand in his.

By the time the weekend arrived, Carrie rediscovered her enthusiasm for the astronomy party and she returned to the campus with Brent. The department planned to observe the lunar eclipse occurring late in the evening, so all telescopes in the department were hauled outside and focused on the planets. Shortly before the event, Brent decided to photograph the event from the roof of the student activity complex and enlisted Carrie's assistance.

"We mounted all that equipment in record time and there's almost two hours before the eclipse," Brent told Carrie as he closed the door adjoining the yearbook office to the roof.

Then Brent's manner suddenly quieted. Anxiously he searched the room and adjacent hallway for signs of other visitors. When he seemed assured that he and Carrie were alone, he offered in a hushed voice, "Have a seat?"

Carrie glanced at Brent inquisitively and sat down behind one of the paper laden desks in the yearbook office. Before sitting down in a chair across the room, he explained further in voice which was barely audible, "There's something I want to tell you."

Now it was her turn to listen to his story. Surprised by his announcement, Carrie looked up at Brent from the assortment of papers and magazines which had caught her eye. She wasn't sure what to expect next, but the expression on Brent's face told her that it was a very serious matter.

"I dated some other girls while I was in Rome," he began gravely, "and became involved in some heavy necking with one of them."

Brent paused in his confession, heaving a weighted sigh. "I regretted it afterwards, feeling that I had gone too far. I didn't intend to become so physically involved, but it just sorta happened. I promised myself that it wouldn't ever happened again," he told Carrie, shaking his head over his self-imposed guilt.

Offering no comment, Carrie cautiously maintained her silent ear. She wondered whether his partner felt the same. Brent continued, "One of the things I look for in a girlfriend is the mothering instinct. It's important for me to find someone who will be a good mother for my children. So far you fit this ideal of mine very closely." Brent stopped speaking for a few seconds and looked directly at Carrie. "I just want you to know that... I've never met anyone like you. Whether you realize it or not, you have all the qualities of a good mother. I can see it from your interactions with people."

Carrie met Brent's eyes, nodding at his forwardness as he quickly pushed his glasses back on his nose. Ignoring his guilt, she felt intrigued by his revelations. No other man she had known admitted using the mother image as prerequisite for a lover. Such desire excluded the creation of a madonna image, an idea which appealed to Carrie. Brent would be too physically attracted to his lover to ever leave her stranded on a pedestal.

Carrie leaned back in the cushioned chair and reflected for a few more seconds. A good father must search for a good mother; Brent had genuinely distanced himself from the child's role by referring to child production.

"I must confess that I consider my boyfriends in light of prospective parenting," Carrie admitted when she turned towards Brent again. "I feel that it is important and it means a lot to me. I get a lot of joy from watching fathers care for their young."

Silence followed her words as Brent and Carrie blankly stared at each other for a few seconds. She wasn't about to reveal the extent of her sexual experience, though limited, exceeded Brent's present level. In spite of the intimacy she and Marty had shared, they had been content with keeping their virginity. Though Carrie preferred men who could lose some control during the heat of passion, she chose those who considered the emotional as well as the physical consequences of sexual activity. Brent evidently possessed these abilities, but he was more naive and innocent than anyone she had ever dated. He seemed to need her guidance, whereas Carrie needed his honesty in their relationship.

* * *

Two weeks later the outpatient therapist suddenly fled home on a flight to Argentina, leaving Carrie in the hands of the psychiatrist. Carrie wasn't as surprised as the psychiatrist by the therapist's abrupt departure. Often Carrie had found the therapist appearing more depressed than herself. Though the psychiatrist apologized for the therapist's abrupt departure and asked Carrie to continue therapy with her, Carrie seized the opportunity to drop herself from the psychiatrist's list of cases. She wanted to regain some of the human dignity which she felt she had lost during her stay in the hospital. Carrie felt that she had nothing to lose in foregoing the visits to the psychiatrist.

The psychiatrist told her, "Your father gave me some information about you that you don't know. You need to stay with me."

Carrie felt angry at the psychiatrist for the deception. Whatever her father and psychiatrist knew about her was something she would have to figure out on her own. She stood up to the psychiatrist.

"I didn't like the drugs that you put me on in the hospital and I didn't like the way my father treated me. I have decided to move on."

The psychiatrist seem flustered by this response. She looked at her desk and attempted to convince Carrie to stay. "You'll need to know it later in life," she threatened.

Carrie shook her head and left the room.

Throughout the summer Carrie continued her studies at a community college and worked two jobs. One job, checking groceries at a local supermarket, enabled Carrie to earn a substantial sum of money in a relatively short amount of time. Despite the high wages, almost one half of the hired checkers quit during the first two weeks because of the high pressure. The pressure didn't seem to affect Carrie and she obtained a second job in the print shop at the community college. Although everyone in the print shop was a hard worker, they made time for practical jokes and watermelon picnics. Carrie blended well with the people at the print shop, and they taught her many things about the bindery and printing business. By the end of the summer, Carrie had saved enough money to realize one of her immediate goals: getting a car.

"It's your color," her mother commented when she saw the blue Toyota two-door.

Grieved, Carrie turned and looked away. She didn't want to be identified with the color blue. At least, not anymore. Carrie had chosen the car for its performance and the smooth running engine tucked neatly underneath the car's hood; exterior color had been an unimportant issue in her mind.

Carrie sighed deeply and looked at the gray cement driveway underneath the car's wheels. She knew that driveway like she knew her own bed, having spent many hours lying on her back to repair the cars parked above her. Carrie had been worried that her mother might become upset and encourage her to immediately get rid of the vehicle. Any move Carrie made for greater self-reliance or independence was never well received at home.

Carrie kept the car, focusing on the many features that she really liked about the automobile. She enjoyed listening to the tape deck and zipping the car's sleek body around turns and into parking spaces. Excited about the feel of the wheel in her hands, Carrie drove the car to the community college during the following week. Usually, she rode her bike, but Carrie wanted to utilize the commute time for joy-riding in her car. Lately, she had been spending her spare moments catching up on her sleep. She always felt tired these days, and she wanted to take the car on a pleasure trip when she had enough energy to make it a pleasant one.

Pulling into a space in the landscaped parking lot at the community college, Carrie quickly turned off the engine and leaned back against her seat. She took a deep breath as she glanced above at one of the thickly leafed trees shading the car. Shaking her head, Carrie felt the heat of the sun melt her into the car's blueness. It would be awhile before she found the strength to resume bicycling the six mile distance to campus in the 100 degree temperatures.

With her mother's words resounding in her ears, Carrie realized the futility of her efforts in trying to ever escape—the heat, the exhaustion, the dark blue... All these thoughts jumbled through her, leading to deeper revelations. Her efforts to escape the conditions of her past and home environment appeared futile and senseless. Desperately, she wanted to touch the fun and exciting people she had encountered through work and school, but her past hospitalization marred her like a growing blue ink stain on a white shirt.

Placing her hands firmly on the car's steering wheel, Carrie turned the wheel freely to the left and right a few degrees. Her eyes measured the amount of freedom in the steering wheel before it caught the safety lock.

Click. The wheel no longer moved. The degree of freedom was minimal. Carrie released her seat belt and heard it roll behind her. Then she left the car.

After locking the car door with her key, Carrie blinked in the sunshine and began walking towards her class. There, on the hot sidewalk, Carrie spotted a large spider laboring across the pavement with only two of its legs. She reflected a few seconds, and then purposely stepped on the disabled insect.

An act of mercy, she thought as she continued her way. Otherwise, the bug would soon become prey or starve to death, having no hope of recovery from its debilitating injury. She remembered all the horses, dogs, cats, and birds that she had known which had been mercifully put to sleep. People were treated differently; nobody ever put them to sleep. Euthanasia was controversial as well as illegal.

Such thoughts haunted Carrie throughout the day. She had always had them for as long as she could remember. They had some connection with the Nightmare that had bothered her as a youngster. Maybe it was due to her own lack of guts that she had never found the strength to let go and end her battles peacefully. Now she felt tired enough to let go as if some permanent disability afflicted her and made her efforts futile. Maybe she owed it to herself—to do the one thing that nobody had the sense to do long ago when the first Nightmare came. Though it wasn't right to die in overwhelming pain, it certainly wasn't right to continually live in it either.

The following afternoon after finishing her morning work at the print shop, Carrie went home and proceeded directly to the bathroom. Holding her arms above the sink, she watched the cold tap water splash over her wrists. For the last several days she had watched the blade of the bindery cutting machine slice through a million stacks of paper. Haunted by the machine's swift cut, she had visualized her escape from the repetitive trauma which seemed to thread her life.

Once her wrists felt numb she grabbed a razor blade from the cabinet. Hoping to finally die in a safe place, she entered her bedroom without closing the door behind her for privacy. She sat down on her bed and curled her legs underneath her in a crosslegged position. Then Carrie ran the blade across her left wrist.

She hated her left wrist, the one which always got her into trouble. Like the swan's wing from the fairy tale, it reminded her of a difficult past. She wanted to cut it off, so she could be allowed to die in peace. Concentrating all the hate and blame that she felt from her present environment on the wrist,

Carrie discovered, however, that she had difficulty getting beyond a scratch. She didn't want to hurt herself.

Like a buddhist monk driven to douse his body in gasoline and burn his meditating body, Carrie decided to complete the ritual by lapsing into a trance. Gazing intently at both exposed wrists, she allowed her consciousness to be swept away by their appearance. As a result of the trance, Carrie realized that she valued them too much to harm them. All the pain and anger were merely reflections of her environment, and not really a part of her. So Carrie imagined a peaceful, nonviolent death, intending to lapse in a trance so deep that her spirit would permanently separate from her physical being.

While beginning to feel her consciousness lightly slip away from its physical form, Carrie sensed the vague presence of her mother in front of her bed. Her sister Samantha had ran for their mother after finding Carrie in the bedroom.

"Carrie, I'll get you some good help," her mother said in her most soothing voice. Noticing the absence of anger in her mother's presence, Carrie tried coming out of the trance enough to listen.

"A friend of mine has a husband who takes the same medication that you do. He really likes his doctor. Says that he's the best in the city. This time we'll get you some good help."

Then she left and Carrie overheard her make a few phone calls. Still feeling lightheaded, Carrie blinked her eyes and looked blankly at her bedroom. She felt encouraged to continue fighting the trance, which she sensed would end her life in only a half hour.

That evening Carrie's mother drove her to a place which had been open for a month. The clinic was operated by a young, innovative graduate from Stanford who approached medical problems from a biological standpoint. Immediately, the clinic took Carrie off all medication and ran a series of blood tests. After a month of tests and observations they concluded that the manic depressive label had been erroneous.

I usually decline to comment on the practices of my colleagues in the medical profession, but the treatment you received is deplorable," Dr. Rick told Carrie after a month. "The medication they gave you adversely affected your biological system and possibly caused the hypothyroidism that you are experiencing now. Your behavior doesn't fit the manic depressive mode and your body doesn't show a biological imbalance. I fail to find any reason for their diagnosis; your EEGs are normal, and the CAT scan appeared normal, showing no evidence of brain tumor or vascular insufficiency."

Then he added, "We want to run some more tests and are waiting for the results of the last blood tests. Hang in there. It will only be another month at the most."

Although the clinic was more humane than the city hospital, it was still had an unconscious depressive effect like a prison. Nonetheless, Carrie felt relieved to learn about the scientific basis for her intuitive fears concerning the medication. The adverse effects were real rather than a product of her imagination, and this knowledge restored trust in her sensory perceptions.

Brent called Carrie at the clinic after she had been there a week. He had recently returned from a trip and wanted to talk to her. He had been visiting a female classmate from the University. She neglected telling him about the circumstances of her admission to the clinic, and Brent never asked for details. The explanation "I wasn't feeling well" seemed sufficient.

"Would you mind if you had a visitor?" he asked, Carrie's present residence didn't seem to phase him in the least.

"Well, actually I'd appreciate that very much," she admitted. Again she decided to take another risk and allow this young man to come further inside her world. Something about his manner assured her that he meant no harm.

Brent visited her almost every single day. Often he'd bring Carrie letters and cards from some of her friends at the University. Carrie looked forward to Brent's visits and always thanked him. Gradually he won her trust through his devotion.

"Rick says that I possess the same blood chemistry as a woman who has just given birth to a baby. Some women experience a mild biological depression after delivery," Carrie rambled to Brent during one of his visits. "Something triggered the chemical response in my body and they are giving me an antidepressant to help kick me out of it. It only takes two months to recover from a biochemical depression, so I'll only be on medication for only three months."

Brent's eyes widened as he listened to Carrie. Regarding Carrie's secrets as privileged information, he responded as if he was eavesdropping on a conversation that belonged to one of Carrie's female friends. His encouragement emboldened Carrie to confide in the hospital staff as well.

The next day during an afternoon pingpong game with one of the nurses, Carrie became suddenly lightheaded. She felt as if her body floated a few feet off the ground. The sensation affected her vision and her focus narrowed on the pingpong ball, making it appear as the only object in the room. Carrie immediately reported these sensations to the nurses and they recognized the sight as "tunnel vision". When they measured Carrie's blood pressure, they discovered that it was extremely low.

The next day Rick came and asked Carrie if he could try hypnotizing her. "Despite what you may have already heard, hypnotized subjects only respond to their internal will rather the will of the hypnotist," he assured her. "Although it does make the subject more open to suggestions, a hypnotist can not cause the hypnotized individual to break their moral code or go against their conscience," Rick explained.

"You show a very high susceptibility to hypnotism which explains the tunnel vision that you experienced yesterday," he concluded. "The occurrence is probably a stress reaction. Were you thinking about the meeting with your mother while you played pingpong?"

"Yes,... yes, I was. I haven't seen her in a while and we had a conference scheduled for the evening," Carrie answered.

"Actually susceptibility to hypnotism is an indicator of excellent mental health," Rick smiled at her. For example, schizophrenics can not be hypnotized. You can learn how to control the trances and have them work for you."

Carrie brightened. It also was nice to know she performed well under duress.

Once the tests were completed at the clinic, Carrie's case was given to Dr. B., who had referred her to the clinic. In addition to the antidepressant, Carrie was given medication for hypothyroidism and the thyroid returned to normal within two years, indicating the dysfunction had been caused by the drugs prescribed by the city hospital rather than natural causes. Dr. B. assumed a father figure in Carrie's life and she saw him about once a month, just enough for him to keep tabs on her and offer advice.

Because he gave Carrie reason to believe in herself, she found his words encouraging. Two months later she brought some of her acrylic paintings to his office.

"Look," she said sadly while showing him one of the paintings. "I must be depressed." The painting consisted of a flaming red sunset viewed from the heights of a mountain. "There's a black abyss." Carrie reasoned as she pointed to the shadowy depths at the edge of the cliff.

"But look," Dr. B. responded. "There's a little bush."

Sure enough, in the darkness of the slope she had painted a small green shrub. Somehow Carrie had overlooked it. She was overjoyed with this insight! How she loved the tiny shrub! She was so happy that Dr. B. had found it for her. It was a relief to learn she wasn't so depressed after all.

He liked Carrie's work and told her how much he appreciated the chance to see her paintings. Carrie was glad she had mustered the courage to bring some of her art to his office. Her paintings were a significant part of her life and she didn't easily share them.

Chapter Nineteen

MacArthur's Park is melting in the dark,
All the sweet green icing flowing down.
Someone left a cake out in the rain;
I don't think that I can take it
'Cause it took so long to bake it
And I'll never have the recipe again,...

"MacArthur Park"
Jimmy Webb

After being released from the clinic, Carrie invited Brent along for a drive to a state park, located only two hours away. He arrived at the house early on Saturday morning.

"What do you call it?" Brent asked when Carrie led him to her car parked in the garage.

"The Blue Mongoose," she replied as she loaded a box of picnic supplies into the trunk. Meanwhile, Brent scanned the perimeter of the car's exterior surface. The car had a cobalt blue body with a silver top.

"I like mongooses," Carrie explained, crawling across the driver's seat to unlock the passenger door for Brent. Brent settled into the bucket seat beside her and Carrie assumed her position behind the steering wheel. Then she started the ignition and backed out of the driveway. Glancing sideways to watch for traffic, Carrie noticed the puzzled expression on Brent's face. She inserted a cassette into the tape player and elaborated further as the music signaled the beginning of their trip, "They're cute, cuddly, and kill pit vipers. Many homesteads in Africa raise mongooses as pets."

Time passed quickly as the Blue Mongoose meandered through the numerous small towns marking the way to the state park. After an hour Carrie and Brent switched positions behind the wheel, allowing Brent to drive the Blue Mongoose into the state park while she gave directions. Once inside the state park, Brent and Carrie chose a three mile trail which interlaced the Brazos River and crossed the park's historical point of interest, the dinosaur tracks lying at the bottom of the Brazos.

Intent upon keeping pace with each other's speed, Brent and Carrie hiked the first mile together in silence. When the trail opened to the river bank, affording a panoramic view of the scenery before them, Carrie relaxed immediately and recalled the day's celebrated magic.

"Did you know tonight was Halloween?" Carrie asked, admiring the splash of fall colors on the Indian summer day.

"No," answered Brent, jumping onto a log to prevent his feet from getting wet.

"Donna is throwing a party tonight. That's why I remembered. Would you like to stop by her suite afterwards?"

"Sure." Brent always seemed game for almost anything.

"This day seems too lazy for it to be Halloween," Carrie remarked. Maybe that's why there aren't very many people in the park. Usually this place is swamped with visitors. In the summer the park has one of the best swimming holes in the area, but I never knew how beautiful the area became in the autumn season!" she exclaimed while foregoing Brent's course across a log for a jaunt over some nearby rocks.

"Yes, it's very peaceful," Brent agreed. He picked up a few stones and skipped them across the river. "After I get my master's degree I'm going to get a farm."

"Really?! I'd like to live on a ranch in the country," Carrie sighed, recalling the details of her dream.

"I want to have Jersey cows because they produce the best cream. I'd raise wiener pigs and the hens that lay colored eggs."

"Colored eggs?! I thought that only the Easter bunny did that trick!" Carrie laughed.

"My dad raised some South American hens that actually laid colored eggs. Besides, I also want some llamas."

"Llamas?! Why llamas?" she asked. Brent was a gold mine of interesting ideas.

"Llamas can be raised as pets and they are good back packing animals for rugged mountain hikes. In addition their coat can be sheared and used like lamb's wool."

Carrie nodded her approval of his pragmatism. Now it was her turn.

"I'd like some sheep, goats, horses, an Irish setter, and two Siamese cats. I like Irish setters because they are so playful... Siamese cats have the most personality."

"How many kids?" Brent asked.

"Oh, probably about four," she carelessly offered. "Two boys and two girls. Kids need lots of playmates." Captivated by the splendor of this ideal day, she granted herself the luxury of temporarily ignoring the issue of world population.

"I'd give all my kids the task of milking the cow in the morning," Brent chirped. "There's nothing like waking up at five in the morning to milk the cow. My brother, sister, and I took turns when we were growing up. Many times I'd awake with my head lying against the warm side of the milk cow, while my hands mechanically performed the routine of squeezing milk from her teats. The milk was warm to my touch and sometimes I'd squirt some of the cats who happened to be wandering around the barn... Never seen happier cats, and they looked so ridiculous with the white milk splashed all over their faces. They licked themselves dry."

"Because this chore strengthens only certain muscles, my arms looked like Popeye's with the forearm being larger than the biceps. My fingers can still remember the motion. It's as automatic as riding a bike." As he spoke Brent demonstrated his skill on an imaginary cow hoisted before him in the midair. Meanwhile, Carrie noted the graceful interplay of the rippling muscles in his fingers and arms.

"I'd teach all my kids how to enjoy the water," she happily announced, recalling the feeling of buoyancy. "I'd introduce them to the water as soon as possible and we'd all swim together like a bunch of ducks."

"I have a difficult time in water," Brent said without realizing that he had implied himself. "Whenever my eyes get wet, my eyelids become crusty and my vision is impaired. I have some special drops that I can use, but I really don't enjoy the water."

"Oh...," Carrie said sympathetically. "Have you tried goggles?"

"No, but I'm still leery of getting my eyes wet."

Carrie shrugged and observed the sand bar under their feet. Brent had indicated that he could be a big baby. She couldn't imagine anyone allowing something to interfere with their swim life. She decided not to hold it against him.

"...And the T.V. set must go into the basement, so that the kids will watch it only when they are willing to brave the cold room...," Brent continued despite Carrie's revelation.

Suddenly Carrie realized that they had unconsciously lapsed into the specifics of raising kids without any formal arrangements. She felt amused; apparently Brent wasn't listening to what he was implying. Rather than call attention to this significant detail, Carrie continued playing with their harmless dreams. She had yet to reconcile with the fact that she was dating a nonswimmer and a man who didn't care much for dancing. How could she even imagine marrying such a man?

"...That's what Daddy did for us. We had to watch Saturday morning cartoons in the basement, otherwise we probably would have watched T.V. all the time," Brent excitedly rambled. His earnestness compelled Carrie to smile in spite of her seriousness.

"I agree. Kids need to learn the value of active play," she continued. "One of the biggest problems today is the fact that we live in a passive society. There's no real interaction with the environment; people wait to let events happened to them instead of exercising some intention in their lives... We'll buy tinker toys and erector sets which stimulate imagination and creativity... and we'll let them have a pet of their own once they become responsible enough to care for it."

"They can have teddy bear hamsters," Brent gleefully interjected.

"Hamsters?!" Carrie protested. "All they do is get fat and have babies. We'll have real animals like cats and dogs."

"Teddy bear hamsters are different," Brent insisted. "I had one that would fit inside my shirt pocket while I did my homework. Sometimes he'd stay on my shoulders where I could feel his soft fur brush against my neck."

"Well OK, teddy bear hamsters..., but only if they help with homework," Carrie conceded.

"Each kid can have their own room and they can decorate it anyway they wish. Parents, of course, have veto power... I painted my room at home blue. I carved a hole in the wall for a secret hiding place and covered it with a plate for an electrical outlet."

Remembering the details of his ingenuity, Brent became silent for several seconds before some insight disturbed his countenance. "I wonder if Daddy ever figured out why that outlet never worked?" he pondered, finally realizing that his secret might not have been as clever as believed.

"We'll have a solar house with a greenhouse for plants," he rebounded. He knew Carrie would agree on this one.

"Gotta have a pool and a basketball court," she added.

"How about a pond?" Brent asked.

Carrie proposed another suggestion: "I like to swim all year."

Soon they became exhausted from fantasizing and contentedly pursued the trail ahead. After rounding several more bends and twists in the trail, Brent and Carrie finally reached the site of the dinosaur tracks.

"Look!" Carrie yelled as she stepped into one of the tracks at the bottom of the river. It had been a dry summer and the water stood only a foot and a half high. "This guy's foot is four times bigger than my own..., but then I have small feet for my size," she acknowledged, closely examining the curvatures in the limestone bedrock.

"A vegetarian dinosaur was eating over there," Brent surmised from notes on a wooden trailhead in front of him.

Then he pointed to an area on the limestone bank. "A carnivore entered the scene from here. He attacked the dining vegetarian. But he ran into another hungry carnivore that happened to be standing there," he narrated.

"Looks like there was a squabble over dinner reservations," Carrie commented when she observed the resulting meshmash of tracks on the other river bank. "Evidently no one was hurt."

"Yah, the vegetarian apparently ran away during the commotion. Once the prey was gone there was no more reason to fight," Brent deduced from the sign's information. Carrie peered at the scenery alongside the Brazos river and imagined its appearance sixty million years ago: vegetation became more lush and green, and the hard limestone transformed into soft mud. Except for these changes, the total appearance of the land was not much different from the present.

Brent snapped a few photos of the area and they returned to the car. Then he helped Carrie haul the box containing picnic supplies to a covered wooden pavilion located a quarter of a mile away from the parking lot. The pavilion sat in a secluded area of the park far removed from the campground area. Several picnic tables existed on the platform, indicating that the shelter hosted many large parties during the summer.

They settled on a table offering some protection from the wind. Dusk came within the next half hour and enveloped the park in fading darkness. Meanwhile, the wind increased its intensity as Carrie and Brent chatted and sorted through the picnic supplies. Under the wind's direction several threatening rain clouds appeared in the sky, forcing Brent and Carrie to pull on their sweaters in the cooler air.

"Tonight, it's tuna and macaroni prepared on the Svea stove." Carrie announced, proudly displaying the Swiss brass stove. She had purchased it secondhand from a friend of hers who was a serious hiker. "This happens to be the first time I've used the Svea. Its the best available in its price range; although, I heard that the stove can be a little cranky at times..."

Thirty minutes and a half a box of matches later, the burner sputtered into a constant blue flame. In another twenty minutes the water in the pot started to boil. Unfurling a red bandanna over the table, Carrie produced a small glass dove and placed it at the center of the cloth.

"I call it my scarlet peace dove," she explained while lighting the candle inside the middle of the dove's body. "It's my favorite candle holder," she sighed when the wind blew out the flame.

"It's the thought that counts," she added.

Carrie glanced at Brent. The wind had stolen the flame from the candle and placed its flicker within his eyes and heart. Staring motionlessly at the transfigured man before her, Carrie became conscious of the force of wind rustling through the tall oaks around them and the rumbling of boiling water from the pot on the stove. Her heart skipped a beat. The pulsating noises carried Carrie's heart away with their vibrating journey, stripping her of all other senses.

"I think the water is ready for the noodles," she murmured. Slowly, Carrie added the final touches to the meal and dished the plates while Brent remained silent. Transfixed by the sounds encircling them, they ate without speaking to each other.

After they finished, Brent and Carrie cleaned their utensils and packed the box containing the cooking supplies. Brent silently helped Carrie spread her sleeping bag over the floor of the pavilion for a ground cover. Without a single word, they took off their shoes and sat down together.

In the evening darkness they kissed. The wind howled in their ears, intoxicating them with its fervor. Soon they were drawn inside the sleeping bag by the chilled night air. Prompted by the enclosed warmth of their bodies, Carrie helped Brent remove the clothes separating them. Wildly, they reached for each other as the sensation of skin rubbing against skin melted them together. Brent quivered as he touched Carrie, finally satisfying a deep longing to hold her close to him.

The wind lifted the sleeping bag across the wooden planks like a tumbleweed tossed on a desert floor. Carrie's heart danced with the rhythm of the flying motion, finding no limits to the rapture she felt under Brent's tender touch. She gently caressed Brent's entire body with her own legs, hands, breasts, and face. Claiming his body with her kisses, Carrie released the deep feelings for Brent that she had held inside for so long. Tirelessly, Brent hugged and stroked Carrie until she surrendered from exhaustion into the net of his long arms.

An hour later, Brent and Carrie left the park in the Blue Mongoose. Still feeling lightheaded from their encounter, she glowed inside like the soft illumined dials on the car's dash. Carrie looked at Brent. He was relaxing in the passenger seat, humming softly to the mellow rock music on the tape player. Remembering the spirit of the evening, Carrie could not recall a more beautiful Halloween night than the present.

Chapter Twenty

I'd rather feel the earth beneath my feet,
Yes I would.
If I only could,
I surely would.

"El Condor Pasa"
Paul Simon

The next month Carrie embarked on a rock climbing trip with a group of students from the state college. She had heard about the club from a friend. The group's destination was Enchanted Rock, a massive igneous complex located in the middle of the Texas hill country.

Frasier Jenson, an accountant for the state department, organized the expedition. When he wasn't working at his nine to five job, Frasier spent the remainder of his life pursuing some form of outdoor recreational activity. His parents were avid hikers and his father had recently climbed Mt. McKinley. They gave their children enthusiasm for the world of nature at an early age; by the age of six weeks Frasier started spending his weekends in a tent. Twenty four years later Frasier still enjoyed most of his sleeping hours in a tent.

Arriving at Frasier's house by eight on Friday evening, Carrie met Stan and Stacy. Two more friends of Frasier's intended to meet the group at the park on Saturday morning. Stan, an electrician, currently shared Frasier's latest interest in kayaking and climbing. Stacy attended the state college and participated in most hiking and camping excursions. After they loaded the bed of Frasier's compact Ford truck, the climbers began the four hour drive to Enchanted Rock with Stan and Stacy reclined comfortably on the camping gear in the back.

The truck traveled leisurely along the old highway which had been replaced by the interstate ten years ago. The highway passed through many small Texas towns famous for their police speed traps; a driver could never be in a hurry in this part of the country. The warm night air amplified the slowness of the drive and they were ready for a stretch of action once the truck rambled over the numerous cattle guards leading to the state park. Frasier carefully forded the river which crossed the dirt road marking the entrance to the campground. Then he quickly selected a site, parked the truck, and immediately exchanged his flip flops for a pair of hiking boots.

"Time for a hike on the summit!" Stan announced as he hopped from the bed of the truck. "Wanna come?"

"Where's the mountain?" Carrie asked noticing that Stacy had declined the invitation. It was about one in the morning.

"I dunno...somewhere in that direction." Stan pointed to a grove of mesquite trees. "Hey Frasier, which direction is the rock?"

"Over there," Frasier assured them and corrected Stan's direction by forty-five degrees north.

Squinting in the dark direction of the adjustment, Carrie failed to find a form even resembling a mountain. Ignoring this minor detail, she decided to take her chances on Frasier's venture. "Sure, OK," she replied dubiously.

Carrie followed Frasier and Stan through the brush, down a gully, and past some more mesquite trees. When they finally struck rock, the men bounded up the steep slope like a pair of rabbits. Carrie played the role of tortoise, keeping the pace in the slippery comfort of her tennis shoes. The moon was absent and she could only see two feet ahead of each step. Carrie reasoned that her best choice in direction was up, provided that she didn't walk over a cliff or drop into a crevice. Occasionally she heard a few footsteps to her right, and made a few turns towards the sound's source. Managing to regain contact with the leaders of the scramble without ever having to utter those dreadful words "wait for me" and spoil the excitement, she reached the summit after an seemingly endless series of upward steps and discovered that it was as wavy as a warped table top.

Stealing a few minutes to recover her wind, Carrie placed her hands on her knees and stooped over the earth. Meanwhile, Frasier and Mark excitedly bombarded her with facts concerning the history and composition of the rock. Carrie only caught some of their information in her exhausted state.

"Look! There's a car traveling on the highway. It must be ten miles away and you can see its headlights from here."

Carrie observed the vague reflection of light sweeping across the rock's surface as the vehicle spun around the curves of the highway. The course grain crystals in the granite rock exhibited a fluorescence, causing the entire mountain to glow underneath the light of the stars. She noticed also that the rock had a particular magnetic quality as if the mountain itself grabbed her ankles and held her feet to its surface. Later, she learned that this endearing quality was known to climbers as the feel of granite. Most rock climbing enthusiasts soon developed a craving for this specific rock. Standing solidly above the competing hills in the region, Carrie sensed no hollowness inside the granite mountain. All their echoes broke the silence and bounced off the smooth granite dome.

The evening wind made its presence felt on the top of the mountain, and Carrie saw some clouds rapidly approaching from the south. In the magic of the moment, she watched the cloud vapor swirl before her like dancing ribbons of mist being led by the wind. Carrie's bare arms felt the ensuing dampness and her nose detected water in the atmosphere. Trapped between the earth and sky by a white film, Carrie waved her arms in the cloud around her to mock the floating sensation. Never before had she felt such a pull to the earth. The mountain bonded Carrie to its breast by the shear force of gravity. If she ever lost her place in the universe, this is where Carrie could find herself. This is where she belonged.

They scurried down the slope and returned to the campsite. Carrie assembled her tent in the dark and dove inside her sleeping bag. As she relaxed in the warmth of her shelter, Carrie tried imagining Enchanted Rock as it might appear in daylight. Failing to conjure an acceptable vision in her excitement, Carrie slept the few hours before sunrise.

In the morning the climbers began an ascent on the northern side of the mountain. The northern face rose almost vertically from the terrain, whereas the other three faces were sharply inclined and promised an arduous walk to the top. After her first glimpse of Enchanted Rock, Carrie realized why it had been so difficult to imagine its appearance. The rock resembled a moon fragment which had broken away and landed on the earth. Carrie was shocked when she reviewed the course navigated during the previous night. From her spot at the campsite, people who climbed the igneous complex appeared no larger than ants. In the wee hours of the morning Carrie had hiked much further and dangerously than she had realized.

Ed, Frasier's friend from college, joined them and led the morning climb. For the first segment of the climb they planned to reach a small ledge on the cliff located twentyfive yards above their starting position. While Ed carefully chose his route over the face of the mountain, Frasier explained some climbing techniques.

"By just holding the rope in your hands and bringing it abruptly to the side like this..., even a five year old child can support the dangling weight of a three hundred pound male," Frasier said as he demonstrated the motion.

"And when you climb, pull your body out from the rock. Be like a spider who spaces himself from a surface with the segmented joints of his limbs. Don't flatten your body against the rock," he advised.

"Every beginner should have at least one test fall to develop trust in the safety rope," added Stan with a shy smile. It helps you learn how to deal with your limits and survive panic in an emergency situation. Learning how to fall safely and recover is tougher than learning how to climb, although a fall is actually easier to perform."

Frasier climbed the slope, replacing Ed at the four inch ledge. He secured the harness around his body to a chock planted in a rock crevice. Then he held the safety rope while Ed began another ascent.

When Carrie's turn came to climb, she fastened her harness to the safety rope and tugged gently to remove the slack.

"Belay up!" she yelled to Frasier.

"Ready!" Frasier responded after adjusting his firm grip on her safety rope.

She chose a small indenture in the curvature of the rock and placed her fingers against its edge. One foot found a small protrusion on the surface. Weighting her toes in the groove, Carrie lifted her body with her fingers. Every muscle strained towards the direction of her fingertips as the balance of her entire stance relied on their force. Carrie pulled her body to a another level of balance, and her other hand and foot searched the rock's face for another hold. Fortunately, she always seemed to find a groove waiting to give support.

Halfway to her destination, Carrie's muscles collapsed from fatigue and she fell. Scraping the rude surface of the rock which had once held her, Carrie swung helplessly in the air.

"Are you alright?!" Frasier hollered.

"Yah!" Carrie answered him. "...a test fall," she reminded herself unconvinced. She had lost her rhythm and her awkward relation to the slope made it more difficult to finger another hold.

It was impossible to quit. Placed beyond the help of another individual, Carrie was forced to continue the upward climb. Though the fall shattered Carrie's faith in her grip, she felt compelled to trust herself again. To compensate for her lack of confidence Carrie pushed her body harder than before and started the climb over again.

Rather than rely on the rock for support, Carrie mastered the skill of using every curvature in the rock to her advantage with a healthy skepticism of all untried reaches. She crawled her way to the ledge where the others sat, dropping her weary body beside the group. Then Carrie eyed the course which she had just climbed with respect.

After the last member of their climbing party reached the ledge, Frasier opened some cans of chicken spread and they made sandwiches for lunch. Drenched by perspiration in the ninetyeight degree heat, they busily passed canteens of water around the group. Ed dumped the contents of his water bottle over his head, shook it rapidly, and showered the group.

Carrie munched on her sandwich in Ed's water spray and thought about her fall. The experience had exhausted her more than frightened her. The idea of hanging on to the world by a string intrigued her. Graphically, this image reminded Carrie of the circumstances delivering her to the clinic only two months ago. Carrie wondered if she could always count on that string to be there. Such a delicate tie to earth seemed too fragile. Could it might be possible to sever the rope and create a stronger bond from the resulting lack of dependence.

These thoughts climbed with Carrie on the final segment. Nature saved the most difficult portion of the climb for last as Carrie had already watched the best climbers of their group slip on the incline. Glancing first to the hazy depths 800 feet below, Carrie scaled the edge of the cliff with the memory of the scene implanted in her mind. If it wasn't so dangerous, the mountain view would have been beautiful. In the exhilaration of the ascent Carrie forgot her scraped knees, bruised shoulder, tired muscles, and sopping forehead. She emerged from the depths with a new perspective, shielding herself from the effects of her grueling efforts. An agreement formed between the mountain and Carrie: as long as she maintained faith in her capabilities and trusted the physical sensations of her body, then she could climb it without any trouble. During her final climb she discarded the painful self doubt that had plagued her from her family and hospital experiences. This self realization of a renewed and stronger individual propelled Carrie gracefully over the threshold leading to the top.

At the top Carrie eagerly surveyed the mountain scenery. What beauty surrounded her!

"Hey, you looked like a natural!" yelled Stan.

Carrie had flown over the ascent with the ease of a winged bird. Entranced by the inspiring view, a part of Carrie's spirit remained climbing the mountain forever. She would always cherish the mountain scene. While the physical strains constantly reminded Carrie of her mortality, she touched immortality through her ecstasy. This interplay of immortality and mortality made motion on the mountain possible, and Carrie never would have been able to complete the climb without having first reached the undying spirit inside herself.

As she surveyed the pastel colored hills in the distance, Carrie felt the familiar pull from the granite dome. The rock harbored her in a renewed presence like a lover. Later she left the summit with the others, feeling that she had won a steadfast friend for life.

Chapter Twenty One

...Honesty is such a lonely word
Everyone is so untrue
Honesty is hardly ever heard
And mostly what I need from you...

"Honesty"
Billy Joel

Spellbound by the wild beauty of Enchanted Rock, Carrie made arrangements to camp there during the Thanksgiving holidays with Brent. Located only two hours away from her grandparents' house, Carrie planned on camping at the park the night before Thanksgiving and spending a portion of Thanksgiving day with relatives. Then she could return to the park and enjoy rest of the weekend in the quiet hill country. These options gave her more time with Brent without overwhelming him with family introductions.

Brent arrived early Wednesday evening and helped Carrie check the engine timing with a new tachometer which she had recently purchased. When they were satisfied with its working condition, they loaded the car and began their journey to the state park. In the ebbing darkness of the night Carrie and Brent took turns driving through the sleeping towns along the country highway, while the familiar soft glows from the car's instrument panel provided a constant light inside the car.

They reached Enchanted Rock at eleven o'clock and felt the wheels of the Blue Mongoose rumble over the cattle guard marking the entrance. After selecting a campsite in the midst of a mesquite grove, Carrie parked the car along the dirt road and hopped out. Without bothering to set up camp, she retrieved her hiking books from the trunk and began putting them on.

"It's a tradition among the best hikers to climb the mountain as soon as they arrive in the park," Carrie informed Brent, who had followed her around to the trunk of the car. "...In spite of the hour."

Brent eyed Carrie curiously and grinned, "You're crazy, lady."

"Yes, I know, but it's fun," she told him, knowing that she had an agreeable cohort. "I climbed it at two o'clock in the morning with the hiking group from the state college. The view is wonderful at night, especially when the Milky Way is out. Just follow me. The mountain is somewhere over there."

Carrie pointed vaguely to her north and Brent didn't question her direction. She noticed he seemed willing to follow her almost anywhere tonight. Reasoning that she could probably find her way to the summit if she wandered through the park long enough, Carrie led Brent through some brush, down a gully, and past some boulders until they struck solid rock. Then they started to climb.

"It's just right over these boulders," Carrie assured Brent as she hurdled over the next incline, relishing every stretch of her road weary muscles. Brent crawled after her, rapidly shortening the distance between them with his lanky frame. When they reached a point on the slope where they could stand upright, they scurried to the top. Thoroughly exhausted, Brent and Carrie sat on the granite dome and surveyed the serene darkness around them.

"Doesn't this pink granite rock have a magical feel?" she asked him.

"I feel like I'm sitting on the moon," he observed.

"Wait until you see it in the daytime. It looks like a giant moon rock," Carrie told him.

The hike down the slope of the mountain was much easier than their ascent. Carrie remembered the way and found the established trail. When they returned from their midnight hike, Carrie immediately began the task of setting up her tent in the dark.

"I brought my tube tent," Brent announced. He ignited the carbide in his miner's lamp and flooded the entire grove with its light.

Carrie paused before the fiberglass poles that she was placing around the circumference of her tent. She glanced at the flimsy sheet of orange plastic that Brent was unfolding from his kit bag. When his hand pulled out a spool of kite string from the bag, indicating the main support for his tent, Carrie recognized his inexperience with the Texas elements.

"I don't think your Vermont tent will hold in this Texas wind," Carrie observed watching the lamp flicker underneath a gust. His camping gear was suited for the sheltered hearth of a pine forest. It would never hold its own in the company of the short, stocky oaks, mesquites, and southern red cedars which withstood wind storms deep in the heart of the Texas hill country.

"I think you're right," he replied, frantically trying to shield his lamp from the breeze. "We can use the tent as a ground cover."

The light from the lamp survived only a few more minutes longer and Brent and Carrie pitched her tent under the light of a small flashlight. Then Brent spread their sleeping bags over the floor of the tent as Carrie secured the remaining gear outside the tent.

"Did you know that in the Comanche Indian culture it is the women who own the tents?" Carrie asked, recalling what she knew about some of the earlier wanderers of the region. "If the relationship didn't work out, the woman simply placed the man's things outside the tent, and the Indian brave collected his things and looked for another woman with a tent. A woman chose a man by putting his gear inside her tent and this signified to the community that he was no longer available," Carrie explained, silently pondering her own feelings about bringing Brent inside her tent.

She entered the tent and crawled towards her sleeping bag. Already, Brent had casually stripped to underwear and arranged his bedroll on the floor. Dumbfounded by his nonverbal message, Carrie watched him coyly slip inside his sleeping bag as if nothing was unusual about his skimpy attire.

She blinked at him in amazement. "Uh, I thought you wore shorts for sleeping...," she murmured.

"No, I always sleep in my underwear," he assured her.

Carrie crawled inside the tent and gave him a long kiss. She needed no further invitation. Encouraged by his scantly clad body, she allowed his hands to undress her during the warmth of their closeness. She felt him clothe her with his soft velvet skin, making her only vaguely conscious of her nudity. Then he lifted her head above his chest and whispered, "You're beautiful."

Captivated by the gentle blue in his eyes, she quietly told him, "You're very handsome." Her glance fell across the contours of his male body as she spoke.

Suddenly some low cries from outside the tent interrupted them.

"Brent, listen! It's coyotes!"

Several mournful howls echoed through the grove, piercing the rustling wind with a lonely bass.

"They must be at least a mile away. I wonder if the ranch owners can hear them... Do the howls bother you?" she asked, curling around in Brent's arms.

"No."

"Me neither, I rather like the sound. It seems comforting in a strange way. Like a baby crying itself to sleep... Do you think they're calling their mates?" Carrie asked as Brent made a trail of warm moist kisses across her lower abdomen. Aroused, she tingled with delight while Brent hiked across her body, causing her to forget the coyotes.

Carrie reached for Brent and rested his head between her breasts as he stroked the inside of her thighs. She held him close, feeling his head rise with every heavy breath until the sensation became unbearable and her body bounced uncontrollably. Feverishly, she drew her hands around his buttocks and tenderly tamed his maleness with her desire. Feeling the energy surge through his body, she released her hold and pulled his body over hers. Together they rode their passion until stilled by the final release.

Throughout the night Brent and Carrie stroked and caressed each other. Catching only a few hours of sleep in the early daylight, they awoke in the middle of the morning. Then they ate a quick breakfast, loaded their camping gear in the Blue Mongoose, and began another hike on Enchanted Rock.

They ventured to the same spot where they had climbed the previous night.

Brent appeared puzzled. "It didn't seem so dangerous when we climbed it last night."

"Ignorance is bliss. I never would have attempted it in daylight," she chuckled.

They continued hiking around the northern face of the mountain and discovered a frog pond. Afterwards they walked the angled slope of the eastern side of the mountain and explored a small cave hidden in the rock's core. Leaving the top of the mountain from the west side, they came across a group of giant boulders scattered on the slope.

"You seem so much more confident and relaxed when you are hiking," Brent commented as Carrie skipped over the nearest boulder.

"I feel much more comfortable being outdoors and away from home," Carrie agreed as she leaped across a few nearby rocks to test her restored physical prowess.

Late in the evening, Brent and Carrie left the park for the gathering in San Antonio. About halfway through the trip the Blue Mongoose began to sputter. A sickening rattle clinked from underneath the car's hood.

"Sounds like a cylinder," Brent suggested, slowing the car to ten miles per hour. Carrie hurriedly analyzed the situation from her passenger seat. They were miles away from a phone and most stores would be closed at this time of night. Help seemed remote for the present.

"If I slip the clutch and drive real slow, then we should be able to continue driving with minimal damage. Also there's the possibility that the heated cylinders might stick if we cool the car too rapidly by stopping."

"OK. Let's continue at a snail's pace. We'll get there eventually," she decided, accepting Brent's solution.

They reached the outskirts of San Antonio by two in the morning. By now the temperature of the car had cooled to a safe range.

"Brent, let's find a place to stop.

"There," she announced as Brent slowed the car. "We can ditch the car behind that sign and pitch the tent beyond those trees. Although we're only a mile away from a major university, no cop will bother us if we hide the tent well. The Blue Mongoose will just look like any other abandoned vehicle rusting away in a vacant lot."

They erected the tent in a live oak thicket about twenty-five yards away from the car. Before settling inside the tent with Brent, Carrie walked back to the Blue Mongoose to check it for the night. Before locking the car, she retrieved a bottle of champagne from the trunk.

"I was saving this for a better occasion, but I decided to open it before life became too complicated this holiday season," she explained. Brent smiled at Carrie's struggle to keep up her spirits. Because she could only find one container, they took turns sipping the champagne from a plastic cup.

"I propose a toast to life's ironies: Celebrate the fun we enjoyed before the car broke," Carrie offered, raising her cup before sipping some champagne. She handed the remainder over to Brent, who returned her salute.

"I'm not looking forward to facing the family," Carrie confessed as she began tearing away at her clothes. "It's not the car that bothers me. Cars are machines, and machines break all the time."

Continuing to pull away everything from her body until there was nothing left to remove, Carrie added, "But I'm not a machine. I don't break; I...," Unable to verbalize her thoughts, Carrie never bothered completing the sentence. Instead she curled her knees into her body, resting the side of her head on top of her folded kneecaps. Feeling the winter air slap her nakedness like a cold shower, Carrie savored its chill. She desperately needed to feel its stark reality. When the feeling became too much to bear Carrie blocked the sensation, allowing the cocky spirit of the champagne to deaden the cold for her.

"My relatives are just waiting for me to break," Carrie grimly stated. "My mother told them that I had suffered a break down before going into the hospital. She never told them the real reason, because she doesn't even want to know it herself. Now I have to muff everything inside so that they don't get upset with me."

"It's rather funny, but I really do feel like crying," Carrie admitted, sadly shaking her head.

Calmly, Brent began removing his clothes. Carrie blinked at him in amazement, feeling awed by his quiet gesture. Without a further word she put away the bottle of champagne. She didn't feel like getting drunk tonight. A slight buzz from the alcohol was enough. Then she laid down at the opposite end of the tent, resting her head on her upright arm. Surveying Brent's body from toe to head, she discovered a special closeness which would have been spoiled by physical contact. His entire body radiated a magical warmth towards her, soothing her bared soul.

"Honesty is a lonely word," Carrie recalled, citing the words of a song by Billy Joel. "...And it's mostly what I need from you..." As she finished the quote Carrie rearranged her position such that she laid her head directly beside Brent's.

"What is honesty?" he asked.

"I never really knew until tonight," Carrie replied like she often did with Samantha, her youngest sister. "I've been remembering the words of a song. I think honesty is like being naked without feeling ashamed or vulnerable."

"Like being naked...," Brent softly echoed before closing his eyes with a contented, knowing smile. He had begun to fall asleep when the discussion grew philosophical. Almost mechanically, he reached out his long arm and pulled Carrie close to his curled body. Once safely nestled in the cavity of his velvet chest, she recalled the loneliness of honesty. Carrie realized that she did not feel alone when she shared her thoughts with Brent.

At six o'clock the same morning, the Blue Mongoose rolled into her grandparents' driveway in time for breakfast. Fortunately, Carrie's grandfather knew a reliable mechanic who could fix the car in town. Brent and Carrie deposited the Blue Mongoose at the mechanic's garage by eight that morning and returned to her grandparents' house.

Meanwhile, an uncle had informed Carrie's mother of the situation while Brent and Carrie were at the garage. When Carrie arrived at the house, her mother cornered her in an empty hallway.

"Now I don't want you getting upset about this," she scolded Carrie. Without altering the amount of venom in her voice she quickly changed the subject, "Tony and I are going to the market this afternoon. Do you and Brent want to come along?"

Astounded by the accuracy of last night's grief, Carrie remained frozen for several seconds. She felt trapped by an inevitable fate. She didn't feel like facing her relatives either. Heading frantically for the nearest exit, Carrie stammered, "Sure, we'll come."

As soon as they arrived at the market Brent and Carrie left her mother and her mother's boyfriend, Tony, and arranged to meet them later. Not interested in shopping, Brent and Carrie bought a few Mexican cookies and sat by a secluded public fountain.

"She responded exactly as you anticipated," Brent observed after Carrie mentioned the morning encounter with her mother.

"Yes," she gulped. Long overdue tears began streaming down her face. Carrie brushed them away and stared blankly at the water fountain. Tossing a few cookie crumbs to some begging pigeons, she watched her fine-feathered friends scurry like slap-stick comedians for the morsels. More tears fell from her eyes.

"Oh no...," she sighed. "Well, I suppose its alright to cry here."

"It's OK," Brent assured her, pulling Carrie gently towards him with his arm wrapped around her torso. She buried her face in Brent's shoulder and sobbed.

"I'm sorry," she said.

"What for?" he asked.

"For the weekend, for the car, for crying...," she meekly blubbered.

Brent whipped a crumpled green bandanna from his pocket, and happily dotted the tears away from her face. Then he held his handkerchief and coaxed Carrie to blow her nose. His fussing made Carrie smile.

"The car wasn't your fault... And it is OK to cry. Girls are supposed to cry. My sister does it all the time. Boys often wish they could cry, but people won't let them... I can tell you about all the cars that I've had with blown cylinders..." Brent's version of the world brought an even bigger smile from Carrie.

"Now look, you're smiling again, lady," he beamed, encouraged by the obvious success of his efforts.

Carrie rested her head on his shoulder and listened to the crystal rhythm of the water as it trickled over the glistening blue tiles. She did not feel like talking anymore as a few more tears escaped her eyes. They threw more crumbs for the pigeons and watched them fall over each other on the slippery tiles like a circus. No finer entertainer could have matched the pigeon's routine; they were the true clowns of the city. In the company of fools, Carrie felt encouraged.

"Well, I'll probably sell the car to help pay for repairs and use the remainder to go away to college. I'd like to finish my physics degree," Carrie ventured, attempting to make the most of the situation.

"Now it looks like something good will come of this after all," Brent brightened, exuberantly wrapping his long arms around her in a mighty hug. Being a Physics major himself, he secretly nourished a desire for Carrie to join him in his academic pursuits.

Carrie slightly smiled and squirmed underneath his arms. Brent's embrace told her that he was someone with whom she could cherish and be honest, an immeasurable worth from her standpoint. It was another benefit of the weekend mishap. This realization shattered any illusions concerning her family. It was time for a change.

Chapter Twenty Two

Freedom's just another word for nothing left to lose
Nothin' ain't worth nothin' but it's free
Feelin' good was easy, Lord when Bobby sang the blues,
Feeling good was good enough for me...

"Me and Bobby McGee"
Kris Kristofferson and F. Foster

One week after the Thanksgiving holidays, Carrie received the following letter from Brent:

Dear Carrie,

Guess I owe you a letter about now. I want to thank you for everything that you have done for me. And believe me it has been a lot.

You know that you have everything going for you. You are mechanically and artistically inclined. You can work on cars or on paintings. Write songs better than Barry Manilow or figure out physics. This ability to operate equally good in both worlds is what makes you very special and unique.

I wish I could put my thoughts down better, but... I just love you. If there is anything I can do give me a call day or night. I have been trying to figure out why I deserve you; finally I just gave up.

Say thank you to your whole family for me. I've never known such a large group like that. Next time (hopefully) I'll be awake and have my wits about me.

As with me, if there is anything you want me to change or you don't care for in myself, please let me know. If I can I'll change it. I'm a very flexible person, but I must know about the things before I can change them. As for you, I like you just the way you are. You can do anything it seems. You have self-motivation. (Something I'm still working on.) You're sexy. (Oh yeah, if I seem to come on too strong in this aspect; just say something. I get a feeling that I did this last time out and I am very sorry. I haven't yet learned how to control myself). You can cook. You can handle small kids—and big ones.

I just don't know, but you seem to be perfect. You fit my ideal very well.

Take it easy lady. I'm setting aside time for you so don't worry about calling.

Bye, I love you
Brent

Brent's letter erased any misgivings Carrie had concerning the effect of the Thanksgiving trip on their relationship. Carrie felt immensely happy knowing that she was one of the best from Brent's standpoint. Meanwhile, her creativity flourished and she pursued her mechanical and artistic endeavors with a painless ease never experienced before in her life. Carrie discovered that she was most satisfied with her work when she felt comfortable in her personal life, and derived a large portion of this feeling from her connection with Brent.

Carrie wrote Brent about how much she enjoyed being with him. Arriving at the house late in the evening, they went outdoors so that they could converse without being overheard by those who had retired for the evening. Finding a secluded pile of leaves in the backyard, Carrie mentioned his letter.

"Brent, don't worry about coming on too strong. I'm responsible also... It's mutual," Carrie told him.

"Yah, everytime I see you I find myself breaking the limits that I had previously set. Then I feel remorseful later. I've finally concluded that most everything is alright except intercourse," Brent admitted.

"With my luck I'd get pregnant in spite of precautions, and I just don't want to take the risk. I've decided I'm not ready to deal with contraceptives, marriage, childbirth, or an abortion," Carrie answered him.

"I have Polish luck," Brent sighed, "which means that you probably would get pregnant even if the probability is only one percent,... and I'm not ready for kids yet. I'm glad we're talking about this stuff."

Satisfied with their discussion, Brent switched to another issue which bothered him, "As for me as a person, is there anything you want me to change?"

Taking a deep breath, Carrie began a discourse with the intention of thwarting any future misunderstandings, "Brent, let me tell you my theory on human character: I believe people don't have faults..."

"Remember the Grand Unified Theory (GUTS) from modern physics in which quarks, the subatomic particles, have the four properties of charm, flavor, color, and strangeness? I believe that people have quirks, a personified version of quarks. Everyone has quirks, otherwise we'd all be the same and the world would be incredibly boring." Pausing for a moment, Carrie earnestly searched Brent's face for signs of comprehension before continuing.

"Brent, I like you just the way you are. It's your quirks that make you special and I accept them as a part of you. Should one of your quirks begins to lose its charm, becomes distasteful, appears off color, or becomes too strange, then I will complain. But don't consider me the absolute authority on the subject. I have my own quirks too. Besides, they say love is blind, so don't rely on me to find fault with you."

"The only acceptance and compassion found in this world is what we give ourselves," she added sadly. "Love stays wherever a place has been made for it. Usually the biggest problem arising between people who love each other is due to misunderstanding. Honesty is important, but sometimes it is hard to find the right words at the right time and place."

"So I just have quirks?" Brent smiled as he pulled her towards him. Resting Carrie on his chest, he laid down on the leaves.

"Yes," Carrie replied, looking down at Brent's face. "You just have quirks. I can't change you and I won't even try." Brent leaned forward and kissed her lightly on the forehead. Carrie dropped her head to the groove inside his neck, feeling the comforting fuzz of his beard brush against her cheek.

"Flattery will get you almost anywhere," she admitted in a whisper. "Your letter overwhelmed me." Then she slowly unbuttoned the snaps on his clothing, chasing away any doubts he had concerning her willingness as a partner.

The following week Carrie sold the Blue Mongoose and enrolled in a state college almost two hundred miles away for the spring semester. Frasier and several other members of the outdoors club were alumni of the east Texas college and they recommended the school for the large number of environmentalists among its student population. Boasting a large forestry department which ranked third in the nation, the college's research played a vital role in the development of the local timber industry. Carrie eagerly looked forward studying forestry along with her physics curriculum.

The Christmas holidays arrived shortly before Carrie finalized her college plans for the upcoming new year. Brent and she spent Christmas day at her grandparents' and then left for a week long camping excursion. They spent three days hiking in the desert near the famous Judge Roy Bean saloon and camped at state park chosen for its historical Indian caves and hieroglyphics.

At night temperatures plummeted down to below freezing from a daytime temperature in the eighties. The Svea stove didn't operate below thirty degree temperatures and they gathered mesquite wood to cook over an evening fire. The mesquite provided a hot smokeless flame and added excellent flavor to their canned meals. Coming quickly with the winter hours, darkness prevailed at the evening meal and compelled Brent and Carrie to retire early. After dinner they took turns tending the fire while the other person showered at the public restrooms.

"You know I could hear "Battle Hymn of the Republic" a quarter mile away from the showers. You're getting better!" Brent greeted as he approached the camp site during one evening. During his absence Carrie succeeded in finding her harmonica inside her backpack and had tried harmonizing with the rustic environment.

"Thanks. Actually I think it has something to do with the desert acoustics. The tones sound more mellow," she said before playing "Dixie" and "Yankee Doodle" for their cactus audience. These melodies comprised the only three songs she knew on the mouth harp. Although Carrie felt more comfortable fingering her guitar, she had left the instrument at home because of its bulk.

On the fourth day they drove through a desolate portion of west Texas and visited the Caverns of Sonora, acclaimed as the most beautiful in the world by the World Spelunker's Association. The caverns did not disappoint Brent and Carrie, and the formations were much more spectacular than any they'd seen at other underground caverns. Leaving Sonora in the early afternoon, they traveled further down the highway until reaching Meridian State Park, an area haunted by local ornithologists for the diversity of bird species inhabiting the park's numerous southern red cedars. They hiked around the park's lake for several hours and spent the remainder of the day lounging in a hammock which Carrie suspended from the limbs of two oak trees.

Having been inspired by the elegance of the caverns, she sang a nonsensical song about the Caverns of Sonora while Brent fell asleep beside her in the hammock.

"Si senor, es siesta?" Carrie asked, nudging Brent gently to determine the depth of his sleep during her concert.

"Mugwumph," Brent responded in his own favorite language with his eyes still closed. Then his arm came around her and pulled her close to his body like a teddy bear. Noting his pleasant smile, Carrie estimated that his nap would probably last at least another hour. So she entertained herself by creating more verses for her song.

Shortly after dusk, they pitched the tent and went inside to escape the night's chill. Carrie awoke in the wee hours of the morning to the sound of a violent thunderstorm shaking the grounds of the state park. For several seconds she listened to the fury of water droplets splattering on the rain fly above her. The incessant roar of the thunder convinced her that the weather would not change any time soon.

"Brent," she said in hushed voice while eyeing the tiny river creeping across the floor of the tent, "I think we're going to have to break camp early. The tent is standing in the middle of a flash flood stream."

"Uh?!" Brent moaned as he rolled over. "Mugwumph!" he answered, settling into another sleeping position. A trickle of water from the side of the tent kissed his cheek. For several seconds he blinked rapidly until attaining consciousness. "It's raining!" he whispered hoarsely as his eyes opened.

"Yes, I know. I don't think that it's gonna stop anytime soon," Carrie replied.

Silently, they laid side by side for a few more seconds, staring blankly at the tent's ceiling. Brent decided to touch the roof of the tent and drain the pool of the water that had collected there.

"Brent, don't touch the tent!" Carrie warned just before his finger reached the surface. "You'll start a leak."

A half-second later, water trickled down Brent's finger from the point of contact with the tent. Brent removed his finger, observing the phenomenon.

"It works!" he happily exclaimed.

"It's due to the cohesive forces existing between the molecular bonds," Carrie sighed, while they watched the increasing frequency of water droplets invade the tent. "I think our best bet is the car," she concluded. "I'm going to get an umbrella and a flashlight."

By the time Carrie returned with the flashlight and umbrella, Brent had already packed several items. He carried a load to the car as Carrie gathered the remaining camping gear. Minutes later he returned and peered inside the tent. "Where are the keys to the Bug?" he politely asked.

Searching for the keys in her pockets, a painful thought flickered from Carrie's memory once she discovered them empty. Alarmed, Carrie ran outside and hurried to the car. Brent followed behind, making valiant efforts to shield her with the umbrella before she finally stopped at the passenger window.

"The keys are lying on the car seat," Carrie groaned. "But don't worry, I'm good at breaking into cars. I get myself out of trouble all the time," she quickly explained. Then she stole an anxious look at Brent, expecting him to explode at her.

"Goody!" Brent said with genuine enthusiasm, gleefully rubbing his hands together. "I've always wanted to break into Maxwell. My brother is an expert at this sort of thing. Everyone should know how to break into their own car. Will you take the umbrella, please, while I figure this out?"

Amazed by his reaction, Carrie stood at the opposite end of the Volkswagen, thoroughly drenched and staring wide-eyed at the bearded character poking at the car's exterior. Completely absorbed by the mental challenge, Brent waddled around the car's perimeter with the comical grace of Charlie Chaplin. Although Carrie often approached aggravating situations with a sense of humor, this man's effortless routine bewildered her. When his antics had convinced her that he really was enjoying himself, Carrie relaxed.

"Brent, I think that we should attack the car from the glove box," she suggested. Initially he ignored her, but after fifteen more minutes of fumbling around the exterior he finally considered her advice. Resolute in his attempt to outshine his younger brother, he obviously wanted no help from the woman he intended to impress.

"My brother would have been in this car hours ago," he sadly moaned while wandering aimlessly over to the front of Maxwell. "He always was much better at this than me."

Under the circumstances Carrie couldn't understand the cause for sibling rivalry; evidently breaking into Maxwell stirred the machismo in Brent's soul. Taking extreme pains to avoid stepping on the male ego masked in this intellectual pursuit, she cautiously continued her assistance. Eventually, Carrie coaxed Brent to remove the glove box and extract the keys from the seat with a coat hanger.

"I did it!" he jubilantly said, dangling the keys before him like a cat with a mouse. "My brother never would have done it this quickly." His assessment of his rival changed relative to triumph.

"Yes, it was good team work," Carrie reminded him and jumped inside Maxwell before he could respond. Although she was relieved that he had not become angry at her over the incident, Carrie wasn't ready to accept any gloating.

"Ah, oh ya, your suggestion to remove the glove box was a good one," he admitted after joining her inside. "Where to now?" he asked enthusiastically, placing his hands on the steering wheel.

"How about the restrooms? I'm freezing and my period came this morning."

Her admission evoked Brent's immediate empathy. Curiously, Carrie watched his response. His blue eyes darkening a shade, Brent reacted tolerantly as if Carrie's period was his period. Carrie knew many men who would have found cause for ridicule or scorn. He won her admiration with his sensitivity rather than his triumph with the car keys.

"You're shivering and shaking like a leaf," he observed.

"I have a low tolerance with the cold. A hot shower would do me wonders," Carrie said, stressing the point that she didn't want his sympathy. Instead, she sought his acceptance of her need to take care of her health and comfort.

"I could use a hot shower too. Let's go. I'm beginning to feel cold."

After spending some time on a shower and a quick breakfast, they left the park and arrived at her mother's house by midmorning the same day.

* * *

Two weeks later, Carrie left for college away in east Texas. Brent had offered to drive her there and she accepted, knowing that the trip would be less stressful than a bus ride or a ride with her mother or Ellen. When Brent and Carrie had driven a hundred miles outside of the city, they encountered hazardous road conditions. Snowfall from the preceding night buried many of the small Texas towns in a white blanket. Lacking the resources necessary for maintaining the highways under these conditions, driving became treacherous until the snow and ice melted. With the most of the car's weight distributed on his rear wheels, Maxwell excelled on the slippery roads.

Much to Brent's delight, the tiny VW bug passed mighty trucks and many cars with four wheel drive that tried crossing the iced hills. Driving in the snow reminded Brent of his home in Vermont, and he seemed to appreciate the exercise in nostalgia as well as the opportunity to boyishly challenge his car in these conditions. When they arrived in town, they found the campus almost void of staff and students. Because of the snow storm, the college had closed and cancelled the first two days of classes. Many students remained snow bound and would not return to campus until road conditions became better.

News of a second impending snow storm limited Brent's stay to only one hour. They said their good-byes at the snow covered parking lot adjacent to her new dorm. Starting to cry, Carrie turned her head away so that Brent would not see.

"It's OK," she said removing the tears that had suddenly fallen. "I'll be alright. It's just my emotions catching up with me. I didn't realize how much you mean to me. I'm going to miss you very much," she explained.

"Ah..., I'm going to miss you too. I'm going to have brownie withdrawals now that you're away," Brent replied as he leaned out the window, sweeping Carrie in his arms.

"That was my strategy," Carrie sniffled. "But I think it backfired."

"What do you mean? You've got me hog-tied and corralled," he smiled, squeezing her tightly.

"Good!" she suddenly burst. More tears trickled down her face.

"I'll write you when I get back to the University," he assured her before he started the car's engine.

"OK," Carrie told herself as she pulled away from his arms and straightened in front of the car's door. "Promise me you'll take care of yourself and drive safely."

"I will," Brent grinned while revving Maxwell's engine. Then he backed out of the snow covered lot and drove onto the main street.

Carrie waved at him and walked towards the dorm. She sensed that Brent and Maxwell would be safe on the icy roads, possibly safer than she in the nearly vacant women's dorm. There was something to Brent's Polish luck. It did seem to have a way of overcoming odds.

Chapter Twenty Three

I can feel the tremble when we touch,
Feel the hands of fate
Reaching out to both of us
This love affair can't wait...

"I Can't Hold Back"
Survivor

Compared to the University, student life at the state college seemed rather sedate. There were few practical jokes performed on campus, and individuals easily conformed to convention. People maintained their distance from each other and the pursuit of learning was viewed more as a business than an active endeavor; classes ended within prescribed hours with minimal rapport between teachers and students. Consequently, Carrie made the adjustment to the large campus with relative ease because the large campus offered much more autonomy. She always had the personal freedom, at least, to make her individualized learning experience as worthwhile as she wished.

Enrolling in a few Forestry courses to satisfy her yearning for the outdoors, she learned how to identify trees by their twigs and cones. The lab instructor led the class on hikes throughout the area to collect samples. For tests he'd point to some unobtrusive stick barely making its way to life from a crack in the sidewalk and ask the class its genus, species, and common name. Although Carrie enjoyed the hikes, the class reminded her that she had difficulty in subjects requiring intensive memorization; she scored much better on Physics tests where she could think her way through problems with minimal amount of cramming.

Soon after classes resumed for the semester, Carrie applied for a job as a Physics lab instructor. The young man who supervised the physics labs was very bright and congenial.

"Ever taught a laboratory course?" he questioned her, rocking back on his chair. Several lures from the fishing hat on his head brushed across his face when he moved.

"No, but I have ten years of experience in teaching swimming lessons," Carrie answered.

"It's all the same," he said straightening in his chair. "They either swim or drown. OK, you're hired."

She enjoyed her job very much, though initially it demanded valuable time from her studies. Eager to proceed with the business of attaining a Physics degree, Carrie jumped ahead in her curriculum without bothering to complete the prerequisites and this doubled the time she spent preparing for her classes.

Brent came for a weekend visit after classes began. He stayed with the boyfriend of Carrie's roommate, John, who rented a house with three other men. The student population verified the existence of a small world: John was the younger brother of a friend whom Brent and Carrie both knew at the University. Brent had stayed with her family during his trip to Houston. In addition, Carrie constantly ran into many old acquaintances from the area high schools in Dallas and Ft. Worth. There were even a few individuals from her grade school. The state champion wrestler who had taken Carrie to the senior prom also appeared on campus one day and they resumed their friendship. Dividing her life into two distinct segments, Carrie discovered she enjoyed studying with the Physicists, but preferred socializing with the Forestry department, the most outdoor group on campus.

Two weeks after Brent's weekend visit, Carrie hopped on a greyhound bus bound for Dallas.

"How's it going, lady?" Brent greeted Carrie as she stepped off the bus at the Dallas terminal.

Without saying another word Carrie threw her arms around the circumference of his skinny body. She felt so happy to see a familiar face among the rogues loitering at the bus terminal. From all appearances, Brent fitted in well with the environment. Wearing his leather jacket and black sailor's cap, Brent's thick unruly hair and bearded face seemed a threat to the rougher looking characters and they carefully avoided him. Hanging onto his arm as they made their way out of the crowded terminal, Carrie felt like she nothing to fear.

"I gotta get back to work soon. There's a program that I need to start running in another hour," Brent announced once they were outside the dingy building. "What are your plans for this weekend?"

Besides his regular campus jobs, Brent worked as a night time computer operator. The position was actually a glorified babysitting job. Brent was required to run a few programs and call the supervisor whenever the computer crashed. He shared the position with two other students from the University, and the position often allowed time for sleep and study during working hours.

"Well, I'm here to see you. I'd just as soon avoid seeing my folks if you don't mind. Mind if I do my schoolwork while you watch the computer. I have lots to do," Brent happily grinned. He certainly would not mind her company during the lonely fortyeight hours he spent operating the computer.

So Carrie enjoyed the entire weekend with Brent on the eleventh floor of an office building. Because Dallas was a city built by commuters, the entire downtown region transformed into a ghost town on weekends and she wandered through vacated streets and offices during trips for hamburgers. The atmosphere of the empty city relaxed Carrie because she didn't have to contend with the hustle and bustle of crowded city conditions. At night she curled beside Brent on the floor of the office and slept between program runs. The machine clanged and whirled computer printouts throughout the night, stopping only when it was time to change the operation. In spite of the noise and discomfort, Carrie was thankful for the time with Brent and accepted the circumstances as a luxury.

Awaking early on Sunday morning, the day of her departure, Carrie discovered Brent missing from his place beside her. She immediately glanced towards the computer.

"He's still here," she sighed with relief when she spotted him laboring over the printer. She remembered that she was no longer in her familiar dorm room; she was in a glassy office building.

Intending to take full advantage of the building's architecture, Carrie rose from the floor and opened the shades on the windows. A brilliant city sunrise greeted her, flooding the room with its brightness and warmth. After having nested overnight on the eleventh floor, Carrie felt a curious sense of homeowners' contentment as she viewed the scenes below with the eyes of an eagle. She considered herself the richest person on earth. Those who inhabited the building during regular office hours didn't know what they were missing. For the first time in her life she felt a bond with another human being that seemed hers for some reason. Although she had spent many nights in many different places throughout her life, never before had she awaken with such a feeling of peace. She had shared a place with another person where she could live without fear of assault or harassment.

When it came time to leave for the Dallas bus terminal, Carrie gathered her things from around the room and packed them in a small overnight bag. Tying the strings around her overnight bag, Carrie felt a sudden sinking feeling seize her chest. Confused by the sudden emotion, she collapsed in the chair behind her as she stammered quietly, "Brent, I feel like my heart is breaking..."

She shook her head over the feeling. It didn't make sense. She could take care of herself. She would see Brent again some other time. However, telling herself these things didn't subdue the swirling sensation which poured from her heart and into her head. The feeling became too much to bear and Carrie began weeping, burying her head in her hands.

She felt Brent come and put his arm around her. After a few seconds Carrie noticed him squatting on the floor in front of her.

Slowly, a realization stirred from her depths. She repeated her vague feelings to Brent, "I..., I don't want to leave you. I can't handle the loneliness of the bus trip... I don't know what's wrong with me," she sobbed.

Nothing seemed logical to Carrie anymore. She couldn't bear the thought of leaving something behind for fear that she might never find it again.

"It's OK," he comforted Carrie, tightly holding her hand in his. Carrie began shaking involuntarily as the tears streamed down her face. He moved forward, holding her close to his body where her face fell against his chest.

"I just feel like crying. I guess I miss you too much," she gasped, feeling bewildered by her emotional state. "I can't go today, I'm too upset."

"It's OK, it's OK...," he soothed Carrie. "How about if I drive you back to school.?" He gently removed Carrie's hands from her face and looked directly at her. Carrie nodded, feeling helpless in the situation.

"Do you mind?" she questioned.

"No," he smiled. "That's what I'm here for," he answered while hugging Carrie tightly. "We'll go after I finish running this program."

The time for departure arrived quickly, and Carrie's tears returned once they started driving. Without speaking, she merely laid her head in Brent's lap.

Brent hummed softly as he watched the traffic, placing his hand around her waist in reassurance. Emotionally exhausted, Carrie fell asleep for the duration of the trip. By the time they reached the campus Carrie felt ready to resume her college activities and leave Brent once more.

Two weeks later, Brent returned to campus to visit Carrie.

"Guess what?! I have a surprise for you!" Carrie told him when he arrived on Friday evening. "I rented a cabin in the National Forest. If this weather ever clears, we can do some hiking."

Unfortunately, the rain persisted throughout the weekend and thwarted their hiking plans. Nonetheless, Brent and Carrie found plenty to do in their cozy environment.

"You must cut my hair," Brent informed Carrie on Saturday morning.

"What?! I don't know how to cut hair," Carrie said dropping her pencil over the physics problem she had been wrestling.

"Mommy always cuts Daddy's hair, and she always cut our hair," Brent told her.

"But I'm not your mother," she answered.

"Well, at the University I'd give one of the women in Siena Hall a bottle of wine for a haircut. I've never been to a barber in my life. I suppose I could go see Karen again..."

"Wait a minute...," Carrie immediately interrupted, "but I have no experience. What happens if I mess up?"

"You're an artist, you can do these sorts of things. I know it... I don't care if you mess up; you should have seen some of the haircuts my mother gave me."

Remembering Brent's sensitivity to tactile stimulation, particularly at the cranial region, Carrie imagined him melting underneath the fingers of another woman and reconsidered her latent haircutting abilities. She schemed to give the man a haircut he'd never forget.

"OK," Carrie conceded, "but instead of giving me a bottle of wine you must do something for me."

"No problem. What is it?"

"You must take off your clothes."

"For a haircut?!"

"You can wear a towel."

"What?!"

"I'm being an artist... Don't worry, I won't wear much either," she consoled him.

"Wait 'til I tell Mom about this haircut," he teased while stripping away his shirt.

Brent sat down in a chair near the kitchen table as Carrie returned from the bedroom half-nude with a pair of scissors in her hand.

"Don't touch the merchandise," Carrie scolded Brent, snipping his hair and moving away from his grasp at the same time. "I might make a mistake."

"You're not merchandise," he grinned.

"I know, but you must not distract your hairdresser."

"I'll take my chances," Brent answered spellbound.

"Tough luck, I am trying to drive you wild. ...You really do have baby cheeks. I noticed them when they auctioned your beard for charity week. Now sit still as I round out your beard, so your face won't look so long."

"I'll be bald at thirtyfive," Brent stated enthusiastically while Carrie layered the upper portion of his hair. "That's why I've started to wear my hats now."

"You wear them because you enjoy them. Face it. You're cute, furry, and irresistible. You can't help it," Carrie told him planting a kiss on top of his head. "With your looks, and my brains, we could really go places, brother."

Then Carrie started singing in her deepest, sexiest voice:

Your furry fa-ace
Is making me blu-ue.
Your eyes are too (two),
Your fluff is the color of cho-ocolate.
Your furry face,
Is making blu-ue o-over you.

"Where did you get that one?" he asked.

"It's something I made up for my cat. There I'm finished. It only took me two hours," she observed, glancing at the clock in the kitchen area.

Brent stood and brushed the loose hairs from his body. "I feel like a new man!" he roared. Then he peered over the top of Carrie's head and asked, "Did you know you have a bald spot right there?"

"What?!"

"I tell that to all the girls," he told Carrie, excitedly lifting her high off the floor. "You're supposed to scream."

"Why?"

"Because that's what Mommy does when Daddy picks her up. She screams, then the children yell, the dogs bark, the cats meow, and we all go 'round and 'round," he explained while twirling Carrie over the kitchen.

"OK. That's it! Time for the showers! Go!" she commanded, ignoring his instructions.

Brent plopped her down in the shower stall, removed her clothes, turned on the water, and joined Carrie underneath the spray. After filling the tub, they reclined in each other's arms for over an hour. Then they progressed to the bedroom where they showered each other with warm kisses and frolicked beneath the sheets. Thoughtfully, Brent drew her closer towards his heart, which thumped incessantly underneath his velvet chest. Within a brief moment's time they were both asleep in the snug embrace.

Chapter Twenty Four

...In a clear blue morning
Until you see what can be alone
In a cold day dawning
Are you still free? Can you be?...
When some cold tomorrow finds you
When some sad old dream reminds you
How the endless road unwinds you...
When that October wind is blowing
And there's nothing left worth knowing
It's time you should be going
While you see a chance,
Take it, find romance;
Because its all on you...

"While You See a Chance"
Steve Winwood

Placing the latest letter from Brent on top of her books, Carrie sank into her desk chair and remembered the time spent with him over the weekend.

She read Brent's letter again. Yes, he definitely was depressed. He wrote about the long hours at his jobs and his worries about saving enough money... *Enough money?! Why does he suddenly need so much money? Now Carrie, you're not dumb. Brent wants to marry you. Face it. Look at what is happening in his life. He was once a carefree college student, and now he complains of a pre-ulcerative stomach condition whenever he drives the school bus. He needs help, Carrie.*

You aren't doing so well yourself. You have a reputation in the dorm for being the first one up in the morning and the last person to go to bed. The only time you ever sleep is when you're with him. Sure, your life would normalize once you quit letting Brent into your life, but do you really want to lose him? What's it worth, Carrie, your books or your love life?

That night Carrie attended a movie on campus with several other women who shared the dorm hall. The movie, a French film with English subtitles, was narrated by a French Psychologist who commented on the case studies of three individuals.

"Every creature is a product of its environment," he began. It has basic drives for food, sleep, and procreation. Environmental stimuli elicit responses from living organisms consistent with these basic drives. If the stimulus is negative, then the animal will respond negatively to its environment," the Psychologist explained.

The following scene showed how rat behavior could be modified through a punishment and reward system. A piece of cheese was placed at the other end of a maze. Every time the rat chose an undesirable path, the animal received an electric shock compelling the creature to choose the correct one. In the second scene a rat received an electric shock every time he tried to eat a piece of cheese, so that the rat associated eating with pain. As a result, the rat suppressed its drive for food and died from starvation, dramatically verifying the Psychologist's behavioral prediction. Next the Psychologist correlated the studies to human behavior, analyzing typical everyday situations in light of the proposed theory. After one scene showed an argument between two lovers, the next clip exactly repeated the encounter with rat heads and tails substituted for the corresponding human forms. All human reactions became the equivalent of programmed rat behavior: anger reacted to anger, insults responded to insults, and negative stimuli evoked negative actions. Other scenes showed how human behavior could be manipulated through a reward and punishment system, using segments from the lives of the three individuals as examples.

According to the Psychologist, these case studies supposedly represented the norm in the human species. One man, numbed by his environment, mechanically assumed the role of businessman, husband, and father with the precision of a programmed robot and the range of feeling of a vegetable. The second individual, a woman, endlessly sought fulfillment through a perpetuating series of love affairs. The third person responded to his environment with the act of suicide. Finally, the movie ended with the Psychologist's summary, which was easily condensed into the title of the movie: "C'est la vie" or "That is life".

Feeling as if the carpet had been pulled from underneath her, Carrie left the theater feeling bewildered by the scientist's assertions.

"That movie depressed me!" roared the Business major in her small town accent, breaking the silence as they walked together towards the dorm.

"I'm not sure I understood it," admitted the Language major, an honor student.

"Ya, all the characters apparently lacked the vision needed to rise above their circumstances," Carrie commented.

"What do ya mean?!" questioned the Business major, wishing to define the issues even further.

"It has to do with the ability of an individual to break the mode of predictable behavior rather than just respond passively to life," explained the Language major who also could speak French.

"Hmmm," nodded the Business major with a grin. Now she seemed satisfied with the interpretation.

Encouraged by the Language major's words, Carrie attacked the movie's theme like a defense lawyer, "If we don't agree with the Psychologist's initial presumptions concerning life, then we can toss out the case studies. They are probably biased anyways... Look, human beings have more opportunities than rats simply because life is not always as defined as a maze. Common sense says that the Psychologist's analogy is not valid."

"Hey, you're right. His arguments sounded so convincing that the plot's basic premise slipped right by me," confessed the Language major, who seemed as relieved as Carrie that the source of the depression had been exposed.

"I feel manipulated," sighed the Business major.

"The whole audience was manipulated by the movie," Carrie observed. "The Psychologist's approach left no room for discussion."

"I suppose that we're so accustomed to accepting these things in our classes that we never bothered to question the movie's plot," the Language major commented.

"Seems that the majority of society as a whole agrees with those views," the Business major added.

Carrie added in amusement, "Tomorrow I could walk into my Modern Physics class, watch the instructor close his book shut, and hear him say, 'Sorry folks, we came up with something else. Everything learned so far has been proven incorrect.'"

Both the Language and Business majors smiled, apparently relieved that they were not Physics majors. Together they spent over an hour rapping about studies, then Carrie returned to her room and continued her homework. Carrie's roommate was out. She spent a major portion of the semester at her boyfriend's house which often afforded Carrie the privacy of a single room. Carrie rather enjoyed the solitude; if she ever desired company, she could just open her door.

Because her thoughts were still concerned with the movie, Carrie was unable to fully concentrate on her Physics assignment. She laid her pencil down and rose from her chair. Staring out the window from her room on the fifth floor, Carrie peered through the silver mist enshrouding the lamps on the parking lot.

"I am not a programmed rat," she thought, feeling her lower jaw stiffen. None of the people portrayed in the movie seemed very happy, and yet, Carrie felt she knew millions like them. She absolutely refused to join them and become a member of the rat race. Where would civilization be today if everyone manifested such prescribed behavior?

Carrie left her window view and walked the few steps over to her bed. Sitting on the edge with both feet on the floor, she rested her elbows on her knees and let the weight of her head fall into her hands. Where would she be today if she had allowed herself to become a product of her environment? According to the Psychologists she should have died long ago, their theories could not account for her existence. What was she doing here anyway?

Carrie's eyes fell to her feet. She couldn't ever live like a programmed rat. There was more to life. Sure, she had endured her share of bumps and bruises, but she had realized personal fulfillment many times in life. Carrie would not have traded her happiest experiences for the world or a million dollars.

She glanced at Brent's letter which remained opened at the far corner of her desk. Feeling a resolute strength stir from her gut emotion, Carrie realized that she had made her decision long ago. Now she knew how she would respond to Brent's letter.

The next night Carrie carried all the loose change that she owned and ran to the pay phone at the nearest drug store. Holding her breath until she heard his familiar voice answer the phone, Carrie greeted, "Hello, Brent?!"

"Hello lady! How are ya doing?" he asked her with the usual vibrancy.

"Ah, Brent, I think we should get married," Carrie softly whispered before regaining confidence.

Chapter Twenty Five

Dream about the days to come
When I won't have to leave alone,
About the times I won't have to say

"Leaving on Jet Plane"
John Denver

"Are you sure? Do you know what you're saying, lady?" he asked breathlessly. His voice inflections told Carrie that he was smiling at the other end of the wire.

"Yes."

He quizzed her, "Do you know what you are giving up?"

"Yes."

"Do you know that I can't offer you much right now besides myself?"

"I know."

"Do you know you might have to quit school for awhile and follow me around?"

"I'm prepared for that."

"Reserve the cabin and I'll arrive as soon as possible on Friday afternoon. We've got lots to talk about and lots of planning to do. Don't worry about anything, lady. Brent is magic; I've got lots of tricks up my sleeve."

"That's why I'm calling, Brent. I wanted to get this issue in the open so that we can work together."

"I've got to run to work now. Take care. I love you."

Late Friday afternoon Carrie heard a knock at her door and rose from her desk to meet the caller. It was Brent. When he stepped inside her room, they threw their arms around each other in a wild frenzy. Knowing that her roommate would be with her boyfriend for the evening, Carrie quickly locked the door as they sank into to her bed. Soon, in his embrace a shared peace stilled

Carrie's senses, rendering her motionless under the weight of Brent's body. He never entered her. The climaxes reached through the intimacy of their touch overwhelmed them.

For a brief, uncertain moment in time Carrie's and Brent's world stopped and a hour passed without their knowledge. When she regained consciousness in their present surroundings, she whispered to Brent, "I think we should probably leave soon."

Brent awoke rapidly from his stupor and hopped to the floor, straightening his attire. Carrie did the same and they left after she grabbed her overnight case. In spite of their feelings for each other, both knew that they would not consummate the relationship before marriage. To Brent and Carrie intercourse appeared as a curiosity, looming ahead in their future like land on a sea horizon. Wrapped tightly in the emotions of their romantic interludes, they remained content with the amount of sex in their love life for the same intangible reason that lovers such as Romeo and Juliet never consummate their feelings until they have reach the right place in time.

When they entered the cabin, Brent placed one knee on the floor and took Carrie's hand.

"Carrie, will you marry me?" he burst with a smile.

"Brent?!" Carrie shrieked. The traditional proposal had caught her off guard.

"I wanted to ask you first, but I knew you were too independent. I was going to wait until I could make you a better offer."

"This is the twentieth century," Carrie pleaded, looking directly into his eyes as he stood. Then she told him, "Yes."

Having completed the traditional formality, Brent sat down at the dining table and Carrie immediately bounced into his lap.

"OK, when are we going to get married? Any ideas?"

"We could elope."

"No, my parents would be disappointed."

"How about just before graduation? You're folks will be there and we could invite our friends from college."

"Sounds great. We have two and one half months to get ready."

"Alright. I'll handle invitations, check into the legalities, and plan the reception."

"...And I'll find a preacher and someone to make the rings. I want to talk with my Dad too. Come to visit next week and we'll call my parents. I want to wait until my assistantship is confirmed."

"I don't want to tell my mother until spring break. I'll need two weeks to figure out how to break the news to her. People will wonder if I'm pregnant."

"They'll figure it out when no baby appears after seven months. Don't worry."

Within the week Brent received written notification of his assistantship at a graduate school in San Antonio where he planned to pursue Solar Engineering. Proceeding with their tentative plans, Carrie took a weekend bus headed for Dallas and together they called Brent's parents from the University dorm. Because Brent's mother was away at church they were only able to speak with one parent. Brent's father greeted their news with only one question, "Shall I make a cradle?"

"No, Daddy that won't be needed for awhile," Brent grinned.

After the phone call Brent explained to Carrie that his father made a cradle whenever a family member expected their first baby. The following week Brent received a phone call from his mother.

"I thought your father was joking, until your letter arrived," she apologized. "All he said was that you were getting married before graduation. You know how your father is. Now I'll have to call everyone and tell them that its true. Daddy gets to foot the phone bill for this prank," she laughed.

Unfortunately, Carrie dealings with her mother weren't as humorous. Carrie told her family during spring break when everyone had gathered around the dining table for lunch. Her mother was not surprised by the news and tried to dissuade Brent.

Her mother began. "She doesn't cook and she does very little housework."

"Boy, I'll say...," interjected Ellen. Ellen rolled her eyes as she spoke, emphasizing the ridiculousness of the entire discussion.

Mother glared at Ellen and continued, "She's more likely to be found underneath the car than in the kitchen. Carrie would not make a very good wife, and she doesn't have much to offer. I hope you know what you are getting yourself into, Brent."

Carrie decided to defend herself with humor. "Ah, Mom," she insisted dryly, "I am very good at making chocolate chip cookies. We'll live on those until I figure out the rest."

Sandy giggled and Brent smiled. Carrie's mother looked very unhappy.

"Well, I know you both love each other," she conceded before her finishing statement. "Maybe it will be enough."

As a result of the tension at her mother's house, Carrie changed her plans for spring break and left earlier than originally intended. The next morning Carrie and Brent drove to the Gulf coast where they camped on the beach with hundreds of other college students. On the way back to school they stayed overnight at a campground two hours away from college. This time, Brent and Carrie decided to vary the evening routine and trade responsibilities.

"I'd rather build a fire than cook anyways," Carrie reflected as began gathering wood for the campfire. Casting aside the pieces she planned to use as tinder, Carrie methodically arranged the sticks so that the pile would light immediately. However, the wood was a little damp and the fire burned slowly when Carrie lighted it.

Brent walked over and rearranged Carrie's smoking pile of tinder. Blowing under the pile, he caused the flame to ignite the rest of the wood. Soon a brilliant fire blazed at the camp site.

Having watched Brent successfully complete her task, Carrie sat down on a nearby log to help fight back her tears.

"Hey, what's wrong?" Brent asked, sitting down beside her.

"Brent, you built the campfire. It was supposed to have been my job," Carrie stammered, rising from the log. Then she walked away from the area.

"I was only trying to help. It was taking you too long to light the fire." Brent jumped to his feet and followed Carrie.

"I never asked for your help. I wanted to do it by myself." She turned her head away so that Brent would not see the tears rushing down her face. Her legs felt so weak that she sat down again, staring off into the space before her. A few seconds elapsed before Carrie closed her eyes and buried her face in her hands; this was the first time they had ever argued.

"Please understand," she sobbed. "I wanted to impress you."

"Ah, that's what I was trying to do," Brent confessed. He sat down on the grass beside Carrie, wrapping his arms around her. She unraveled from her tight curl over her knees and clung to his embrace.

"We were so busy impressing each other that our intentions crossed. Look, Brent, I want to do these things for myself. It's important to me."

"Ya, I never was a patient teacher like my father, and you would rather stew over a Physics problem for several hours than ask my help. It's your Irish stubbornness, one reason why I'm marrying you. I wish I had your drive."

"Sometimes its a hindrance. But it has helped me out of a few rough spots. It's one of my quirks," Carrie smiled, lifting her head.

"You must help me learn how to teach you. I want to be prepared for our kids."

"How about if you tell me rather than take over the task,... and we go much slower?"

"OK."

"And I'll try to ask for your help much sooner," she promised.

* * *

Next week Carrie bicycled to the gynecologist's office. Before the examination she mentioned that she had skipped her period for the last two months.

"It kicks out under stress. It's somewhat hereditary," she informed him. "My great aunt, an army nurse, lost hers in World War II."

"Have you ever had intercourse?" he questioned her as she laid down on the exam table.

"No."

"Anything violent quite some time ago?..." he asked with anger and irritation before his voice trailed off.

Carrie scarcely heard his words and his sudden change in tone puzzled her. Because this was her first visit, she was unfamiliar with the standard questions and procedures. Looking up at him, she merely shook her head as he gently reached inside her. He nodded his head once his findings answered his own question, and Carrie knew that he believed her.

"Bring your fiance when you return in two weeks to pick up the prescription for the birth control pills. We'll know the results of the test by then."

When Carrie brought Brent along on the following visit, the doctor ushered them inside his office. On one of the walls was a large black and white poster of a half nude boy carrying a daisy in his hand. Carrie studied the poster with the other objects in his office and surmised the doctor's affection for children. He was young, having completed his internship only two years ago, and perhaps his dedication to the youthful results of procreation was what had called him to this particular field of study. He asked Carrie and Brent a few questions about their future plans and answered questions concerning birth control. It appeared that he just wanted to see Brent and Carrie together. Although most of the conversation seemed rather inconsequential, Carrie welcomed the opportunity to involve Brent who appreciated his inclusion in a world often cloaked by feminine mystique.

"I'm now a man of the world," he happily observed after they left the medical building. "Even the guys at school treat me with a different sort of awe and respect."

Carrie laughed. "It's within my best interests to keep you informed about these things. I may need your support and understanding sometime." Then she remembered her encounter with the physician and seriously added, "Brent, what if for some reason I'm unable to carry a child?"

Brent looked at Carrie and answered softly, "For all I know I may not be able to get you pregnant. We can always adopt; children are children."

"Good," she acknowledged, noting their agreement on this issue. There would be no problem with whatever happened.

Carrie's appointment with Dr. B. also proved inconsequential. Although she resented her mother's insistence, Carrie really did not mind sharing the good news with Dr. B. He was the best substitute for a parent she could find.

"What brings you here? I told you that I didn't want to see you in my office again," he smiled.

"I'm getting married to Brent and my mother wants me to check it out with you. She thinks I'm sick."

Dr. B. grimaced and looked down at his desk for a few moments. "There's something about the capacity to love which measures sanity," he quietly murmured. Facing Carrie, he met her eyes and stated emphatically, "The problem is your mother's."

Hearing Dr. B. speak the unspeakable, Carrie understood vaguely what he meant. He confirmed her own private suspicions concerning her mother. Abruptly resuming his professional demeanor, he straightened the papers on his desk and stated in a businesslike voice, "If she questions you further, have her call me."

Another matter crossed his mind and peered at Carrie with his eyes opened wide. "Uh,... I understand your conservatism and religious upbringing as well as your own personal sense of morality..., uh... have you and Brent been... uh, ...intimate?" he asked, pausing for a moment to search for the right descriptive words.

Intimate?! Carrie swallowed hard and braced for a lecture on fornication. "Yes, but we haven't gone all the way. We're happy just being together."

Dr. B. blinked, and shuffled some more papers around his desk.

"Good! Good!" he happily exclaimed. "Intimacy is very important in a relationship. One should feel comfortable with their partner before choosing to spend the rest of their life with them."

Though, she could not imagine marrying a man without having been intimate with him, she couldn't believe she was getting this much support from a man older than her father. She nodded at Dr. B. She had sensed the importance of intimacy and had never fully realized its value until now.

Chapter Twenty Six

Let me not to the marriage of true minds
Admit impediments. Love is not love
Which alters when it alteration finds,
Or bends with the remover to remove:
O no; it is an ever-fixed mark,
That looks on tempests, and is never shaken;
It is the star to every wandering bark,
Whose worth's unknown, although his height be taken.
Love's not Time's fool, though rosy lips and cheeks
Within his bending sickle's compass come;
Love alters not with his brief hours and weeks,
But bears it out even to the edge of doom.
If this be error, and upon me prov'd,
I never writ, nor no man ever lov'd.

Sonnet CXVI
William Shakespeare

Carrie spent the morning of her wedding day cleaning the swimming pool in her mother's backyard. No one else in the family knew how to operate the filter pump, and this activity happened to be one of Carrie's favorite chores. Feeling the sun warm the bare skin on her back, Carrie methodically ran the vacuum over the sides of quiet pool. It had been raining all week and the pool was a mess. The yard wasn't much better, but fortunately the sun was rapidly drying up the spring puddles.

Briefly, Carrie stopped and watched the rays of the sun refresh the earth with a lingering mist. She sniffed, trying to catch the enchanting swirls of vapor. Of all the things she could have done before the wedding, cleaning the swimming pool was the most gratifying. The afternoon reception would be held in the backyard and a clean swimming pool would help soothe her giddiness during the festivity.

However, a year's supply of acorns had clogged one of the filter pipes during the winter, and the job took longer than expected.

"Shouldn't you be getting ready for your wedding?! You only have two hours," Carrie's aunt giggled when they arrived and found her outside.

"I suppose I should start thinking about changing into a wedding dress," Carrie grinned goodnaturedly.

"Here, I'll finish the pool," one of Carrie's uncles offered. "They can't start the wedding without the bride."

"Aren't you nervous?" another aunt asked.

"Nope," Carrie replied as she waltzed inside the house. Marrying Brent seemed the most natural thing in the world on such a sunny day as the present one, even if she did have to exchange her bikini for a fancy dress.

Two hours later, about sixty people crowded the rose garden of the city park. Carrie made her way down the stone stairs towards the water fountain at the base of the hillside. The sight of Carrie in a long flowing white gown walking down the rose-covered hillside caused Brent's heart to skip a beat. She was carrying a red rose and wearing a garland of daisies around her thick blond hair.

Soon Carrie climbed down the last few steps and her eyes met Brent's. A friend played guitar and sang the final verses of the "Wedding Song" as Carrie took Brent's side before the pastor. Clad from head to toe in white, Brent's dark glasses and curly brown mane made him look striking in a white tuxedo. Their preacher, the only clergy who agreed to marry them with two month's notification, was a good friend of the pastor at the church in Brent's hometown. He officiated in a concise and meaningful fashion, and nobody became bored with the proceedings.

"Let me not to the marriage of true minds admit impediments...," Samantha began, reciting the Shakespearean sonnet in the middle of the ceremony. Carrie was relieved that Samantha had toned down her melodramatics considerably from her private rehearsals in front of the bedroom mirror. Ever since being asked to read the sonnet for the wedding, Samantha had been spouting the poem as flamboyantly as possible, often having her audience rollicking with laughter by time she finished. This time when Samantha finished nobody laughed; instead, the listeners thoughtfully nodded their heads. The pastor added to Samantha's spell with a few final words, and then Michael's rich voice resonated through the park. Strumming his guitar with slow deliberate fingers, he solemnly chanted the wedding song from "Fiddler on the Roof".

Placing their arms inside the other, Brent and Carrie walked away from the fifty or sixty people who had congregated for the wedding. They followed the stone steps towards the fountain in the middle of the rose garden. When they arrived at the fountain, Brent and Carrie stopped and turned around. They watched the cluster of people at the base of the hillside slowly come to life as if they had been frozen by some magic enchantment. Instead of immediately leaving the site, most people began conversing with the person standing next to them.

"When are you going to get married?" People overheard Professor Max ask Dr. C. The young fair-haired professor blushed. Until today few realized Professor Max's deep affection for the sweeter passages in life, once lavishly celebrated in his Romanian homeland. As the crowd began strolling through the rose garden, Brent and Carrie posed for a few pictures. Then they were chauffeured from the park by Donna's father. For the next few minutes Carrie and Brent stared at each other in awe. They still couldn't believe that they had just been married. At the reception Brent and Carrie forgot their awkwardness and enjoyed celebrating with all their friends and relatives. Carrie delightedly noted that the pool was cleaned and the backyard was festively decorated.

"That was the best wedding ceremony I've ever attended," commented Carrie's grandmother, a hardened veteran of many wedding ceremonies. "It was the most meaningful."

"We didn't want people to get bored," Carrie told her with a smile. Until her last final scarcely two days ago, Carrie had wondered if it would have been better to dismiss with the formalities and elope. Somehow all the tensions had disappeared in the last few days, including those within her former family.

"You're glowing," remarked Jerry when Carrie joined the cluster of students on the patio. Carrie had spent part of one semester at the University being infatuated with Jerry, her Physics lab instructor. Whatever Jerry said was scientific enough to be true. Carrie looked down at the patio cement and pondered his observations for a few seconds: if getting married to Brent had caused her to glow, then this must be what it felt like to be a bride. It was a subtle change with major implications. Like a freedom which is suddenly granted legal sanctity, the change arrived with a sense of maturity and relief. Now she and Brent could belong to each other as husband and wife.

Dispensing with any further formalities, Brent and Carrie exited the reception before her relatives decided to toss her in the pool according to their Irish version of a Polish custom. Carrie knew them well enough to consider their threat seriously; her relatives were notorious for their wedding pranks. Together Brent and Carrie dashed to the VW bug though a crowd of people shouting and throwing rice. Hurriedly, Brent and Carrie jumped inside the decorated bug to escape further pranks. Insulating themselves from the crowd, they locked the doors and kissed each other before starting Maxwell's engine. While driving away from the neighborhood, Brent adjusted the window shade to avoid the sun's glare. Millions of computer paper dots floated down from the shade.

"Fred Morris is responsible for this one," he laughed as he brushed away the dots that had collected in his lap.

"He always uses computer dots," Carrie chimed.

Wait 'til he gets married!" Brent roared excitedly as he accelerated towards the highway.

They breathed much easier once they safely stepped inside the honeymoon suite of the hotel. Feeling assured that the pranks were over for the time-being, Brent and Carrie looked at each other and wondered what to do next. Brent began talking about his overwhelming experiences at the wedding while Carrie inspected their surroundings in the room. Sitting down on one of the chairs, Carrie watched Brent who currently stood just a hair inside the doorway explaining how to put on a tuxedo.

"Brent, are you nervous?" she asked, smiling at his excited antics.

Without another word Brent violently nodded his head.

"This does seem rather awkward," Carrie agreed. "Funny, we've dashed for each other so spontaneously in the past... Maybe we should have done this sooner. Its such a change of pace from the ceremony of the day."

Brent nodded his agreement without moving an inch closer from the doorway.

"Let's start with the champagne," Carrie suggested.

Relieved at having finally found something to do, Brent popped the cork off the bottle and poured two glasses. He walked over to Carrie and silently handed her the drink.

"I think we should get on with the order of consummating the marriage," Carrie suggested, taking a comical swig from her glass of champagne.

Appearing more comfortable after Carrie had mentioned the unspeakable, Brent again nodded. "I'd like to get out of this monkey suit. Can you help me?" he asked, referring to his tuxedo.

Carrie put down her glass and assisted with the complications. Then Brent unzipped the back of Carrie's dress and lifted it high over her head.

"My knees were knocking so much at the ceremony that my best man had to hold me up. I never would have made it without Sullivan," he told Carrie as he kissed her.

"Yah, I only tripped over the train of my wedding dress twice," She added before becoming serious. "Hands are my favorite parts of the human body," she quietly told him. "I could lose any one of my five senses, but I would mourn most the loss of a hand. They are the most expressive; they do so much and feel so many things."

Carrie had never seen Brent's eyes so blue and she watched his face as she firmly tightened her grip on his hand. He entered her as her hips rolled with him. Their breathing grew heavy, then suddenly Carrie felt something rip inside her. Brent fell on top of her with the deeper penetration.

"Are you alright?!" she heard him whisper hoarsely.

"Huh?! Oh that was great, Brent!" Carrie responded. She felt too dizzy to even lift her head and she sensed a numbness in the lower half of her body.

"You passed out on me. Scared me to death. I thought I had killed you."

"No," Carrie replied, slowly recovering her senses. "The feeling really is different!"

Brent looked at her dubiously.

Searching his face earnestly, Carrie answered as if she was playing him in chess, "It's your move."

He resumed his motion inside her, but lost total control within a matter of seconds. She squirmed in response to his rigorous movement until they both stopped abruptly, and her lightheadedness returned. Having spent all his energy, Brent collapsed beside Carrie catching his breath. They slept soundly for the next seven hours and at two o'clock in the morning sent out for pizza. For the remaining two days they enjoyed the time together as much as two lovers who had become one, their lives centered around the timeless activities of sex and sleep.

Chapter Twenty Seven

...When the night has been too lonely
And the road has been too long
And you think love is only
For the lucky and the strong
Just remember in the winter
Far beneath the bitter snows
Lies the seed that with the sun's love
In the spring becomes the Rose...

"The Rose"
Amada McBroom

Slowly, Brent and Carrie resumed interaction with the world of dates and schedules that they had known before the wedding. After attending Brent's graduation exercise, they cruised to the Northeastern United States in a miniature motor home that belonged to Brent's father.

During the first evening of their trip Carrie guided Brent to a State Park south of the Red River.

"This will be our last night in Texas for a while," commented Carrie before she jumped out of the motor home as soon as it stopped.

She walked a few steps towards the brilliant blue lake before them. A strong wind gently brushed the loose strands of blond hair from her face as she gazed across the lake. She belonged here in this flat land where everything could easily be seen for the way it stood. A warm gust of wind sailed over the crystal blue waters and drew strength into her legs. She felt solidly planted on the earth.

Later that night, only a few hours after she and Brent had fallen asleep in each others arms, Carrie awoke and fully opened her eyes. For several seconds she laid motionless as her eyes outlined the shadows inside the motor home. She heard the incessant beat of bullfrogs and crickets outside the screened window and turned towards Brent. He remained sleeping between her and the window. It was hot inside the motor home and Carrie felt restless. To avoid disturbing Brent's heavy slumber, she put on a pair of shorts and a T-shirt and made her way outside.

She felt much better in the open air, underneath the bright white light of the moon. Lying down on the picnic table near a mesquite grove, Carrie raised her knees and stared at the night sky. As her head began swimming with the shadows of the evening's darkness, Carrie recognized the familiar restless feeling of a long, forgotten Nightmare. She wanted to get away, but she couldn't. She wanted to be smart enough to figure things out, but she wasn't. She wanted to explain her feelings to Brent, but she didn't know how.

Carrie sat up and glanced at the woods on her left. Maybe she should enter the tangled brush and disappear like a magician. Would anyone notice that it really wasn't an act? That she would disappear and not come back? She didn't want to bring anyone into this other part of her world, much less Brent. She had always sheltered those she knew from it.

Carrie rose from the table and walked towards the motor home. She decided to ignore these sensations once more and fall asleep beside Brent as if nothing else had happened tonight. This was what she wanted most.

Inside the motor home she took off her clothes and slid underneath the sleeping bag next to Brent. Less than fifteen minutes later, Carrie left the bed to throw up in the restroom.

"What's up?!" Brent asked her as he watched from the doorway. He had a dazed look on his face, but he immediately sized up the situation. Without saying another word, he gently held Carrie upright as she emptied her stomach. Tears rolled down her face and her body shook with the emotion. For a few seconds Carrie stopped and leaned against the walls in exhaustion. Another wave of nausea hit her and she leaned forward. This process repeated itself several times until Carrie finally sank into the hollowness inside the pit of her stomach. Then she went limp and Brent gently lowered her to the floor.

"I hope I haven't grossed you out," she gasped, weakly looking up at Brent.

"Not at all," Brent said slowly. He had been deeply moved by the experience. "Let me carry you to bed," he pleaded.

"After I brush my teeth," she replied.

Brent supported her and Carrie brushed her teeth. Afterwards he carried her to bed where she slept until dawn. Early the next morning, Brent pulled the blocks away from the tires of the motor home and began the second day's drive. Alert and aware of her surroundings, Carrie remained in her prone position and chatted animatedly with Brent between naps. She felt dizzy whenever she stood, and contented herself with watching Brent's activities. Throughout the course of the drive Brent excitedly directed Carrie's attention to points of interest along the highway and she raised her head to look out the window. They maintained an easygoing, light-hearted pace during the trip. Whenever Brent become tired of driving, he would stop the motor home a small distance away from the highway and visit Carrie in the back.

"Did you see the Rockies?" he excitedly asked her on the third day of the trip. He sat down on the bed next to her, leaning forward to kiss her softly on the lips.

"Those are the Rockies?!" she questioned, perplexed by the present scenery around them. "They don't look real from this distance."

Brent kissed her again. He seemed like a dream to Carrie, who had been slipping in and out of waking consciousness for the last few days. She pulled him closer to her. She wanted to love and hold him forever. Swayed by the intensity of her feelings, Brent met her passion and they made love.

For some length of time he rested by her side and then rose to return to the wheel. "How do you feel now? Can you sit by me in the front?" he whispered.

Eagerly, Carrie lifted her head towards him. Her dizziness returned, and she sadly fell back. Without saying a word, she shook her head. In her dreamy existence she had forgotten her physical state.

A feeling of helplessness flooded Brent's eyes when he realized the gravity of the situation. "I don't want to lose you," he suddenly sobbed.

Carrie held his head over her breast and stroked his hair. "I'm not planning on leaving anytime soon. How could I leave you now that I've finally found you?" Carrie gently dried his tears and rocked him in her arms. "Your tears are safe here. I love you even more for sharing them with me."

Rubbing his head against her, Brent gasped, "God, I love you so much."

"I have a hard time believing I can affect someone so," Carrie remarked. Then she promised Brent, "I'll be OK. It's probably just due to the stress of finals, the wedding, and the fact that I've lived at sea level all my life. I still think the snow-covered Rockies look like a movie backdrop. There's something unreal about having snow in the scenery."

Brent began laughing. "I bet you've never seen snow greater than two inches."

"Actually, one year we had three inches of that funny white stuff," Carrie grinned.

"Wait until you see Yellowstone and the Grand Tetons!"

By the time they reached the Grand Tetons two days later, Carrie felt well enough to attempt a three mile hike. Although there was over five feet of snow on the ground, the weather was too warm for even a jacket.

"The sun is melting all this snow into run-off water," Brent observed as they crossed over a stream which was rapidly thawing. "Be careful. It's pretty slippery."

Heeding his words, Carrie followed him. "Brent, did you really used to hike through this stuff when you were little?"

Clump. Clump. Phuff! Carrie stepped into a snow drift near a tree and fell in over her head. Covered by snow, she noticed that her feet had not yet found the bottom of the pile.

"This stuff is like quicksand," she commented, groping for a sense of familiarity as she struggled to get out of the drift. She had experienced quicksand while hiking around her cousin's place in Texas.

Oblivious to her predicament, Brent continued hiking ahead of her. When a chipmunk scampered across the trail, he turned around. "Where did she go?!" he murmured, puzzled by her abrupt disappearance.

Quickly, he traced the tracks in the snow and found Carrie stranded in the snow drift. "Oh you poor Texan!" he laughed as he helped her crawl out of a hole in the snow. "Nobody ever taught you how to walk on snow."

"You mean this funny white stuff?!" she retorted. "I just haven't found my snow legs yet."

"Stay away from the trees," he instructed.

"How about if I go first?" she begged. "It's hard to see over your head."

"Good idea... that way I won't lose you to the snow drifts," he added, nudging Carrie forward.

Several snow drifts and a mile later, Brent and Carrie returned to the motor home and drove to Yellowstone. This time she rode with Brent in the front portion of the motor home and stared wide-eyed at the snow deposits towering above the vehicle's roof. After two good nights' sleep in Yellowstone, Carrie seized the wheel one afternoon and bumped Brent into the passenger seat. Delighted, he explained the vehicle's operation to her and she shared the driving for the remainder of the trip.

After spending a week at the farm of Brent's parents, they left Vermont and drove Maxwell back to Texas. The week had given Carrie a chance to see the home that Brent talked so much about as well as rest up for the return journey. She continued experiencing dizziness, and took time out for naps whenever she became too tired.

Chapter Twenty Eight

I bought a ticket to the world,
But now I've come back again.
Why do I find it hard to write the next line?
When I want the truth to be said
I know this much is true

"True"
Spandua Ballet

In the warm, congenial atmosphere of the Physics and Engineering graduate program, Brent and Carrie created their first home together. Because the two departments were closely associated, Brent and Carrie had adjoining desks in the same student office on the third floor. Like the other students in the department, both married and single, they helped establish the interdisciplinary associations into one family. During the summer following the school year, Carrie instructed a Physics lab and earned class credit for her independent research in electronics. She increased her physical stamina to the point where she could play on the women's intercollegiate soccer team in the fall semester. She also enrolled in some advanced Geology courses and made lasting friendships with a few of the other students.

One of these friends was a Geologist named Don. He was a triathlete with the body of "David" and the artistic pathos of Michelangelo. Though his sculptures were of wood, he threw himself into the study of rocks with fervency unknown to most scientists. Slightly dyslexic, Don met Carrie when a professor recommended her as a Physics tutor.

"Teach him Physics, Carrie, and he'll be your friend for life," Brent encouraged her after Don left the student office one afternoon. Like some of the other graduates in the room, Brent had been listening to their latest Physics lesson.

"I think that he'd be a good friend for life," Carrie acknowledged. Brent possessed an intuitive sense about people, almost like an art curator with a painting. Carrie trusted his judgment. "In many ways he reminds me of myself, although I'm not near as verbal. I've had my own share of learning disabilities to get over."

As the semester progressed, Don introduced Carrie to his friends in Geology and Carrie and Brent formed close friendships with them as well. Don's girlfriend was captain of the soccer team and Carrie enjoyed helping Don pick out gifts for her. One weekend, Brent, Carrie, Don, and some other Geologists went camping at a nearby state park. Because everyone had so much fun, this weekend solidified the burgeoning friendships. Towards the end of the year, Don invited Carrie to join the study group at the duplex that he shared with his housemate Jack. He wanted Carrie to love Geology as much as he did. She found that these devoted Geologists gave her a different perspective on science as well as life.

* * *

"OK, Jack, what is a geosyncline?" Don asked in his most serious voice, while his mustached grin betrayed his playfulness. As soon as Jack gave the correct answer Don continued with his study questions for tomorrow's Stratigraphy test.

"OK, Jack, what time in the morning do you get up to go duck hunting?"

In the later hours of the night, both the questions and answers rapidly became the same.

"Duck hunting?! I gotta get my hat to answer that one!" yelled Jack. Both housemates ran from the table and returned quacking to the living room wearing their fur-covered caps.

"Five o'clock in the morning, Don," Jack insisted after the two men settled at the table like a prepared comedy routine.

"Correct. OK, Carrie, draw a thrust fault on the chalkboard," Don demanded as he fluffed the fur on his cap. Jack mimicked Don's actions and they drew a smile from Carrie before she walked over to the board hanging on the dining room wall. She appreciated the softer side of these muscled men. Tonight Carrie noticed that they seemed rather anxious to express their sensitivity. Perhaps it was due to the stress of the tomorrow's test.

"Does it matter what color chalk I use?" Carrie teased, admiring the selection of chalk at the board. The remark gave her more time to think about her answer, especially since Geologists were more precise about these details than Physicists. It had never occurred to her until now that the pursuit of science could be an artistic endeavor.

"No," Don firmly decided. "Jack, draw an anticline. Use the correct colors for the ages of the rocks."

Meanwhile, Don himself, waddled over to the board. "...And I'll draw a syncline. I just know Dr. Wilson is going to ask these questions on the test. Quack. Quack."

"Did you know Karen is looking for another apartment?" Jack asked Don while he drew his Geologic structure on the board.

"Oh, really?!" Don said without conviction. Then he angrily threw his piece of chalk at the base of the chalkboard and straddled his seat at the table. "I can't blame her, especially since they haven't caught the guy who raped her roommate."

"He held a knife to her throat. She couldn't escape," Jack shuddered. "Shoot, I wouldn't move either if someone stuck a knife at my throat."

"Richard and Larry are on the lookout for that critter. He's gonna be one sorry man if they find him before the police. How can anybody do such a thing? I hope he gets caught."

"Some people are strange, Don... just like our peeper," replied Jack.

"Did Jack and I tell you about our peeper?" Don asked Carrie excitedly.

"No, you didn't," Carrie answered after having curiously listened to the men's open discussion of the rape as if she was a fly on the wall. Their heartfelt support for the victim surprised her.

A knock on the door interrupted her thoughts.

"Come in!" hollered Don before he stormed into his bedroom.

Tall, burly Jim Henderson walked inside the living room. "I'm returning your Geology notes," he announced, handing the papers over to Don. Don, who had just retrieved his pistol from his room, took the papers. He laid the pistol on the table in front of big Jim.

"What's that for?!" Jim cried, shocked by the gun openly displayed in front of him.

"I'm gonna use it to scare away our peeper," replied Don. "I don't want him peeping around here."

"Find the one who raped Karen's roommate," Jim growled. "There's getting to be too many of those kinds of people in this city. No one is safe anymore."

Don picked up the gun and felt the trigger with his shooting finger. Then he sadly shook his head and looked directly at Carrie with compassion for her gender. She backed away from the recognition and Don turned his head away. "I don't know what this world is coming to," he said softly.

"Well, if you shoot someone don't forget to drag the body inside the house and place the gun in the dead man's hand. You don't want to be the one thrown in jail. The laws are pretty funny these days," remarked Jim.

"I'm not sure I could shoot someone except in self-defense," Don decided as he glanced towards Jack, consulting him as if Jack was his conscience.

"There was a fellow in my high school who shot a burglar in his house," Jim recalled, leaning back on his heels. Feeling the weight of the memory, his shoulders slumped forward as he stared at the floor. "...And the boy was never quite the same afterwards."

"I could do it," Carrie quietly stated, walking confidently towards the pistol in Don's hands. She remembered the encounter with the Knights of Oblivion and her decision to rise and fight. She felt that she could answer to her own conscience.

Still fingering his pistol, Don smiled and studied her for a few seconds. Then he nodded his belief. After a few minutes of silence Jim left. Jack peered through the shades and watched his car roll out of the driveway. Minutes later another car arrived in front of the duplex.

"Our neighbor has a goodlooking woman with him," Jack announced as he peered at through the front window.

"He's too ugly to have a girl like that," Don rejoined indignantly from his position beside Jack. Carrie couldn't be sure whether the roommates concerns were fatherly or out of jealousy. A pounding noise erupted from the other side of the duplex wall. Don and Jack echoed the pounds from their side. Carrie deduced that they were probably fraternity brothers. She wondered what the woman thought about the primitive manner in which these men communicated.

"Good luck on tomorrow's test!" Carrie shouted above the din as she hurried out the front door and hopped inside Maxwell. She didn't care to stay and meet the neighbors. Her garage apartment was only a few blocks away and she wanted to be asleep before one o'clock in the morning.

When Carrie arrived home, she discovered that Brent had already quit studying for the night. He had left the light on in the kitchen for her before going to bed. Carrie stepped across the stones on the walkway leading to the apartment and brushed past the bamboo lining the path. In comparison to the fraternity duplex, she felt grateful for the quiet, familiar sounds and lights of her own home. She entered the house, securing the locks behind her until she had made her way to the hide-a-bed in the studio room.

Undressing in the dark, Carrie quickly slipped under the covers beside Brent. She watched a smile flicker across his face in the moonlight as he unconsciously acknowledged her and pulled her close to him. She planted a kiss on his lips and watched his body wiggle slightly. Then she caught another smile in the moonlight. Carrie knew that he would not remember their silent conversation in the morning. Brent was a heavy sleeper and any dialogue between them during the night never registered on his waking consciousness. Carrie settled into his arms, feeling secure inside their peaceful home.

.

Chapter Twenty Nine

Doctor, my eyes have seen the years
And the slow parade of fears without crying
Now I want to understand
I have done all that I could
To see the evil and the good without hiding
You must help me if you can
Doctor, my eyes
Tell me what is wrong
Was I unwise to leave them open for so long
cause I have wandered through this world
And as each moment has unfurled
Ive been waiting to awaken from these dreams
People go just where there will
I never noticed them until I got this feeling
That its later than it seems
Doctor, my eyes
Tell me what you see
I hear their cries
Just say if its too late for me
Doctor, my eyes
Cannot see the sky
Is this the prize for having learned how not to cry?

"Doctor My Eyes"
Jackson Browne

"Carrie, Carrie... where are you?" she heard Brent shout when he discovered that she wasn't in bed. It was about two o'clock in the morning.

Carrie heard his voice but didn't answer.

"Carrie?!" he panicked.

His alarm shook her loose from the fragments of a dream.

"Brent...," Carrie sobbed.

"What are you doing there?" he moaned reaching for her underneath the bed.

"I feel safer here," Carrie's voice cracked.

"Just relax. It's OK," he soothed Carrie, meeting her under the bed.

"Promise you won't hit me?!" she cried in fear. Every muscle in Carrie's body tightened with emotion.

"Ah, I won't hit you. Please come out."

Hanging her head, Carrie crawled from underneath the bed and curled in Brent's lap like a tiny kitten. He held Carrie's wet face in his hands, rocking her gently until she quit trembling. "I don't know what happened," Carrie said as soon as she found her voice. She peered anxiously at her surroundings. "I had a bad dream. They are getting worse... All I remember is that I had to get away. I still feel scared."

Brent carried her to bed and placed her beside him, staying awake until Carrie fell asleep in his lap.

A few days later Carrie told Dr. Mitch, a college counselor, about the Nightmare. She had sought Dr. Mitch's advice during the previous week when similar uneasy dreams and feelings began disrupting her sleep at night. In addition she told him about him about a baby blue negligee that her father had sent over the holidays. "It bothered me and I threw it away. It doesn't fit our relationship. When I called and asked him about it, he said that his wife had helped him pick it out. I asked him not to send anymore presents."

"Did your father ever molest you?" he quizzed her.

"Not physically, but in many other ways. The threat was always present. I learned how to anticipate his actions and kept a safe distance. His overtures were strong enough for my mother to notice though,... I don't understand the connection with the Nightmare?"

"Well, what do you think about these dreams?"

"I think they're crazy," Carrie replied without thinking.

"You're crazy if you don't believe them!" he growled.

Stunned by the emotion behind his words, Carrie gulped, "Are you sure?"

He leaned forward and stated bluntly, "It's obvious that some traumatic event occurred in your childhood that you still remember. It is probably much worse than what you are able to recall. These are powerful feelings. Facing and understanding them is the only way to prevent them from controlling your life."

Somewhere, buried deep under her present consciousness, Carrie sensed a flicker of relief, though she panicked at the thought of the reality. Carrie concealed her emotions from Mitch and left the office as soon as possible. She hurried across campus to meet Brent for lunch.

Blinded by a whorl of sensations, Carrie walked briskly on the wooded pathways unaware of the birds, squirrels, and live oaks marking her steps. The lifeless form of a lone infant surrounded in darkness appeared in her mind's eye. This infant had long blond hair and wore a light blue dress. Suddenly Carrie stopped, shuddering at the recollection. She caught her breath and walked on.

"Mitch believes that I was sexually assaulted as small child," Carrie explained to Brent over lunch in the student lounge. Without further elaboration, Carrie looked down at the red checkered table cloth on the table and threw her sandwich aside. What else could she say to Brent? What was there to be done? All the confused pieces of the puzzle fitted together easily in conclusive horror.

Carrie took a deep breath and sighed, "Want to pick me up at three thirty or so? I need to work on a computer program for Opstein's graduate class. It's an easy routine and I've already done one like it for another class."

"Are you sure you don't want to go home?" questioned Brent. "You seem a little out of it."

"I feel a little bit out of it," she admitted. "But I think I'll be OK. Finishing the assignment would boost my spirits."

There were only a few people left in the department that afternoon. Carrie unlocked the door to the computer room and welcomed the seclusion. The room gave her pleasant vibrations. Various colors and thicknesses of wire laced the walls and desks like crepe paper decorations for a party. Computers and computer hardware were scattered throughout the room. Each computer station revealed its own story about the project by the way it had been left or moved by professors and students. Carrie happily recognized several components of her past projects scattered across the room, each still possessing the same fascination and level of excitement that she had earlier enjoyed.

By coincidence one of the computers was dubbed the SELF-1 Microprocessor. She had programmed the microprocessor in assembly language in order to use it as an analog-to-digital converter. Assembly language was simple; it used a binary code of either yes or no, open or close, 0 or 1, black and white.

If only life could be this clear, Carrie thought as she inserted her disk and logged on the personal computer. Sooner or later, the basics of events could be reduced to either life or death, "to be or not to be". Was it really always a choice?

The events of the day echoed in her head as Carrie began editing her computer programs. Thoughts of the encounter with Mitch drifted into her head. She recalled the discussion at Don's house several months ago. The men discussing the rape of one of their friends had been more kind. In comparison, Mitch was an academic with expert knowledge instead of heart-based knowledge. What could a student expect from a Harvard trained PhD? These thoughts overrode the mental challenges of the homework assignment.

She sighed. Time to stop and get out of this mental loop. She could not concentrate on her work. Carrie took a deep breath and freely typed any thought that surfaced. She glued her eyes to the portable computer in front of her as a wet tear rushed down her face.

HELP flashed across blue screen.

A series of questions followed the message: *Why do little birds have to leave the nest just because they are touched? Why do mother birds kill baby birds when they are touched?*

Piercing her like a knife, the questions related to an incident which had occurred when she was six. It had happened on a warm spring day while she was playing alone in her backyard. She had heard commotion from underneath a tree in the front yard.

"Carrie, Carrie," the neighborhood children shouted frantically at her through the fence. "Please help us!"

Carrie turned her head towards their voices. She walked towards them as they directed her to some object at the foot of the fence. A baby blue jay laid motionless in the grass.

"It belongs to us," the older children told her. "Would you hand it to us? We're taking care of it."

Carrie scooped the tiny blue jay in her hands. She gave it to the children on the other side of the fence just before her mother called her inside the house.

"Don't ever touch another bird!" her mother yelled and came out of nowhere. "Mother birds can smell the touch of a human on their babies. They kill the babies who are touched because they don't like the smell. Now the mother will kill it, because you touched the bird." Then she left Carrie alone in her bedroom. Carrie felt crushed. She had only wanted to help the young bird, not kill it.

Suddenly, a sharp cry penetrated the sanctity of Carrie's bedroom from outside her window. It was the mother bird shrieking at the rest of her young lying on the ground. Carrie ran to the south-facing window and glimpsed the fury of claws and feathers. Turning quickly away from the horrible sight, Carrie heard the violent shrill of the mother bird admixed the innocent chirps of her babies. One call cried for life; another screamed death.

Bam! Bang! Bam! Carrie hurled her head against the closet door as the attack continued outdoors. She felt like the giant in the biblical "David" story that the teacher had read that day. She would rather die than hurt that tender little bird. Bam! Bang! Bam! She used the wall as the stone for her head. Bam! Bang! Bam! The stone... the stone... Carrie hurled against herself.

Then she stopped. It was quiet outside. The attack was over. Some tears fell from Carrie's eyes; she didn't feel like hitting her head anymore.

Baby bird wants to die... wants to die... Baby bird hurts too much. Mother bird abandons baby bird. Father bird gone. Mother bird doesn't like baby bird. Mother bird drives father bird away. Kill bird... Kill bird...

But baby bird lives. Baby bird wants to fly... wants to spread wings ...

Surprised, Carrie recognized the baby bird in the story that flashed across the computer. The stark logic behind her intuition shocked her. Carrie cried no tears although she felt them inside. She could not touch them and make them surface.

"Brent, do you have time for a walk? I need to talk," Carrie asked him when he appeared in room.

"Sure," he answered her with a smile and hug. "Tough day, huh?!"

"I didn't get too far with the homework assignment."

Carrie took Brent's hand as they left the building. Without speaking, Carrie and Brent followed a winding sidewalk path which eventually led them down a wide staircase. At the base of the stairs stood a private patio shaded by tall, verdant ash trees. It was early spring and the roses surrounding the enclosure were ready to burst with their loaded buds.

Carrie and Brent sat down on the stairs surrounding the patio. Breaking the silence, Carrie cried "Brent, the abuse is true. Look at what is coming out," she told him as she handed over the computer print out. "What should I do? I can't study with these thoughts invading my work."

She closely watched Brent's face while he calmly read her story. Having only read it twice herself, she found that she still could not read it objectively; the words stung her too hard. Trapped in a never-never land where the lines separating light and dark focused into a pronounced blur, she had no control over the dream which haunted her life. Nothing seemed real; she was only a ghost.

In her mind's eye Carrie saw the ghostly figure of a small child motionless on the floor in extreme pain. Marked for the world of the dead, Carrie felt no bond between her and the infant. Yet, the child was hers, a part of Carrie that she could not deny. Carrie refused to abandon it. Glancing at Brent after he finished reading the computer sheet, Carrie noticed the mist in his eyes. She moved towards him. Silently, he folded his arms around her.

"I believe something happened," Brent replied, "But I don't know how to help you. Clean the paper a bit. Remove the computer commands so that it reads easier. I can help you with that."

"Brent," she addressed him before admitting, "I don't feel the same anymore. I'm living a bad dream over and over again and I can't even cry to save myself... I need to be treated as a human being."

"I believe you," he repeated, squeezing her lightly a few times to assure her.

Chapter Thirty

If I could read your mind, love,
What a tale your thoughts could tell.
Just like a paperback novel, the kind the drug stores sell.
Then you reach the part where the heartaches come,
The hero would be me. But heroes often fail,
And you won't read that book again
Because the ending's just too hard to take!

"If You Could Read My Mind"
Gordon Lightfoot

Carrie procrastinated on calling her friend Jane, instead she diverted her attention to cooking dinner and cleaning the kitchen. She studied until she felt sleepy enough to join Brent in bed.

"Brent, I'm going to call Jane. Do you think it's too late?" Carrie whispered in the darkness at eleven o'clock. She had finally realized that she would not be able to sleep until she contacted Jane.

"No," he assured Carrie. "You know she's a night owl. You two sometimes talk on the phone until two in the morning."

Carrie dialed Jane's number and counted the number of phone rings with bated breath. Jane answered on the second ring.

"Hello Jane, this is Carrie. Sorry to bother you this late," Carrie apologized. "Are you busy? Do you have time to talk?"

"Can you come now?" Jane asked. "I need to be in bed before two o'clock. Pam is at the library, but Ricardo's sister is staying here. We'll have to be quiet when she goes to bed."

"OK. I'll be right over."

Carrie grabbed an old shirt and put on some gray sweatpants. Leaning over the bed, she lightly kissed Brent before she stepped outdoors. "I'm going over to Jane's . Thanks for your help."

"Take care," he said quietly before snuggling underneath the blankets with the contentment that only sleep can offer.

When Carrie arrived at Jane's apartment, Ricardo's sister ushered her inside. The place was bright and cheery in its usual state of happy disorder, and Carrie felt relieved to find that nothing had changed within the last few days. Jane busily hummed about the apartment, settling her guest from Peru and making a place for her to sleep.

"Care for some tea or coffee?" Jane asked once her guest had retired in the adjacent room.

"No thanks," Carrie answered. Her stomach would not accept anything now. Carrie sat down at the dining table stacked with the various books and papers, reflections of the hectic lifestyle of a student. Jane entered the room from the kitchen and sat down across from her.

"This is difficult," Carrie began, hanging her head over the table. "I feel like crying, but I can't."

"I could tell that you were upset this afternoon."

"I didn't know what to do," Carrie sighed, suddenly dropping her hands on the table in a wave of anguish.

"Hey, it's OK," Jane pleaded, lightly touching Carrie's wrist. "Everyone needs to talk. Pam does, I do, Ricardo does, Cindy ... After I saw you, I finished my errand for the office. When I returned, the director noticed that I looked upset and asked me what was up. I told that I had run into a friend who was on the verge of tears. The woman was very understanding and told me that I could bring my friend into the office until she felt better. Another woman in the office even offered the empty studio room for refuge... I wished you had stayed."

"It hurts too much to talk about it. So I wrote it on the computer in sort of an allegorical form," Carrie offered breathlessly. Still feeling unsure of herself, she persevered with her intentions. "Can I show you the print out?"

Carrie quietly placed the rewritten copy on the table.

"Brent helped me rewrite it. I'm going to give a copy to the counselor tomorrow. I don't want anyone else to see this."

Jane sipped her coffee as she curiously eyed Carrie. Then she started reading the print out. Carrie glanced at Jane's facial expressions, but Jane ignored her and concentrated on the material. After reading only the first two lines, Jane cried, "Oh Carrie!" with tears filling her eyes.

Carrie turned her head away. She had not expected such an intense reaction. She shook her head in bewilderment.

Jane stopped reading and reexamined Carrie's appearance as if she had just put on a new pair of glasses. Immediately Jane correlated Carrie with the main character in the story. Meeting Jane's stare, Carrie instantly saw that she had dressed very well for the part, though the attire could have easily passed for current college fashion. Before leaving the house she had absentmindedly thrown on an old blue shirt that she had worn as a teenager. For some reason, it had never occurred to Carrie to throw the shirt away like the others. She was attached to it. In addition, Carrie had forgotten to brush her hair before leaving home tonight, making her thick wavy hair seem more tousled than usual. She appeared as torn and tattered as she felt inside. The recognition seared Carrie's memory, forming the haunting image of the battered child in her mind's mirror. She buried her head inside her folded arms so that she couldn't see this disturbing reflection. Meanwhile, Jane read the print out, sobbing as she poured over the paper. Curiously, Carrie watched her.

"Carrie, you were such a little girl," she commented softly.

"About two," Carrie slowly nodded. Lifting her head, she explained, "The incident occurred when we lived in the brown house, which means that I was anywhere from one to three years old. Also I know it happened shortly after the birth of my younger sister, because there is some connection between her birth and the attack. There's only a difference of one and a half years between us."

"But why would anyone want to do such a thing?"

"I don't know. I've been wondering the same thing for a long time."

Finally free to verbalize, she listened to every word she told Jane. Unlike the child in her memory, Carrie could speak.

"The attacker was an uncle in law. Initially he and my aunt were childless. They adopted a baby girl several years later and my aunt gave birth to a girl of their own the next year. Somehow my father was indirectly involved," Carrie recalled, pausing for a few moments as she probed the painful wisps of her understanding. Jane remained silent, trying to assimilate the information and her feelings. Carrie became quiet too.

"It's getting late," Carrie quietly said after an unexpected calm had settled in the room. She felt tired enough for sleep now. Any further discussion would disturb her chance for a restful night.

"I feel better," she told Jane. Carrie rose from the table but her legs wobbled beneath her. Shrugging off the physical difficulty, Carrie recognized the sensation as a familiar ally. She could guess the amount of her emotional stress by the toll it exacted on her physical body. Carrie thanked Jane for the evening and they exchanged warm hugs. Then she departed into the night.

As she drove the only car on the road at this hour, Carrie watched the morning fog envelope the city and create halos around all the street lamps. Tonight the pickup cruised through the residential section of town as if it already knew the way home. Parking the truck in the driveway, Carrie made her way through the bamboo shadowing the entrance to their garage apartment. In the darkness of the studio room she removed her clothes and laid beside Brent on the bed. Brent immediately sensed Carrie and moved closer to her body in his sleeping state. Without even an eye flicker he whispered, "I love you."

☆ ☆ ☆

The next day Carrie met the counselor in his office and related her findings with the computer exercise. "Look at what is coming out," she said as she handed him the computer print out.

"Do you mind if I show this to an associate of mine and get her response? It's very poignant," the counselor commented softly as he skimmed over the paper. After a moment's reflection, he asked, "What's the name of the file on disk? ...And the command for adding or deleting a file?"

"Bird," Carrie answered. "The commands for adding and deleting are save and kill."

"Kill Bird," he instructed her as she rose to leave his office. Carrie quickly stepped out the door. His response differed greatly from Jane's. Jane had helped her understand and assimilate the information, whereas Mitch seemed more alarmist. Mitch's approach scared her because it was so vague.

Chapter Thirty One

I'm woven in a fantasy.
I can't believe the things I see
The path that I have chosen now
Has led me to a wall
And with each passing day I feel a little
More like something dear was lost
It rises now before me, a dark
And silent barrier between.
All I am, and all that I would
Ever want to be
It's just a travesty, towering, marking off
The boundaries my spirit would erase.

"The Wall"
Kansas

After the visit with the counselor, Carrie went home and gardened for the rest of the afternoon. Even though he seemed harsh, Carrie felt no malice from him. As she firmly patted some snapdragons into their place in the ground, Carrie thought about what it meant to kill the bird file.

"Trust the intention and the rest will follow. This is what the flashbacks are revealing more than anything else: it's the spirit of the act which counts... one of the major differences between sex and rape. Young children and animals, despite their inabilities to communicate in speech and writing, can read people's hearts and know their intentions. In order to save my child, I must remember how to communicate with it," she told herself. *"The intention must be followed by clarity of action. It is not enough to just have the intention. You have to take those next steps even if it seems like baby ones."* Then Carrie gathered her gardening tools and walked inside the house to cook dinner.

Brent arrived home soon. From the kitchen window Carrie spied him sailing down the driveway on his ten-speed. Within a matter of seconds she heard his familiar thumps inside the entry hall.

"Going back to school tonight?" she asked, hugging and kissing him at the front door.

"Yes, there are some instruments I need to check," he told her.

"Great! Can I catch a ride?" she asked. "I have a few things I need to do."

"How about eight o'clock?" he answered. He happily dropped his backpack in the hall's corner and returned Carrie's hugs. "We'll have time to relax at home."

After dinner Brent and Carrie returned to the Physics department. Carrie deposited her books in their student office and started walking towards the computer room.

"Good luck," Brent told her before she left the office. "I'll be in the lab if you need anything."

Pushing the buttons on the combination lock of the door leading to the computer room, Carrie flipped on the light switch and brought instant brilliance to the room. She saw the computer waiting for her at the opposite end surrounded by an odd assortment of microchips, soldering wands, and multi-colored wire. She took a deep breath and approached the computer. Would killing the bird file "kill" her too?

She reminded herself that a computer was just a magic box created out of years of scientific research, consisting of an enclosed cathode ray tube connected to a microprocessor. In fact, she reassured herself, she had unraveled the secrets of the 8080 microprocessor chip only last year in her electronics class. She knew how to make the chip work for her. Carrie loaded the disk and typed the command "KILL BIRD". The computer hummed as it searched for the file on the disk. After she heard a click, the file disappeared.

Carrie scanned her internal feelings and found a profound since of loss aching inside her. She wondered what to do next. Suddenly she heard some footsteps echoing in the hallway, Carrie glanced towards the source of the sound. Ricardo and Jane appeared in the doorway of the computer room. Ricardo was Jane's boyfriend. They knew that Carrie often studied here late at night while Brent worked down the hall.

"Que paso?!" Ricardo smiled, before Jan interrupted.

"I've been thinking of you and I wanted to see you. Ricardo offered to take me here. He is on his way to the library to study for his U.S. medical exams."

"How about a shot, Carrie?" he teased, pretending to be a doctor as he gently turned his finger into Carrie's arm like a syringe.

The words instantly triggered a memory which pumped tension throughout Carrie's entire body.

"Don't hurt my baby!" Carrie burst sobbing into Ricardo's arms. Throwing herself at him like a shield, she immobilized him in a tight embrace in order to protect an imaginary baby behind her.

The intensity of her response silenced everyone. After a few moments, Ricardo rearranged the embrace into a hug. He began softly rubbing her shoulders as he assured Carrie that he had not meant to hurt her. Carrie relaxed with his warm assurances. Then he quietly left for the library while Carrie collapsed in a nearby chair and stared into space. Jane grabbed an adjacent chair and placed it in front of Carrie. Then she sat down.

"Carrie," she softly called, moving closer to get inside Carrie's vacant stare. "You've held this story inside for a very long time. Nobody should have to carry this much alone."

Carrie felt tears welling in her eyes and turned her head away so that Jane would not see.

"Are you sure?" Carrie asked. She had not expected Jane, though her timing had been impeccable.

Jane nodded. "When I was a young child, I spent a few days in the hospital to get my tonsils out. I met a little boy who had his arm wrapped in bandages. His parents had burned him. I felt for his little arm. He was the nicest boy. All he would do was smile at me because he was so happy to finally feel safe."

A tear escaped Carrie's eye.

"Oh God!" she cried, covering her face with her hands.

Jane reached out and peeled Carrie's hands from her face. Avoiding Jane's eyes, Carrie rested her gaze on the wall beyond Jane while tears streamed down her face. The cold weight of twenty year old grief passed with each tear, marking a sharp division between life and death.

"Tell me what happened," Jane prompted her.

"My mother... my mother left me," Carrie quietly recalled, her gaze remaining fixed on the green blackboard ahead. "I remember hearing her shout "don't hurt my baby" to the assailant."

"What happened after the assault?"

"The people in white came and took me away."

"People in white?!"

"The ambulance attendants. I was in some dark enclosure, a closet, lying in a mess of blood, urine, and vomit... I felt cold. My blue gown was all torn. A man in white came and carried me away to the flashing red and yellow lights. He had thick black fuzz on his arms. I remember his warmth for me."

Taking a deep breath before continuing, Carrie explained, "They thought I was going to die in the hospital. I threw up often and didn't want to eat. There was a thick bandage on my head. Someone had cut my hair... I didn't want to have anything to do with anyone at the time. The only person who really mattered to me was my mother and she was gone. A nurse got it through my head that my mother would be terribly upset if I didn't get well. I lived because I didn't want to upset my mother."

Carrie trembled, "My mother rejected me in many ways. It was like she had been programmed to kill the memory along with me. She seemed unable to deal with it and me as well."

Carrie continued, "Every time my parents argued I felt responsible. During one confrontation with my father, my mother left me alone in the bathtub when I was three or four. I became entranced by a razor lying on the rim and ripped my face and limbs. I felt so upset that I made razor marks all over my body, mimicking the results of the attack. I couldn't forget the trauma; I felt marked. It was a living death."

Carrie sighed and leaned back in her chair. These past experiences seared her as she recalled the perceptions of her childhood with the eyes of an adult. Stripping the meaning of her entire life to its bare essence, Carrie paraded the truth before her. Other memories which had been formerly buried with Carrie's emotions came forth, finally making sense for the first time. Instead of the baby bird and infant, her reflection stood before her like an exposed rock section consisting of a series of transparent overlays with each overlay representing a period in time.

"Carrie?!" Jane implored, breaking Carrie's blank stare at the computer board. "Did you ever see the rapist... again?!"

Carrie answered with more burning tears, "I saw him again. He and his wife invited us to dinner when my aunt became pregnant. Throughout the course of the evening, my mother made several stinging comments, but nobody else said anything. Before we left they made me hug him. When I hugged him it was like disappearing into an oblivious blank space, nothing. When I was eight we moved to Texas and the attacker visited our house about every other year. He always arrived late at night after everyone except my father had gone to bed. Often he'd leave behind samples from his business for my father to show us in the morning."

Something inside Carrie flickered, returning life to her expression. She turned towards Jane and looked at her. Blinking a few times, Carrie explained, "Once he left an object called a "Love Light" which consisted of a red votive candle enclosed in a wooden frame with four red glass balls suspended in front of the light. The brochure said that owning the "Love Light" would create a romantic atmosphere and peace and love in the world. My mother threw it away after my cat broke two of the red balls," Carrie mused, recognizing how her cat protected against the prolonged assault on her life. She clenched her fists for a moment, immediately releasing the tension in frustrated sobs a few seconds later.

"I didn't know enough to cry about it then. The physical pain stayed with me. There was no place for feelings. I saved all my emotions until I could freely sort through them in a safe place."

Her anguish subsided and Carrie felt a simple peace fill its absence. She had wanted to understand these events which had hurt her so deeply.

"Was the attacker ever tried in court?" Jane asked.

Carrie gave her a quick glance and shook her head as she leaned back in her chair. "My father knew who did it, but he and the assailant covered it up. They made some sort of deal."

Carrie heaved a deep breath. She could breathe much easier now. For several moments Jane and Carrie sat in silence until Ricardo returned from the library. Brent strolled in the room a few minutes behind Ricardo. No more words were spoken. The men picked up the mood of the women and nodded. Everyone seemed ready to go home. They turned off the lights and locked the door to the computer room.

Later, Carrie told Brent about her encounter in the computer room. "My memories of the assault are creepy. No wonder I felt so bad when I was a child; I was living with it! I'm still having difficulty believing it. I am so different from my parents."

"That's for sure," Brent replied as he began undressing. "Samantha was your baby."

Carrie walked two steps away from him and thought for a moment. Then she looked sideways at Brent and nodded, "Whenever my parents exploded inside the house, I'd run outside with her. Almost every night, Samantha wanted to sleep in my bed. She was scared. That little twin bed became pretty crowded at times, especially when my younger cousins came over. I'd tell them stories about the cat, who was always tucked underneath my right arm."

"How about getting some sleep now?" Brent asked, sitting upright in bed and patting Carrie's place on his right side.

"I'll try," she sighed. "I still feel scared. Can we leave a small light on or something?"

For his answer Brent rose and turned on a lamp in the nearby hallway. Satisfied, Carrie hopped in bed and curled underneath Brent's arm, a place where she usually felt safe. "I'm gonna ask the counselor about a quick way to get over flashbacks."

* * *

Two days later Carrie walked across campus to meet the counselor in his office.

"How's it going?" the counselor asked.

"Not so good," Carrie replied. She explained how memories of the assault were interfering with her life. "I still feel as if I'm in an altered state of consciousness; it's like being in shock, except that I never come out of it."

Carrie looked hard at Dr. Mitch, the counselor, to be sure he understood the gravity of the situation before continuing.

"I called both of my parents and asked them whether anything out of the ordinary had occurred when I was two years old. My mother immediately knew that I was referring to an assault. She questioned me about the identity of the attacker, expressing surprise that it wasn't my grandfather because she had always been afraid of him."

"On the other hand, my father told me to "examine the reality today as opposed to the past", saying that I "could not possibly imagine what it was like to be in the shoes of certain individuals so long ago"."

Carrie stopped and wondered if Dr. Mitch thought she had imagined her story. Breaking the silence, Dr. Mitch looked at Carrie out of the corner of his eye and commented, "Well, it's obvious you have to deal with this issue on your own. Did you really expect any support from your parents? What are you going to do now?"

Stunned, Carrie realized the depths of the counselor's cruelty. Compared to her parents, the counselor seemed unstable. He really wasn't with her either. He wanted to control her like a puppet just as her parents had done. Regardless of his intention, Carrie seized the opportunity to learn from her mistake. She had been conducting her investigation without stopping to check in with her emotions and intuition. Instinctively departing from the counselor's approach, she retraced her steps. Her mind craved more information, more data points for understanding. It was the grit in life that created pearls of wisdom. It had never been her intention to elicit parental support; she had given them up years ago. She had merely sought validation of her own conclusions. Their confused, distorted replies had helped her piece together the truth. Unlike Dr. Mitch, she had found her parent's comments encouraging because it showed that she had finally escaped the quagmire of her former existence.

"Well, it is my own life...," Carrie started slowly, "and my choice is to deal with this issue regardless of the decisions of my parents."

"In order to gain control of the flashbacks, you must give yourself the opportunity to remember the event as a whole," Dr. Mitch continued, missing Carrie's subtlety. "Traumatic events from the past can be recalled by a technique known as hypnotic age regression. Because of your abilities in self hypnosis, you are a good candidate for this process. However, age regression involving particularly traumatic events can be very dangerous, so I am reluctant to try this method with you. It is something you must consider seriously."

Leaning closer towards Carrie, he cautioned her further. "I saw a video of a case where a competent hypnotist regressed a woman to an incident which had occurred at the age of six. In the trance state the woman acted as if she was six years old. Apparently the six year old had urinated in class once and the shame of the experience left her psychologically devastated. The woman relived the experience so completely that she actually urinated in the physician's office. Because of the amount of trauma involved, the hypnotist could not bring her out of the trance. Her psychological equilibrium could not be restored," said Dr. Mitch seemingly terrified by the results he had witnessed on video. Staring at Carrie, he did his best to exude authoritarian fear and terror.

Carrie evaded his stare. She looked towards the series of books lining the walls of the office. They were an illusion. These symbols of a learned mind contrasted with the counselor's tactical scare drama. She shrugged inside, though she never physically betrayed her feelings. Had Dr. Mitch been brainwashed or educated by the establishment? In her Physics studies, Carrie had learned that life was what you made it. Intention, or logos, had a lot to do with it. Like the set up of a Physics proof, people tended to manifest the products of their intentions. She didn't want to carry the counselor's load of irrational fears. Though she felt mentally strong enough to handle a first grade accident, reliving a sexual assault might be challenging. Purity of intention was essential.

"Think about it," he told her, "and tell me next week."

Chapter Thirty Two

Someone saved my life tonight, sugar bear.
You almost had your hooks in me didn't you dear
Altar-bound, hypnotized, sweet freedom whispered in my ear
You're a butterfly, and butterflies are free to fly
Fly away high away bye bye.

"Someone Saved My Life Tonight"
Elton John and Bernie Taupin

After leaving Dr. Mitch's office, Carrie bicycled home. As she pumped her way up and down the hills of the city, the counselor's fears echoed in her mind. His lack of faith bothered her. In some ways he was helpful and and in some ways he seemed almost hostile. She felt demonized in a manner similar to the past assault at the University by the Knight's of Oblivion. Dr. Mitch's face matched the frozen look on the men mechanically casting stones at the dorm window. It didn't make much sense to her. In comparison, those who prohibited her recovery seemed no better than the crazed assailant. Who was the real victim? - the demonized or those who were captivated by the serpents of their own minds. She would have to succeed without Dr. Mitch's blessings, just as she had done with her parents and the University.

The next day Carrie hunted for Ricardo and Jane in the cafeteria. She had come to rely on Jane's overflowing sense of warmth and compassion, which complemented Ricardos' quiet heartfelt acceptance of life in general. After peering through the lunchtime crowd for several minutes she spotted them at a table near the fire exit. Jane saw her and excitedly motioned for Carrie to join them.

"I need to ask you two for a favor," Carrie smiled wryly, feeling out of place. The lunchroom was the site for lighthearted small talk and college pranks, not for issues of life and death. Nonetheless, Carrie plunged forward with her request, "Will you help me with reliving an assault?"

"What?!" Jane answered with excitement. Ricardo looked perplexed. Jane turned towards him and began conversing in Spanish. Glancing at Carrie, his eyes brightened as he nodded his comprehension.

Of all the people Carrie knew, Jane seemed the most comfortable with her feelings. She lovingly embraced everything in life associated with being human, relying on natural curiosity for her sharpest insight in human affairs. Because such a humane perspective enabled Jane to see beyond the worst of any human experience, Carrie sensed that Jane would be able to help her.

"Sit down and tell us about it," Jane encouraged Carrie when she finished translating to Ricardo.

After Carrie made certain no one could overhear her above the din of the cafeteria, Carrie started explaining the need for a sort of regression. She mentioned the dangers associated with such an undertaking and repeated Mitch's story about the woman who became permanently trapped in her memory.

"I feel that I can handle it if you can," Carrie continued, "I need to view the assault as an entirety. It's the only way to gain control over the flashbacks. Otherwise, they will come on their own without my direction."

Jane consulted Ricardo in Spanish. They wanted her to come after a barbecue on Saturday night. Some of Ricardo's friends and family were throwing a party. Later in the evening they could drive over to Carrie's apartment together. Carrie agreed and they finalized the arrangements and exited the cafeteria with their arms around each other. Many people smiled at their carefree attitude as Ricardo, Jane, and Carrie skipped across campus. No one suspected that they had just finished discussing the consequences of rape and child abuse, much less guessed that Carrie had decided to test her psychological limits.

On Saturday Brent walked with Carrie over to Jane's apartment. He remained only a few minutes and then returned to his graduate office. Many of the guests at the barbecue were from South America and most conversation was spoken in Spanish. Carrie spoke with some of the visitors using a little Spanish and many gestures, while the American hosts busily prepared dinner using frenzied English. Then she chose a quiet seat on the black iron steps of the apartment's tiny back porch and watched the brilliant pink and orange sunset from the second story. From her height all the trees and shrubs displayed their shiny new green leaves as the birds and katydids disjointedly hummed their tunes. She could hear Ricardo slap barbecue sauce over the many chicken pieces, patiently working the meat over the coals. New leaves, katydids, birds, and barbecues always reminded Carrie of spring, the promise of summer and renewed life.

After viewing the scene below again, she grew uneasy. Everyone and everything seemed so content in its environment except Carrie. Her friend Cindy offered her a beer, but Carrie refused the alcohol. Carrie didn't feel like drinking anymore; the slight buzz from the previous party that afternoon had worn into seriousness and Carrie wished that she had never drunk those two beers, having partied at the other gathering with the zest of a sailor about to depart for a five year sea duty. Her head began to ache and her stomach felt tied in knots. She rose from the stairs and stopped Jane in the hall.

"Is there a place where I can lie down for a moment? Carrie whispered below the level of the surrounding commotion.

Jane looked at her and nodded. Quickly leading Carrie to the room that she shared with Pam, Jane ushered her inside. Carrie collapsed on the twin bed with the fewest items on it and rolled on her back.

"I'll wake you when Ricardo and I are ready to leave," she promised Carrie, closing to the room.

Carrie felt relieved to be left alone in the darkness with her thoughts and listened for a moment to the muffled noises of the party. No matter how much she desired to brush aside the pressing concerns of tonight and join the festivities, she could not change her feelings. Right now Carrie seemed as alien as the different experiences of her childhood. Perhaps someday soon, Carrie thought, I will be able to laugh again and have fun with the rest. Carrie knew that she must endure tonight's trial if she ever wanted to successfully break her isolation.

Carrie's head responded to the alcohol. Only on certain occasions did a minimal amount affect her in such a great degree. She felt irritated with herself for not having abstained. However, sobriety would have made little difference, because tonight Carrie was also sensitive to the alcohol on people's breath. A tear trickled down Carrie's hot face as she opened her eyes in the darkness. A line of brilliant white light shone underneath the door and Carrie could distinguish the shape of the dresser at the opposite end of the room. The moonlight reflected off the white window shades making the room seem less black than initially. She lied down on one of the beds in the room and rested.

Aware of the distant sounds of the party again, Carrie awoke and noticed that the noise level had quieted. A sizable amount of time had elapsed since she had left the vicinity. Her stomach felt less tense and Carrie felt ready to mingle with the group again. Cautiously, Carrie entered the living area.

"Ready to go, Carrie?" Ricardo asked as he warmly slipped his arm around her, hugging her waist.

"I think so," she replied. "How about you two?" Jane was absorbed in a conversation across the room.

"Pretty soon," replied Ricardo as he nodded towards Jane.

Fifteen minutes later, they cruised down the main city streets in Ricardos' car. Occasionally Jane and Ricardo interrupted the silence with a mixture of English and Spanish. Carrie sat in the back seat hoping to glean some encouragement from the bright city lights. At the expense of her innocence, she felt that she was paying for a crime which she had not committed. Her life in the physical world had reached its limit. There was no more that she could do on a conscious level. Forced to allow her subconscious to take over, Carrie hoped that her inner sense of direction would not fail her. In the past it had always ultimately directed her to a relatively sane and healthy answer. She knew that she could no longer live without remembering the assault; because of this, Carrie was convinced that direct confrontation was the best approach.

When Carrie stepped across the threshold to her garage apartment, she immediately felt confident as the familiar surroundings spoke to her, reminding her of things she needed and valued. Carrie retrieved a Mexican Indian blanket and placed it in the center of the living area on top of the blue carpet. The blanket was her favorite because it consisted of a weave of thick cotton threads arranged in a blue, purple, red, and white striped pattern. For comfort and safety Carrie threw a few pillows on the blanket. She turned off the ceiling light and turned on another lamp in the room with a softer light. Lighting a hurricane lamp which Brent and she had received as a wedding gift. It held significant value for Brent and Carrie. They used it during power shortages as well as celebrations. This night the lamp would guide her attempt in confronting the nightmare.

Ricardo and Jane sat on the blanket and watched her with many questions in their eyes.

"I need something to drink. Do you have any of that mint tea left?" Jane asked.

"The stuff from Brent's farm?!" Carrie answered.

Jane eagerly nodded.

"Let me brew some. It will only take a moment," Carrie chimed, walking towards the kitchen. Although, she didn't feel thirsty herself, Carrie enjoyed brewing mint tea for company.

Jane left Ricardo alone on the blanket and joined her in the adjacent room. "How are you doing?" she cornered Carrie.

"I'm not sure," Carrie responded. "I feel a little scared, but I am anxious to get on with it." Carrie handed Jane a cup of tea and together they entered the living area.

"One more thing," Carrie announced, reaching for Mitch's card from her purse and placing it beside the phone. He had handed Carrie his phone number last week with the request that she contact him if needed. "Call him if there is an emergency. There's a first aid kit in the bathroom closet."

Carrie never intended to call Dr. Mitch, but she began to doubt herself. Carrie looked across the blue carpet at the blanket where Jane and Ricardo sat, and imagined the blanket slowly moving away like a ship leaving a crew member adrift at sea. Glancing at their faces, Carrie realized that they were patiently waiting for her to come aboard. They were still with her. Carrie noticed that she had not scared them away like Dr. Mitch had done with her. Carrie approached the blanket and knelt at the far corner. She felt unsure whether she really wanted to join them and proceed with the agenda.

"Come on closer," they encouraged her. Carrie edged forward until she completed the circle. There were many things that she learned from Jane and Ricardo. Human attributes such as compassion were devalued in academia. Compassion wiped out fear and discouraged trauma-based learning. It was the type of knowledge that could only be taught through demonstration. Those who hadn't mastered compassion could not teach it because the learning of compassion required cognition rather than memorization. Both teacher and student had to be ready. This level required substance or the ability to derive meaning from one's existence. It was based on value, a notion that life was worth living. The compassionate understanding gained from this experience would help Carrie safely detonate the explosive memories haunting her.

Her salvation remained in the ability to trust herself. She stared at the flame inside the burning oil lamp, visualizing herself becoming a part of its soft consistent light as a reflection of the light within her depths. Carrie sensed the reassuring warmth of the flame while she searched for her inner strength and direction. As soon as Carrie felt that flicker of confidence center her physical body with its own nature, she verbalized her intention to achieve a consciousness without being self destructive or harmful.

For the moment, the level of consciousness remained mild and the information Carrie sought readily came to mind. Noticing a pen and paper lying on the nearby desk, Carrie reached for them and began drawing the design of the house which had been the scene of the assault. Mapping and drawing was an easy way for Carrie to start. She enjoyed drafting and the familiar run of an instrument over paper assured Carrie of her ability in self expression.

"I believe the assault occurred in this section of the house," Carrie said. "The memory of the region is dark and fuzzy compared to my recollection of other rooms in the house. I have a sinister feeling associated with the area."

"My newborn sister stayed in this room. The exterior of the house was painted brown and my family referred to the residence as the brown house. The house had a big backyard."

Carrie stopped and looked at her drawing. The front of the house consisted of a bedroom, living room, dining room, kitchen, and bathroom. The back of the house which possibly included two more bedrooms and a half bathroom remained a void. Carrie slid a little bit further from the circle. Sitting now on the edge of the blanket, she turned away from the group and stared at the light one more time. Carrie's gaze fell to her feet again as she commenced with the story.

"It was a humid, warm evening in the spring of the year. Some of the fans in the house were on. My father was away. My mother was at home. After she put me to bed in the early evening, I laid awake for some time and slept lightly with the sounds of the house. I awoke fully when I heard a knock at the door and the noises of a scuffle taking place. The noises made their way to my room until I saw my bedroom door open."

Carrie paused for a moment while Jane translated her words into Spanish for Ricardo's understanding. Initially Carrie felt annoyed at the interruption, but realized that the break actually prevented her from lapsing into a deeper trance. It also gave Carrie the chance to examine the memory's effect on her physical state. She realized that the verbalization of her story was a critical indicator, showing that she was at a safe level in her consciousness. She wished to avoid hypnotizing herself as she wanted to naturally maintain control of the flow of information.

"Both my mother and uncle stood in the doorway," Carrie continued after Jane finished speaking. My mother struggled weakly with the man. She cried, scratched, even tried biting him, but he was much stronger. In one hand he held the broken wooden handle of a broom or mop. He walked towards me with the wooden stick. He wore a white shirt with black pants. Tonight he wasn't wearing his glasses. I heard my mother cry "don't hurt my baby"."

Jane translated again for Ricardo. Carrie felt touched by their desire to understand.

"I can't remember what exactly happened to my mother," she explained. I've partially blocked the memory. I panicked when she ran out of the room."

By the time Carrie had finished her sentence, something very painful clicked inside her. Her mother had forsaken her. Immediately overwhelmed by the emotions associated with the event, the recollection threw Carrie's body on the blanket between Jane and Ricardo and she squirmed in pain and anguish. Carrie's legs made crawling motions on the ground, but she never moved anywhere. She wanted to get away, but the bars of an imaginary crib trapped her.

Quickly, Carrie began calming herself with her thoughts, "This is just a surviving emotion. Detach yourself. You never chose your mother as your identity. Remember, you always have yourself. You can speak for yourself now."

Gradually, Carrie regained control over the memory and her expression became verbal instead of physical. She sat up on the blanket and narrated further, "As I tried to crawl away I noticed that my bear didn't move or try to help me. He stared idly into space and didn't get hurt. My uncle grasped the stick in his hands with enough intensity to support the weight of his entire body. I saw the anger in his eyes. I realized that he was really angry at something else besides me. I was just in the way."

Again the emotions became too much to verbalize and Carrie's body fell down on the ground, resuming the muscle contractions. She calmed herself again, "Carrie, Carrie, don't even try to figure this out. A crime never makes sense. Just report it to the satisfaction of your own authority, in the least painful way possible. Authorities know what to do with this information."

"I could not understand why he wanted to hurt me," she said to Jane and Ricardo. "I thought that he had loved me," she gasped. "Before the assault he often played with me when they visited. There was an intense pain in my chest as if my heart had broken. I felt very empty and sad that he wished to hurt me."

"He pulled my hair while I tried to crawl out of the crib and turned my body over." The sheer force of the memory jerked Carrie's body around and she started thrashing wildly at an unseen foe. She began perspiring heavily as her heart pounded with a two year old rhythm. Jane began speaking to Ricardo in Spanish. Carrie quieted at the sound of the language. By the time she finished, Carrie had regained her composure.

"I became angry and he pounded my head against the side of the crib," Carrie added.

Then the memory intensified and she lapsed deeper into the trance. "No, no, no,...," Carrie cried at the unseen attacker. A tear escaped from Carrie's eye as she listened to her own words, "He raised the stick and rammed it inside me... it bit me inside... it hurt because it was so big and I was so little."

Jane gasped. The outburst briefly startled Carrie, projecting her deeper into the trance when she realized the reason for the outcry. Carrie began fighting for her life! Wrenching with pain as she remembered the wrathful thrust into her abdomen, Carrie tried to crawl away. Her thrashing became so violent that Jane and Ricardo rolled her in the blanket as if she was a burn victim. Once again the cocoon feeling of the blanket around her calmed Carrie and she continued verbalizing her thoughts.

"Something happened to my wrist," Carrie observed. She paused several seconds, because she could not presently differentiate between her right and left side. So Carrie raised the hand that felt injured. Turning towards the raised side, Carrie was stunned by the recognition. Her left wrist hung in a contorted position over her arm. It was her "swan wing", the one Carrie had once hated and had tried to cut away. Carrie couldn't bear to look at the disfigurement and quickly laid the wrist down beside her.

"He hit me on the head," Carrie said without emotion, "and he gave me a bloody nose. He kept ramming the stick inside me. I fought hard to maintain control over my bladder, but the force of the stick was too much and I lost control... it killed me inside," Carrie said quietly.

"Instantly I felt numb below the waist. My sense of human dignity had been taken away from me. So I became like my teddy bear who sat motionless beside me."

Jane translated to Ricardo. By now Carrie felt completely exhausted.

"Later I regained consciousness and discovered that I was alone in a small dark room. In a strange sort of way the darkness comforted me. I felt cold and hungry, but I was too sore and weak to move around. I heard voices from outside the room. The people in white came and took me away."

Jane spoke with Ricardo for several minutes as Carrie left her position on the floor and began straightening her hair, which had fallen loose. She picked up the clasp from the floor and walked to the other side of the room.

"That's all I need to remember," she told them from where she stood, tying her hair back. This trivial, mundane, activity seemed a natural way to end the trance.

"Carrie, do you think that the assailant had been drinking?" Jane asked her, remaining deep in thought on the blanket.

Carrie paused and reflected for a moment. Matching the memory of the assailant's smell to her sensitivity to alcohol, Carrie identified the cause for concern. "Yes, I think so," she answered softly.

Dumbfounded, Jane shook her head. Carrie shrugged. There were more important issues. Now that the ordeal was over she felt unsure of herself and maintained her distance from the group. Carrie wasn't in the mood for anymore tears; she had already grieved too much for a past which she never understood until now. Having successfully survived tonight's experience, Carrie only wanted the safe, warm contact of another human being.

Ricardo leaned against the sofa, patting the floor beside him. Carrie smiled sheepishly and hopped beside him. He placed his arm around her and let his head drop on Carrie's shoulder. Sharing his exhaustion, Carrie allowed her head to fall on top of his. If either one of them moved, the other would have fallen over. Jane turned around and sat on the other side of Ricardo, completing the human arrangement like the leg of a triangle. In light of this mutual support Carrie felt reassured.

Ricardo and Jane stayed until Brent arrived. Relieved to see that Carrie had survived the ordeal, Brent wrapped his arms around her in a mighty hug.

"You're still in one piece!" he smiled.

"Yes, I'll tell you all about it tomorrow," Carrie promised. "Let's go to bed; I'm tired."

That night Carrie dreamed about the infant in the crib. She was the small child who rose and leaned over the railing, waving her contorted arm.

"Mom...momm, mom,...mom," sobbed the small child in desolation. She felt that her mother would never come back. Her heart was broken.

A soft blue light bounced in front of the crib and interrupted her painful moans. The child watched the light dance in the air like a brilliant bubble. The bubble stopped and a blond fairy in a blue gown appeared in its place. The child reached for the blue fairy beyond her reach. The wooden rail slipped its latch and the toddler tumbled over the dropped edge onto the floor.

"Mom.., momm, mom..., mom," continued the child as she crawled towards the blue fairy in the air above her. The blue fairy led the way to a small dark closet at the opposite end of the room. Standing upright, the toddler rose and made bloody handprints over the closet walls. This distracted the girl from her painful circumstances. Exhausted by the effort, the small child fell asleep inside the confines of the dark walls.

Chapter Thirty Three

Lost and lonely
Now you've given me the will to survive
When we're hungry...love will keep us alive
Don't you worry
Sometimes you've just gotta let it ride
The world is changing
Right before your eyes
Now I've found you
There's no more emptiness inside
When we're hungry...love will keep us alive...
...I was standing
All alone against the world outside
You were searching for a place to hide

"Love Will keep Us Alive"
Eagles

A few days later Carrie met with Dr. Mitch in his office to let him know that she had managed the age regression with some friends. She could not determine whether he was surprised by her news or if he expected it. He did not ask for any details.

Instead, he straightened in his chair and asked Carrie, "...But tell me, why would anyone do such a thing?"

His question bothered Carrie. She didn't think that there was any excuse for such a heinous attack. The attacker had been like a rabid dog without a mind. She could only imagine the poison inside his head. He assumed that her attacker had been acting rationally in venting his violence on her. At this point she didn't want to get inside Dr. Mitch's head either. She felt that she could understand Dr. Mitch and the attacker, but she could not make excuses for their lack of cognition and inability to connect with themselves. Like the attacker, the counselor appeared impotent in his connection with his own humanity. In their blind insatiable drive to grasp the situation in carnal terms, they were left with nothing but a reflection of their own devastation where she remained invisible, perversely killing the very thing they craved. This separated them from Carrie. Despite their crude attempts, they could never reach her.

Instead of agreeing with Mitch or confronting him, she offered her impression, "As a child... I sensed that the man's instrument was very much like the wooden stick he rammed inside me. He held all his anger in that stick, depending on the use of the stick as if it supported all his weight."

"He-e... was impotent?!" Mitch guessed. He seemed happy with the bone Carrie had thrown him as a decoy.

Carrie nodded, "I think so. He and his wife had difficulty producing children for several years."

Mitch appeared satisfied with her answer, and did not question her further on this issue. Abruptly, he changed the topic before their time ended. "How are you coping with the stress of finals and graduation? There's medication available that will ease the strain."

"My grades have slipped some, but I'll pass all my courses even if I flunk my finals. I don't do well with drugs," she told him.

In spite of Carrie's answer something still seemed to bother Mitch. She could tell that she had not convinced him. He continually pursued answers outside of himself, which led to insatiable consumerism. She reasoned that he would never be satisfied.

"Look, I'm scheduled for an annual checkup in a few days. Dr. Leibniz will tell me if any medication is needed."

Glancing at the floor, Carrie added, "There's a scar and I want to know if it has affected my physical capability for childbearing. I want to know if it has healed properly."

Mitch dropped his recommendation for the drugs after he heard this response. He acknowledged, "I know Dr. Leibniz well and she's a fine doctor."

Anticipating Dr. Leibniz's reaction, he instructed Carrie accordingly, "Tell her...," he began while looking directly at Carrie, "...that you were the victim of a violent sexual assault at a very young age. Tell her you've been receiving counseling under my care."

Carrie shuddered at Dr. Mitch's brief statement. He was still trying to own her. She wondered where Dr. Leibniz stood. Was Dr. Leibniz fooling her too? Though Dr. Leibniz probably was familiar with the scar from past examinations, she had never mentioned the mark to Carrie. Carrie made a few closing remarks and left the office quickly. Neither of them suggested meeting again.

Once she stepped into the daylight outside the building, Carrie sighed relief and began walking towards the southern portion of campus. The discussion with Dr. Mitch disturbed her and she wanted to clear her head before meeting Brent.

She had hoped that Dr. Mitch would be different from most counselors. It must be their training, which amounted to psychological bloodletting. For some reason they always left her with the feeling that she had been responsible for the assault. Dr. Mitch proved no exception. She couldn't understand how being under his care suddenly made her acceptable to the medical establishment. Hot burning tears began flooding her eyes as she walked away from the main campus. Remembering the assault had not been enough. She had to learn how to protect herself. Regardless whether the flashbacks subsided, the threat of another sexual assault remained. Every month at least two more assaults occurred on campus, and the academic environment was safer than the city. Unfortunately, the authorities acted as if all the victims had deserved the crime and provided little protection. Reliance on uncooperative authorities was almost as taxing as surviving the crime itself.

The amorphous presence of the blue fairy seemed to warmly envelope Carrie even in her conscious state. Carrie imagined that all she really needed as a young adult was a hug and a pat on the back. She could not understand why such a simple affirmation was so hard to find and difficult for some people to give.

Carrie's feet echoed her thoughts as she plodded past the buildings and towards the athletic fields. Pounding the spring grass underneath her steps, she passed the baseball dugouts, metal fences, and powdered white lines on the ground. Not bothering to think about her direction, she walked to the portion of campus where she felt mysteriously drawn.

Suddenly Carrie stopped. Realizing why her feet had carried her to this place, she brightened. She never wanted to harm herself, despite the programming of her environment. She had arrived at the bleachers on the same green field where she first started playing intercollegiate soccer last autumn. The magic of the sport still attracted her.

Carrie whiffed the slight breeze from across the turf and climbed the bleachers to the highest bench. Sitting down, she leaned back on the splintered wood and studied the field. Carrie never could remain content with watching sports; she always had to play them. Recalling the first practice, Carrie remembered worrying about whether she possessed the required physical stamina and strength. Somehow her uncertainty had disappeared by the first hour, and never returned. If she could only get back some of that confidence, then she'd play these emotions like a black and white soccer ball.

"Meet the ball in the air, bounce it off my head, dribble it between my feet, roll it off my gut, steal it from an opponent, race with it down the field," she thought, before adding, "Then drive it past the goalie!"

How she could remember these moves! They were still inside her! Having learned them, she could use the skills to her advantage. With a bit of practice she'd soon be able to assimilate her feelings of the assault, learning to play off them.

With these thoughts Carrie rested on the bench for a moment. She felt like a spectator for the first time all season. Recalling all the teams that they had played on the field, she imagined the soccer games being replayed before her. She had never just watched; she had been so busy playing. Dribbling an imaginary ball between her toes as she ran plays in her head, she remembered the sensation of constantly hooking the ball with her feet to keep it underneath her. It wasn't a matter of perfection; it was vigilance. Glancing at the goal posts at the end of the field, Carrie clarified her own goals. She aimed for wholeness rather than for perfection. Together the inner team of experts and friends helping her heal represented parts of her psyche. Something had been missing in her life and these people provided mirrors of her own reflection. Some appeared as animals and represented the instincts. Puddy, the cat that lived in the garden outside had a habit of gracefully wandering in her studio apartment when Carrie wanted to work outside. The cat would purr and demand to be caressed. The cat reminded Carrie that cuddling the cat was as important as smelling the roses. All these pieces of her mirror instinctively formed the archetypal divine presence she sought.. Like the blue fairy of her dreams, their presence warmed and illuminated her.

Then she rose from the bleachers and stretched her arms and legs. One more piece was missing. One of her friends, Liza, was not only the toughest person Carrie knew — she was nice. In the past Carrie had confided in Liza on several occasions. She decided to see what Liza was doing this afternoon. Near the end of the soccer field stood a pay phone where she could call and inform Brent of her whereabouts. If she hurried, then she might be able to talk with him before he went to his afternoon class.

"What's up?!" Brent asked cheerfully when he heard Carrie's voice.

"I'm going to visit Liza. Could you meet me at her dorm room after you finish your class? I'll be ready to go home in about hour."

"Liza's a good person," Brent told her. "Go for it."

"OK. Bye," Carrie quickly replied.

"Goodbye," Brent answered as if he had all the time in the world.

After hanging up the phone, Carrie walked over to Liza's dorm room. Liza, a Geology major, was one of the most down-to-earth people Carrie knew. All the Geologists, particularly the women, hung together like cowboys on a desolate range, driving their internal stock with a devoted sense of business.

Inside the dorm's lobby, Carrie turned down the hall to her immediate left and knocked on Liza's door. Within a few seconds Liza greeted Carrie with an eager smile. She had her wooden rifle tucked inside her right arm as if ready for action. Liza had resumed drilling with the rifle after the rape of the students in the Geology department. Liza sent subtly clear messages.

"Come on in," she invited Carrie, swinging the door wide open.

"Do you have time to talk?" Carrie asked her. Turning around, Carrie watched Liza put aside the imitation rifle which had been smartly tucked in her right arm. Attune to the spirit of the Alamo located two miles away, the pretty, slim, blond resident assistant defended the first floor of the dormitory with her high school drill team rifle. Carrie understood Liza's need for the rifle which equipped her psychologically for any attack. Though the rifle would be useless in a real confrontation, it might sufficiently fool an assailant. Both Liza and Carrie believed that there were some things worth fighting, even if the odds of winning appeared dim.

"Sit down," Liza said softly, offering Carrie the Mexican Indian blanket on the floor. The blanket resembled Carrie's favorite at home, except the colors of the stripes were more earthy.

Taking off her shoes and socks, Carrie sat on the blanket. After Carrie had made herself at home, Liza joined her on the floor. Facing each other like a pair of Indian braves, they leaned forward as Carrie began their serious discussion.

"... It has something to do with the assault that I've been working through lately."

Liza raised her head and glanced beyond Carrie as she quietly recalled their last discussions. Both of them regularly informed the other of the events in their lives. In a few seconds Liza lowered her head, nodding her sympathetic understanding.

"Well, there's something that's been bothering me lately, and I need your answer," Carrie stated.

"...Liza, is it okay to be angry?" Carrie asked her in a low voice. Carrie felt as if she was missing something.

A sudden painful thought stirred from Liza's depth's and flickered across her countenance. Liza mumbled something, staring at the floor. She seemed unable to respond. Confused by her reaction, Carrie watched her in awe. Glancing at Carrie, Liza's eyes immediately turned a shade bluer. At that moment Carrie realized how much Liza cared about her.

"Liza," Carrie whispered, leaning back as Liza stared at the floor again. "Have you ever known anyone else who has been raped?"

From Liza's reaction Carrie imagined that Liza might have had a similar experience. But Liza murmured, "One of my friends in high school was cornered in an alley and raped by a gang of boys. Her mother and my mother were good friends... My mother told me much about it."

"Liza," Carrie whispered again as she leaned forward to confer. "Did she turn out okay?"

"She married a minister. She helps him run his parish in Austin."

"Is she happy now?" Carrie pressed.

Slowly regaining her confidence, Liza rose and rocked on her bare feet as she realized the answer to Carrie's question, "Yes."

Looking down at Carrie with a half-smile on her face, she answered further, "And yes, it is okay to be angry."

Looking into the space ahead of her, Carrie quietly nodded as if repeating Liza's response to her own inner depths and giving the feelings permission to exist. Meanwhile, Liza retrieved a teddy bear from one of the shelves above her desk and handed it to Carrie.

"Here, hold this," she said.

Immediately, Carrie reached for the teddy bear and drew it close to her. After holding the teddy bear for a moment Carrie asked, "Where's yours?"

"Mine's the Pink Pig," Liza acknowledged brightly, already halfway to her bed to retrieve the small stuffed animal.

"...the Pink Pig," Carrie repeated in mild awe.

Carrie watched Liza tuck the Pink Pig in the arm opposite from the one which usually handled the rifle. Raising the teddy bear in the air, Carrie examined it away from her. Even Jane and Pam owned stuffed animals.

"I feel too old for stuffed animals," Carrie decided after a few seconds. "I have Brent."

Carrie stretched out on the floor. Carrie lined her body on the teddy bear such that her head fitted on the stomach like a pillow. This position reminded her of all the times she spent resting her head in Brent's lap to gaze peacefully at the sky above.

Feeling slightly uncomfortable, Liza stared at Carrie from the corner of her eye. Finally she joined Carrie on the blanket, putting her head on a pillow from her bed and holding the Pink Pig close. For few seconds Liza mimicked Carrie's thoughtful stare at the ceiling, then she wrinkled her nose and posed a rhetorical question.

"I've always wondered... what do you do with your hands when you're lying next to a man?"

Not wishing to insult Liza's intelligence, Carrie softly assured her, "You'll figure it out when you get there."

Liza carefully considered Carrie's answer.

"O-Ohhh!" Liza suddenly whispered. Following with slight a chuckle, Liza felt flattered that Carrie had not insulted her intelligence on this question.

"Liza," Carrie slowly interrupted with a shy grin. "I'm working on a scientific theory that women marry men who remind them of their stuffed animals." Carrie explained, "The last time I held a stuffed animal was at the age of four... He was a long, skinny mouse about three foot in length, and had big floppy pink ears. His ears were so big that Mr. Mouse, which was his name, could hear all the secrets of everything in the world. I consulted Mr. Mouse from time to time in the same manner that Benjamin Franklin consulted his mouse. My Mr. Mouse had brown corduroy fur that he kept soft for cuddles and hugs, making him even more knowledgeable about the world."

"Well, it so happens that Brent is a tall, skinny fellow who likes to eat cheese," Carrie continued. "He has brown velvet fuzz on his body and loves to be hugged. Brent gives me all sorts of wonderful ideas on physics and how the world works. Sometimes I call him "Mr. Mouse" and he calls me "Mrs. Mouse"; together we live in a house."

Peering down at the stuffed animal beside her, Liza chuckled, "I wonder what this means about the man I'm gonna marry?!"

Liza had never considered her Pink Pig as husband material. With delight she hugged the Pink Pig, soon forgetting her former worries.

"Well, I bet that he'll have a really sweet disposition, possibly on the heavy side," Carrie speculated. "He'll like Polish sausage and be hog wild about his woman."

Carrie smiled at Liza who was happily embracing the Pink Pig. At the moment the Pink Pig seemed very real.

A knock was heard on Liza's door. Rising to answer, Liza opened the door with the Pink Pig tucked in her arm. A young man, one of the dorm's residents, confidently stepped into the room and asked a series of questions about general affairs in the dorm. Rather than distract from the order of business, the Pink Pig inconspicuously appeared as part of the answer to the young man's concerns. The Pink Pig soothed him.

Brent strolled into the room a few seconds behind the young man and Carrie hopped to her feet. Walking suavely around the younger man, Brent puffed up his chest as he observed the stuffed animals in the women's arms. Liza noticed Brent's debonair stance and flashed a knowing smile at Carrie with her steady blue eyes. Now Liza could recognize the Mr. Mouse in the man, which became more obvious every time Brent straightened. With a subtle nod Carrie placed the teddy bear on Liza's desk and walked over to Brent. Casually, Carrie curled her arm around Brent's waist.

"Ready to go?" Carrie quietly asked him. For his response Brent gave her a big cheesy smile. "See ya later, Liza," Carrie announced over the words of the young man who was trying to captivate Liza with his questions.

"Bye," Liza said with a weak wave from the fingers on her left hand. Taking care not to disturb the Pink Pig in her other arm, Liza resumed giving the young man her attention.

As they strolled out of the room together, Brent squeezed Carrie tightly a few times and questioned her, "How's it going?!"

"Much better now. I think that everything is going to be alright, no matter what happens."

* * *

Later in the week, Carrie met with Dr. Leibniz for a medical check-up. She was direct with the physician.

"I've been working through memories of a sexual assault. I'm seeing Dr. Mitch. I'd like to know whether the scar is healed and whether I'll have any difficulty with childbirth."

"Yes, I know Mitch. He's fascinated with the studies on hypnotism."

"Yes, I know. I seem to have an ability to create my own altered states."

"I think that it is more common than people think. I have one patient that remembered arriving at a particular destination while forgetting how he got there. Apparently he got in the car and drove without any problems, except that he doesn't recall how he got from point A to point B."

After the physical exam Dr. Leibniz remarked, "The scar has healed nicely. There is a tiny mark on the cervix and we will continue to monitor it for signs of abnormalities. You should have no problems getting pregnant or delivering babies. Your pelvic structure is ideal for carrying babies."

Carrie thanked her and left. The encounter with Dr. Leibniz had been refreshing. She had not pulled a power play. She appreciated Dr. Leibniz's attitude. Rather than blame Carrie, she merely helped Carrie deal with the pain by assessing the situation. She gave Carrie the information that she needed to take care of herself.

Chapter Thirty Four

...Climbed a mountain and I turned around
'And I saw my reflection in the snow covered hills
'Til the landslide brought it down
Oh, mirror in the sky
-What is love?
Can the child of my heart rise above?...

"Landslide"
Fleetwood Mac

When Carrie later related the story of the assault and Dr. Leibniz's findings, Brent's reaction was as unemotional as Carrie's bland description. Being two scientists, they automatically collected data and analyzed results. Now they were using these skills to minimize the impact of the trauma in the present.

"I'm beginning to be concerned about finals," Carrie announced. During the last week her interest in her studies had declined. "I am so glad that I took an incomplete for the computer course; I'd never have the time for my other four classes if I had not put the program aside."

"Ready for a back rub?" Brent asked, interrupting her and waving Carrie towards the bed. She took off her blouse and bra and laid beside him. Kneading the muscles on her back, Carrie's mind continued to wander over the events of the past two days.

"What are you doing?" Carrie questioned him when Brent abruptly discontinued his massage. She noticed that he was examining her as if she was his beloved bug underneath a microscope.

"Just looking at this three inch scar on the side of your back. Where did you get it?"

"What scar?! ... I don't know," Carrie sighed, wondering whether the mark was related to the assault. "I was rambunctious in my youth. I got a lot of scars just from playing outside."

A few seconds later, Carrie added in a quiet, serious voice, "Brent, there's another scar which I know is related to the assault. Though I've been vaguely aware of it during all these years, I've never seen it until today. At the base of my vagina there's a inch and one-half mark."

"I've never noticed it," Brent confessed, looking perplexed.

"You don't wear your glasses when we make love," Carrie replied with a wry smile.

Brent brightened, blushing slightly.

"Does it make a difference?" she asked him.

"No," he answered honestly, the perplexed look returning to his face.

His hands stopped moving as he shifted his position around Carrie. She turned over and clasped his hands inside hers.

"Good, because I want to feel you inside me again," Carrie said, removing the rest of her clothes. "It's been two weeks," she reminded him as a matter of fact. The reality of her world was that she was young, in love, happily married, and loved her present life. Nobody could tell her otherwise. This was all that she really knew. It was all that mattered to her. As a young mother with an infant that soon forgets the traumas of the birth, the Nightmare would disappear as Carrie gave birth to her own story. The Nightmare was just glimpses of the past that needed to be integrated in her growing understanding of herself and world. She could congratulate herself on having come so far. Her life was a celebration.

At first Brent hesitated. But when he realized that Carrie was serious, he allowed his desire to rise. All he knew was that his wife had a high libido. Carrie embraced him, while enjoying the familiar rhythm of their moves together. She could not deny her sorrow and the sense of loss. As much as it scared her, she had learned to embrace the pain until it soothed. Carrie wrapped her arms around him. Poignant tears fell from her eyes. She loved this man who wanted to be with her. Soaring past barriers of pain and fear, Carrie erased the travesty of her life. Her passion for life surpassed any walls or limitations, which merely transformed to boundaries marking her path.

She let Brent's warmth lift her into world far away from pain and fear. His heart thundered incessantly beneath his chest and it stirred her. Without words he called for her and she went to him. Inside him, she found the beat of a different drummer that led her to herself. Together they savored the comforting glow of the love that enveloped them before contentedly falling asleep in each other's arms.

Afterwards Carrie dreamed that she went back to the crib and followed the trail to the closet. The amount of blood and destruction left her aghast. She peered inside the closet and found the child. There were bloody handprints on the wall that the child had made before collapsing on the floor.

The child was dead. Carrie sat down beside the child and cried in despair. Suddenly she quieted and looked at the child again. A light beam had fallen across her, illuminating the small figure. The child was alright now. She gazed at Carrie. The child was wrapped in a soft blue blanket and wore a light blue nightie. She held a white rabbit fur hat in her hands because it was soft. Carrie noticed that the child had been cleaned up and didn't appear to be hurt. She saw the child smile at her.

* * *

Later that same year, on a clear day in late September, Brent and Carrie left for a brief camping trip in Colorado. The prospect of hiking in the Rockies excited Carrie, especially after completing her Geology course. Brent had visited the region as a boy and he wanted to hike the mountains again. They took a quick vacation before resuming their college studies later that fall.

During the first day of the hike, Brent and Carrie ascended over five hundred feet for every mile. Following the switchbacks through canyons and over steep hills, they reached an alpine meadow by early afternoon.

"Did I tell you about the letter I received from Don?" Carrie asked him as she looked over the cascading bluff on the far side of the trail. In her haste to catch the airplane flight, Carrie had retrieved the letter from her mailbox and packed it in her suitcase. She had forgotten about the letter until this morning when she repacked her gear. The alpine meadow seemed the perfect setting for savoring a letter from a friend.

"What did Don write?" Brent questioned her.

"Well, he sent me the latest results from his studies on bluebirds. His family hung over sixty birdhouses on their farm in east Texas. His findings are pretty interesting."

Pausing a moment to balance as she stepped over a boulder, Carrie continued, "If a baby bird falls out of a nest, Don returns the young to the birdhouse. He says the parents don't seem to mind his assistance. They even let him inspect the nest as long as he doesn't leave the lid open too long."

Glancing over to her shoulder to be sure that Brent heard her, she added, "Don has even found places for lost baby bluebirds in other nests. Other parenting bluebirds accept the homeless young and care for them without any problem. According to Don, the idea that birds reject those which have been touched by humans is false."

"I thought so," said Brent. "That's been my experience on my parent's farm."

"Really?!" Carrie replied in disbelief. After thinking his words over for a moment, she commented, "I don't think that all animals have the same instincts. The healthier ones ensure survival of the species." ·

"It makes sense," Brent observed. Then he added, "Let's stop for lunch, I'm hungry."

"There's a nice flat granite rock around the next bend," Carrie suggested. It caught my eyes several yards ago."

"Looks good," Brent announced when they reached the rock. Taking off his forty pound pack and dropping it aside, he settled on the rock like a swami with a straight back. Immediately, he devoted himself to the task of spreading the picnic items in a order known only to himself.

No matter how many years she spent with Brent, his picnicking style fascinated her. Sitting down on the rock, Carrie rested against her pack and watched him. From the corner of her eye she spied a tiny, furry striped creature scurrying towards them. "Oh Brent!" she exclaimed. "The chipmunks have come to see us!"

"And we're being invaded by camp robbers!" Brent laughed as several masked birds landed in the surrounding pines.

Brent extended his arm in the air. A camp robber swooped down from a nearby tree and landed on Brent's fingers. With a fixed cheesy grin Brent looked at Carrie from the corner of his eye. He kept his arm motionless, so that he would not disturb the small jay. Amazed by the sight, Carrie froze. She wanted to ask Brent so many questions about touching the bird, but she remained speechless. Instead, she breathlessly watched the camp robber casually hop to the middle of Brent's palm and look around. Brent gently stroked its soft feathers as his bold touch eventually cradled the jay. The camp robber did not leave for almost a minute.

"Brent, do you think I could try it?" Carrie asked in a whisper. "Would they also come to me?"

"Sure," Brent confidently soothed her, still grinning.

Trying to contain her excitement, Carrie quickly opened her palm. She hoped that the camp robbers would not notice that she was shaking inside. A small bird landed in her hand. In one brief instant Carrie forgot everything that she had painfully learned as a child. She petted the jay. Carrie could feel the small bird's quivering body. It did not hurt. The camp robber stayed as she bent her elbow to draw it closer to her. Then she stroked the bird with the cup of her palm. Surprised to feel the bird's heart beating faster than hers, Carrie took a deep breath and relaxed. She realized that touching the bird seemed as light as the wind; a person could feel it, but not hold it. Finally, when the bird had decided to fly away, Carrie felt the abrupt force of its spring into flight.

Higher and higher, the camp robber flew towards the snow capped mountain and soon disappeared into the background. Sitting secure on the gray granite, Carrie sensed that she would always be able find its spirited flight if she ever looked into the clear blue sky.

3105393